THE REBEL

THE ASSASSINS GUILD, BOOK #2

C.J. ARCHER

❃ Created with Vellum

"Why should you love him whom the world hates so?"
"Because he love me more than all the world."
— Edward II, Christopher Marlowe

CHAPTER 1

Hampshire, July 1599

*L*ucy Cowdrey knew the man walking across the meadow barely ten feet from her was not a local. She'd made it her business to meet everyone in the village of Sutton Grange and surrounds in the two months since her arrival, and none looked like this man. He was broader across the chest and shoulders than most and very tall. Lucy couldn't see much of his face, covered as it was by his wide-brimmed hat, but the little she did see was enough. No one in the little corner of Hampshire she now called home was as dark of complexion. His skin wasn't Moorish, but it was certainly a deeper tone than sun alone could achieve. He was a stranger.

And he was trespassing on her brother's land.

She knew she ought to confront him, but she was no fool. If he were there to steal cattle, she would not be able to stop such a large man. Perchance he was only passing through anyway.

Lucy gave him a wide berth, but kept him in her sights. He did not look up and went on his way without a nod or greeting in her

1

direction. Not only was it odd, but it was impolite too. If she were a man with nothing to hide, she would have at least tipped her hat.

They passed each other with nothing but grass and wildflowers between them, yet she could not keep her gaze away. She watched him over her shoulder, and promptly stepped into a rabbit hole.

"God's blood!" she cried as she fell onto her hands and knees.

Before she could right herself, two big hands gripped her arms and helped her to stand. The man had reached her remarkably quickly. "Are you hurt, ma'am?" He squatted and wrapped one of his big paws around her ankle and gently massaged. "Roll it for me." His voice had the deep, rumbling quality of someone past youth but not yet into middle age. There was a rough, undefined edge to it, and the accent marked him as not from Hampshire.

She twirled her foot and almost lost her balance. She clutched at his shoulder to stop from falling to the ground again. Once had been embarrassing enough, but twice would be utterly humiliating.

His muscles rippled beneath her fingers. "Well?"

"It's fine, thank you."

He let go of her foot and stood. "Then I'll be on my way." He still hadn't revealed his face to her. All she could see was his square jaw and firmly set mouth. The hat, a large straw one like farmers wore with a black feather tucked into the band, covered his eyes, nose and cheeks. He wore a jerkin over his shirt and a dusty pack slung on his shoulder, a rolled up blanket or cloak tucked beneath its strap. He was likely a laborer. He was dressed like one, and only the demanding physical nature of hard work could form such a magnificent figure. She'd seen it many times in the farm hands who'd come to her father's farm in the north as scrawny lads and left it as brawny men.

None had been quite like this man, however. There was something about him, aside from his size, something altogether more powerful that had nothing to do with mere measurements. A man like that could easily harm a lone woman, but he had not. Indeed, he'd come to her aid.

It was that which gave her the courage to confront him.

"Are you going to the village?" she asked. Sutton Grange was only an hour's walk past Stoneleigh, the estate where her friends the Holts lived. Lucy had just left them. The man would be off Cowdrey land and onto Stoneleigh's once he passed the hedgerow.

"No." He touched the brim of his hat in farewell and began to move off.

"A moment, if you please. May I ask you some questions?"

"Depends on the questions."

She blinked. Why was he being unnecessarily defiant? If he had nothing to hide, he would gladly answer her. And remove his hat.

"Can you take off your hat, please, so I may see your face?"

"Is that one of the questions?"

"No, it is a request that you remove your hat."

"No."

No? What was wrong with this man that he'd refuse a simple request? "Why not?"

"I like my hat where it is."

"That's no reason not to remove it when speaking to a lady."

Silence. Not even the leaves in the nearby wood rustled. Lucy's nerves strained, but she was determined not to break the deadlock. The man may not think her a lady, and perhaps she wasn't compared to the likes of Susanna Holt, but she *was* gently born. Well, perhaps not gently *born*, but certainly bred. Thanks to her father's wealth, he'd been able to obtain a coat of arms and declare himself a gentleman. He'd sealed his new status by educating all of his three children, including Lucy, to a level where they could easily interact with their betters and show no country ignorance. The only thing her father lacked was the right connections to elevate Lucy and her brothers further still. Particularly after her engagement to Edmund Mallam ended so sourly.

"Is that all the questions you have of me, ma'am?" he asked. Lucy thought she heard a hint of amusement in his voice, but it could have been sarcasm, or just plain rudeness.

"No. You're a stranger to these parts. I know everyone for

3

several miles, from farm hand to lord of the manor, but I do not know you."

"You have not seen my face," he said. "How do you know I'm a stranger?"

"I can tell from the rest of you." Her gaze swept down his body and back up again, settling on that impressive chest and shoulders. "There is no one built quite like you around here." Her face heated, but the man couldn't have seen with the hat over his eyes.

"Is that a reason to distrust me?"

"You are on my brother's land. If any cattle go missing—"

"You think a lone man could steal even a single cow unseen in the middle of the day?"

She crossed her arms. He was insolent and rude. "You are a stranger to these parts and should be identified. We don't want trouble." Lord knew there'd been enough of it, all thanks to Lucy's God-awful relatives. Because of them, she had not expected to be welcomed by the Holts, but it was clear from the first meeting that the pregnant Mistress Holt and her husband did not blame Lucy for her cousins' actions. Even now, months later, she still couldn't believe her own cousins—albeit ones she'd never met—had tried to murder the beautiful Mistress Holt and her charming husband. It seemed so unreal, like the sort of tale her older brothers told her as a child, right before one of them leapt out from behind a door and shouted, "Boo!"

But it wasn't a tale, it had been very real. Thank God that rotten branch of the Cowdreys had been lopped off before it could do any damage. It was up to Lucy and her brother Henry to prove to the people of Sutton Grange that not all Cowdreys were alike. She was determined to prove it. Determined too that no harm should come to the Holts' doorstep again.

"I'm an innocent traveler," the man said, palm raised in surrender. "There's no need to see my face because I haven't caused any trouble. Nor will I. And if I did intend to, then don't you think your insistence is a little foolish?"

"Are you calling me a fool?"

"I said a *little* foolish."

"Is that a slight on my size?"

"No." He thrust out his chin, but kept his hat brim down. "You have nothing to fear from me."

"Then why not show your face?" If she were foolish before, then she was even more foolish to continue. So be it. He had proved he wouldn't harm her, but that didn't mean he was an innocent.

"Perhaps I'm ugly," he said.

She stared at his mouth to see if it curved into a smile, but it did not. It remained grimly set. It was, however, a very handsome mouth with its perfect bow shape and full lower lip. "I doubt that."

"You flatter me." There was that amused tone again, the one that she couldn't determine whether it was genuine or mocking.

"It was an observation, nothing more."

"You think yourself observant? Then you will recognize me anywhere, hat or no." He touched the brim again in farewell.

He had a point. She would know that powerful frame anywhere, and that mouth. "I think we've both wasted enough time in idle chatter," she said. "Good day to you."

She walked off, and his only response was a grunt that she couldn't interpret. She did not look around to see if he left immediately or watched her departure, although she dearly wanted to. She headed home to the farm and was pleased to see Henry striding toward her as she neared the barn. She saw him so rarely of late. Brutus, her hound, barreled past him and greeted her with licks as she bent to pat him. His body fairly quivered with excitement.

"How's your patient?" Henry asked.

"Susanna isn't my patient. She's Widow Dawson's. I'm simply offering my support. She's quite well, thank you." Lucy looked up from Brutus and received a lick under her chin, then he bounded off toward the house, scattering hens and geese in all directions.

"Henry," she said, walking arm in arm with her brother, "am I foolish?"

He burst out laughing, bending his knees and tilting backward so that he was in danger of tipping over. She jabbed him in the ribs with her elbow and he smothered the laugh, although one corner of his mouth betrayed him. "Is this a serious question?"

"Yes."

"Do I have to answer it?"

"Yes."

"With honesty?"

She put a hand on her hip.

He sighed. "Very well. As your older brother, I feel a burning desire to tell you that you're the most dim-witted female I've ever met. But since we're adults now, and I have no other company here but you and the servants, I suppose I'd better be honest and say no. You are not particularly foolish. Indeed, you're one of the cleverest women I know."

"Do you know many?"

His eyes twinkled. "London is teeming with them. Few write better than you. None play the virginals as well, and their knowledge of history is limited. You, my irritating little sister, are far too bright for your own good. If you weren't, you wouldn't be asking me this question."

Lucy narrowed her gaze at him. She hadn't the slightest idea what he meant, but she suspected it was a compliment, and she wasn't one to shrug those off, even from a brother.

He laughed again and removed his hat to run his hand through his blond hair. "What's brought on such an odd question?" His gaze softened. "You haven't been thinking about Mallam again, have you? You're better off here without him."

Very true. It was better to be far away where Edmund's new wife and nasty tongue couldn't destroy the last shred of dignity Lucy had left.

"Forget I said anything." She strode toward Brutus and the kitchen entrance at the side of the house. Until the renovations were complete, everyone had to use the servants' entrance. It had bothered her at first, until she'd seen that Susanna and Orlando almost always used their kitchen to come and go from Stoneleigh.

Lucy had been disappointed upon her arrival at Cowdrey Farm. Although all the buildings were sturdy and in excellent condition, the main house was a rather drab, rectangular building with few pleasing features. Lucy had suggested a new entrance be added at the front, directly in the center and jutting out several feet from the main wall to break up the flatness. Already it looked better, despite the network of scaffolding covering the upper level. Once the entrance and rooms above it were completed and the vines Lucy had planted along the walls on either side grew higher, it would be quite a lovely house. Not as large as their father's in the north of the county, but something she would be proud to live in.

That's if she got to stay. It would, of course, depend on whether Henry found himself a wife, and if that wife wanted a sister-in-law underfoot. There was also the chance Lucy might wed and move away, but with so few suitable men in the neighborhood, that outcome was not looking likely. Besides, after her experience with Edmund Mallam, she was not at all keen to venture down the matrimonial path.

Henry caught up to her and shortened his stride to keep apace. "Has Mistress Holt said something to upset you?"

"I'm not upset. And she is the kindest neighbor, Henry. If you visited the Holts more, you would know that."

"How can I when I'm so busy here?" His harsh tone made her pause mid-step. Was he still bitter about being wrenched out of London and his legal studies to manage Cowdrey Farm for their father? She knew he had been at first, but surely not anymore. It was *his* inheritance ultimately, after all.

"So why the foolish question?" he asked, striding ahead.

She had to run to catch up. "That's not at all amusing."

"I couldn't resist." He took her by the elbow and gently halted her alongside the kitchen garden. The scent of pennyroyal was particularly strong, but not as delicious as the smell of roasting mutton from the kitchen itself. "Come, Lucy, tell me what's wrong. It's not like you to doubt your virtues like this."

She patted his arm and gave him a reassuring smile. There were small lines around his eyes that she hadn't noticed before, and shadows too that hadn't been there before arriving at Cowdrey Farm. Henry was tired. Not surprising since a farm of Cowdrey's size required a lot of work, and he had never been master of his own estate before. Cowdrey Farm had been an unexpected inheritance that their father had given to his second son to manage with the aim of bequeathing it to Henry outright upon his death, which, God willing, was many years away. Lucy's oldest brother, Simon, would get the main family farm in its entirety. It was a neat arrangement, but Henry did not seem overly grateful. He'd grown up believing that, as second son, he could almost do as he pleased. And what pleased him was studying law at the Inns of Court in London.

"It's nothing," she told him. "Don't worry. I met a man on my way back from Stoneleigh. He was harmless but ill-mannered. He got me thinking, that's all."

"Lucy, should I be worried about something?"

"No, of course not. It's nothing. You know how we females get these things into our heads."

He frowned fiercely. "You are not the typical female."

She entered the house before he could question her further. She was determined to dismiss the stranger from her thoughts entirely. It was a beautiful day, and she wouldn't let an upstart ruin it. After their midday meal, she would go for a walk and pick cress to use in a purgation for one of the maids who'd been up coughing all night. She needed to do something useful, helpful. Something *worthy*, to take her mind off the rude man with broad shoulders and a mouth that invited all sorts of sin.

ole hadn't meant to kill his target in quite so public a place as The White Hart tavern in the village of Larkham. The plan had been to attack after Renny left, away from the other patrons and shielded by darkness, but the fool had gotten so drunk he could barely walk. He could, however, pick a fight.

For some reason known only to himself, the prick picked a fight with Cole. He couldn't possibly have known that Cole had been sent to assassinate him. The vicious rapist who liked to leave his mark on his victim's chest in the form of two crisscrossing knife slashes had come to the Guild of Assassins' attention through a letter penned by the father of one of those unfortunate girls. At least the families could sleep easier now knowing Renny had paid the price for his crimes.

"I'm happy to see you, Cole," Orlando Holt said, leaning on his rake and regarding Cole from beneath the brim of his hat. "I truly am. But why did you come here?"

Cole removed his hat and nodded at Orlando's wife, Susanna, reclining on a chair in the shade of one of her orange trees, her feet propped up on a crate. "I brought a gift. For the baby," he said. The three of them were alone in the walled garden, which contained some shrubs, two mature orange trees and a dozen saplings. The saplings had been planted to replace the ones maliciously chopped down last autumn. Cole remembered that awful day. Susanna had been devastated, Orlando coldly furious.

But that may as well have been a lifetime ago. There was an air of contentment around the couple now, of happy expectation as the birth of their child neared and their orange trees grew. Even the house looked fresher, with new panes in the ground floor windows and proper shutters over others. Orlando had been busy.

Susanna gave Cole a drowsy smile. "That's very sweet, Mr. Cole."

"It's just Cole," he said, stroking the black feather in the hat's brim.

She rubbed her large belly and turned her smile on her husband. As if he knew, Orlando switched his attention to her. The secretive glances they exchanged conveyed an unspoken message, but what that message contained, Cole couldn't guess.

"*You* brought us a gift?" Orlando said to Cole. "No, really, why are you here?"

"Orlando," Susanna chided.

"You don't know him like I do. Cole doesn't form friendships with people outside the Guild, and even those of us in the Guild don't truly know him. For instance, he's just Cole to everyone. Is that a last name, first name, or something else altogether? Maybe Hughe knows more. Maybe he doesn't." He spoke to Susanna but watched Cole the entire time. No doubt he hoped to draw out answers with his teasing. He should have known better. "He likes to keep things simple, his circle tight. I thought he'd washed his hands of me when I left the Guild." Orlando shrugged. "I'm glad he hasn't," he added softly.

Cole kept his gaze on Orlando, steady and unblinking, hopefully giving no sign that his heart had just delivered a solid blow to his ribcage after his friend's admission. A bee buzzed near Orlando's head, but he didn't bat it away. He matched Cole stare for stare, the smile on his face a challenge to defy him, prove him wrong, or right.

"It's very sweet of you to bring a gift for the baby." Susanna's voice broke through the taut silence. "May I see it?"

The smile on Orlando's face grew wider. Cole broke their connection and rummaged through his pack. He found the rattle and handed it to Susanna. She gasped as she inspected the handle and the hollow sphere wedged on top. A delicate pattern had been carved into of the wooden sphere, giving a tantalizing glimpse of the tiny, solid balls inside. They plipped and plopped as she turned the rattle over.

"Oh, Cole, it's beautiful and much too precious to give to a baby to play with."

Too precious for a baby? Cole frowned. "If you don't like it, I can get you another one."

"No!" She cradled it against her chest. There were tears in her eyes. "I didn't say I don't like it, just that a baby might lose it, and it's much too valuable to be lost somewhere out here. I mean, look at the fine carving on the handle. And how did those tiny balls get inside? It must have cost you a considerable sum."

"Cole doesn't give a whit for the cost of things," Orlando said, sounding pleased to be imparting some knowledge about Cole. "He gives away money as if it were as freely available as water." He cocked an eyebrow at Cole, challenging.

"Hughe pays me too much," Cole said. "I have no need of it all."

"Thank you," Susanna said. "You may not value the rattle, but I do."

Cole hadn't said he didn't value it. He did, just not in a monetary sense. He'd spent three weeks making it after not finding anything in the London shops that he'd liked. Most had floral patterns on their handles, which was much too feminine if the babe were a boy. More important, all the rattles he'd seen had balls or bells dangling on tiny chains or leather strips that seemed too easy for little fingers to remove and little mouths to swallow. His design was sturdier too, not easily broken, and would last several generations. He rather liked the idea of his gift becoming a family heirloom.

It wasn't necessary to tell Susanna and Orlando any of that, of course. Let them think he'd bought it. It made no difference to him.

"It's very sweet of you to deliver it in person," Susanna said.

Orlando squatted at his wife's feet. She handed the rattle to him. "You were sent here by Hughe, weren't you? Or not here, precisely, but nearby."

Cole said nothing. He wasn't allowed to discuss his work, even with a former Guild member, and he certainly didn't want to discuss it in front of a woman. He was surprised Orlando didn't consider his wife's feelings, although Cole knew she was aware of what her husband used to do for a living, and what Cole still did. Orlando had made that clear when they'd all been together back in November.

It was the last time Cole had seen them. Hughe had returned once to check on their former colleague and to attend the wedding. Cole had not. Orlando was no longer a part of their crew. He'd chosen a new life away from his friends, and Cole wasn't one for dwelling on the past. Better to cut ties, move on, and not drag that anchor around.

Nevertheless, it seemed a pity to be so near and not come to visit. Besides, he had a rattle to deliver.

As if she sensed Cole's discomfort, Susanna rose and walked as elegantly as a lady in her condition could down to the last of the saplings—out of earshot, if Cole and Orlando spoke quietly enough.

"Why didn't you tell her you made this?" Orlando asked.

"What makes you think I did?"

"You use this leaf pattern on a lot of your work."

Cole shrugged. "You can tell her, after I'm gone."

"She'll be annoyed that I didn't mention it while you were here. She'll want to thank you."

"She already has."

Orlando turned the rattle over and appeared to be inspecting the bird perched on the top of the branch carved into the handle, but then he said, "You killed someone, didn't you?" He set the rattle on the chair his wife had vacated and stood.

There was no point hiding the fact. Orlando wasn't a fool, and he would find out sooner rather than later. "In Larkham."

Orlando swore. Larkham was very close to Sutton Grange, after all. It was likely he'd seen the man on market days. "What for?"

"He said he didn't like the look of me."

Orlando grunted a laugh. "I don't like the look of you, but you've never killed me."

"Never say never."

"It was Hughe's orders, wasn't it? What was the man's crime?"

"I can't tell you that."

Orlando sighed. "Have it your way. At least you were discreet? No one saw you?"

Cole watched a yellow butterfly dancing in the air near one of the orange trees, flitting around as if it couldn't decide which lush green leaf to settle upon. It was peaceful in the garden, cut off from the world by the high brick wall. He could see why Susanna liked it so much.

Orlando swore under his breath when Cole didn't answer. "You'd better tell me what happened. And don't insult me by speaking untruths." When Cole hesitated again, he added, "I can deflect questions away from you if someone happens to mention a stranger passing through."

The persistent wench in the meadow came to mind. At first Cole had been bothered by the fact he couldn't remove his hat in her presence. Long-entrenched manners were hard to break, and many years of living the rough life of an assassin had not destroyed the habits drilled into him as a boy, but by the end of their blessedly brief conversation, he was glad he'd kept his hat on, if only because she'd been so determined that he should remove it.

And because she could indeed identify him if he had.

"I didn't mean to kill him." The words slipped out of their own accord and took Cole by surprise. He hadn't meant to tell Orlando anything. He had no right to know. "Not then and there."

"How can you not mean to kill someone?"

"His throat got in the way of my knife. I was aiming for his shoulder, but he lunged."

"Is that a joke?"

"Have you ever known me to jest about death?"

"I've never known you to jest about anything. Your sense of humor is as black as your hair."

And my soul.

"So now everyone in Larkham knows you're an assassin," Orlando said.

"No. Everyone knows I'm a killer."

"You realize the village is only ten miles from here." It wasn't a question, so Cole didn't bother answering. "Someone from Sutton Grange may have been there yesterday and seen you do it."

"Then I'd better not show my face around here for long."

"You'd better not show your face around here at all." He sighed heavily. "I'm sorry, Cole, but I don't want trouble brought into Susanna's life. Not now when everything is going so well."

Cole conceded the point with a nod. He picked up his pack. "I was just passing through."

Orlando bowed his head, heaved a sigh. "Wait. I didn't mean for you to leave right this moment. Come inside, eat. Cook will pack you some provisions for your journey and you can be off before nightfall."

"I'll accept the provisions with gratitude, but I'll leave immediately." Orlando was right. Cole didn't belong in the peaceful little valley with its dancing butterflies and promise of new life.

He didn't belong anywhere.

"Did anyone see you come here?" Orlando asked as he watched his wife inspect a leaf on one of her young trees. His eyes were half closed, the smile never far away from his lips as he followed her every languid move.

Cole's stomach clenched into a tight ball. The domestic scene was so tranquil, so pure, it hurt to witness it. He looked away. Three people in a walled garden was one too many. "I met a woman in a meadow just over the way," he said. "She asked— ordered—me to remove my hat."

Orlando turned his attention away from Susanna and focused on his former colleague. A frown scored his forehead. "And did you?"

"No."

"Why weren't you in disguise?"

"I was. In Larkham. I changed out of it when I left."

"You didn't hear her coming? You're slipping, Cole."

"I heard her. We avoided each other until she fell into a hole. I wish I'd kept walking. She was a very meddlesome woman, and foolish."

"In the meadow you say. Was she pretty with pale red gold hair and freckles?"

Cole hadn't seen her face properly, not with his hat pulled so low, but he'd seen enough of her figure to know her bodice fit snugly over her chest. Very snugly. "Who do you think it was?"

"Lucy Cowdrey. She left here not long before you arrived." He chuckled. "I disagree with your description of her. She isn't foolish or meddlesome. Lucy is a good woman, gentle natured, always helping others. She takes food to the poor and visits the sick with no concern for her own health."

"Sounds foolish to me."

"Foolish, no, naïve, yes, and a little too eager to make amends for her cousins' actions."

"Cowdrey. She's related to that brother and sister who tried to kill you last autumn?"

"Distantly. She and her brother have taken over the farm. I assure you, they are nothing like their cousins, although she left her previous home under something of a cloud."

He didn't elaborate, and Cole didn't press him. If anyone understood another's need to keep a secret, it was him. Besides, he cared nothing for the Cowdrey woman's problems.

"Susanna adores Lucy," Orlando went on. "She's been an excellent companion for her in this latter part of the pregnancy. My wife would have gone mad with boredom if it weren't for Lucy, and Heaven help us all when Susanna is bored."

It couldn't have been the same woman Cole encountered. That shrew had a sharp tongue and a blunt mind. "Is she likely to mention she saw a stranger passing this way if someone asks?"

"She may." Orlando's mouth twisted in thought then he nodded. "Indeed, I think it likely. Lucy would consider it her duty. The fact you refused to remove your hat will make her remember you all the more."

"Ill-mannered people bother her that much?" Cole was glad he wasn't staying to meet her again. She sounded exactly like the sort of woman he avoided. Not that well-bred gentlewomen with soft hearts and high morals were throwing themselves at him. They seemed equally happy to avoid him as he them.

"Have you been into Sutton Grange?" Orlando asked. "Can anyone there identify you?"

"No, and I've met no one else."

Orlando picked up the rattle. The balls tumbled inside the larger one, and Susanna looked around at the sound. She smiled and approached, slowly, brushing her fingertips over the leaves of each tree as she passed. "Good," Orlando said, watching her.

"Worried about me?" Cole asked.

"A little."

"I can take care of myself."

"In that case, I'll have you know I'm more concerned for the virtue of the ladies of Sutton Grange than your neck. You have a habit of leaving broken hearts in your wake, and we have friends in the village. I wouldn't like to hear how you'd kept their beds warm only to disappear before dawn without saying goodbye."

"Goodbyes aren't always necessary. And I don't break hearts."

Orlando rolled his eyes. "Yes you do."

"You're mistaken. Heart breaking is your area of expertise. The women of England and half the Continent went into mourning when they heard you'd wed."

Orlando slapped him on the back, hard, then took his wife's arm as she joined them. He kissed her forehead and rested a hand on her round belly. If she'd heard Cole's comment, or knew about her husband's previous reputation, she made no sign of it.

"Come," Orlando said to Cole, "let's go stock that pack of yours so you can be on your way."

THE AFTERNOON SUNSHINE was as potent as the strongest wine. Cole felt drowsy after walking most of the night. The fast pace had been relentless, but at least he'd gotten far enough from Larkham by dawn that he would be ahead of a vigilante pack, if one were after him. It was possible that the villagers didn't particularly mind having their local rapist murdered by a stranger who'd managed to slip out of the tavern in the ensuing commotion and disappear into the night before they could raise a hue and cry. Renny, the target, had made two young women from the village his victims, but they and their families had been too frightened of the influential alderman to confront him publicly, hence the letter to the Guild of Assassins.

The man would not be missed, except perhaps by the family he'd left behind, who presumably had no notion of the crimes their husband and father had committed. It was why Cole had deposited a leather pouch full of coin on their doorstep before he went to the White Hart to watch Renny. They may not have been poor if their grand house was any indication, but without Renny to provide for them, their situation would quickly deteriorate.

Cole had wanted to stop only long enough to rearrange his pack when he left Orlando's house, but the lure of the sunshine was too much. He lay down on a soft bank of grass in the shade of a hedgerow, yawned, and closed his eyes.

He woke up to the sound of a woman humming. Through the

gaps in the hedgerow foliage, he could see her bending over in the meadow beyond, collecting wildflowers. The basket over her arm was filled with cress and primroses. She would see him if he stood up, so he rolled onto his side, propped his head on his hand and watched.

Bending over like that, it was difficult to tell how tall she was, but her voice was light and warm like a summer's breeze. It suited the day. It was as if this woman was exactly where she should be—collecting flowers in the sunshine.

Cole ought not to watch. It was wrong. It made the innocent activity sordid. He wanted to leave, but that would draw attention to himself. He was about to lie back down and close his eyes, block out that voice, when she straightened. God's blood! Even with her back to him, he knew it was the woman he'd encountered earlier. She wore the same tight gray bodice, had the same trim figure.

Lucy Cowdrey, according to Orlando. It must be her. Tendrils of pale red-gold hair had worked free of the pins and her hat and fell in delicate wisps past her shoulders. The ends curled and bounced as she moved. He wondered how long her hair would be if those curls were teased out. Probably down to that slender waist.

He remembered the way her breasts had filled out her bodice and wished circumstances were different and he'd met her in the village at another time when he wasn't in haste. If she wasn't a virgin, he'd happily take her for a tumble in those wildflowers. If she could keep her mouth shut, that is, and keep her questions to herself. Would she let him leave his hat on?

He snorted softly. His fantasy would have to go unfulfilled because Lucy Cowdrey was most likely a maiden in every sense. Her sort always was. If she had any secrets, they would be buried as deeply as her sense of fun and adventure.

In which case, she would be very much like Cole.

The irony amused him, but he didn't smile. He just watched and wondered what her face looked like. Orlando said she had freckles. With hair that color, it wasn't surprising. But freckles on just her nose, or did they cover her entire face? What about her shoulders?

The image of her smock slipping off one shoulder, revealing a smattering of freckles across pale skin, came unbidden into his mind. No matter how hard he tried, he couldn't dislodge it.

Damned woman. He was going to have to walk away with that itch unscratched.

He closed his eyes and listened to her humming until it faded into the distance.

He must have fallen asleep again because he didn't hear the footsteps until they were surprisingly near. He felt for the blade strapped to his forearm, more out of habit than concern. Judging from the lightness of the steps, it was a woman for certain. Lucy Cowdrey. She wasn't a danger, merely annoying. He opened his eyes and sat up, twisting to reach for his hat to hide his face.

The blow hit him hard. Pain exploded through his skull. Everything blurred, but not before he got a glimpse of his attacker's boots. Sturdy boots. *Men's* boots.

Cole swung his fist, but his movements were sluggish, and he connected with nothing but air. Only one punch hit something solid. It felt like a stick and was probably the weapon that had been used to crack his head open. Warm, sticky blood seeped from the wound, into his hair, onto the grass.

He couldn't keep his eyes open. Couldn't stop the blackness as it rolled in like an Arabian dust storm and swallowed him whole. He was going to die behind a Hampshire hedgerow with only his killer as witness. No mourners nearby. No family.

Odd that he should think of them now when he hadn't thought about them in so long. Would Hughe bother to tell his father of his youngest son's death?

The last thing Cole knew was more white-hot pain, this time in his ribs and stomach. He couldn't even fold up to protect himself from the kicks.

Then he didn't even feel those.

CHAPTER 3

*L*ucy had been gone longer than she'd intended, but the day was so beautiful and the flowers so pretty down by the stream. After briefly dipping her stockinged toes into the cool water then drying them in the sun, she'd finally set off home. The warmth made her drowsy, her mind slow, which explained why she failed to see the man until he sat up.

She gasped and dropped her basket, scattering flowers and cress over the grassy mound. Embarrassed at her skittish reaction, she bent to collect them, keeping one eye on the man. He looked at her. He wasn't someone she recognized. She should ask him what he was doing on her brother's land. Or perhaps she should just walk off in the other direction and hope he didn't bother her. One encounter with a stranger per day was quite enough. Her fingers tightened around the handle of her basket as she watched him surreptitiously. He didn't seem in any state to harm her. His gaze was unfocused, blank, and… he was bleeding!

She approached, albeit carefully. "Are you all right?"

Dried blood covered the side of his face and the grass next to him. He continued to stare at her with that unsettling blankness. A small furrow creased his brow. "I'm sorry. I don't think I know you." He spoke with the round, crisp accent of the upper classes, which she hadn't expected based on his simple country clothing.

"We've never met." She knelt beside him and inspected his wound. It had stopped bleeding, but the gash above his ear was long and deep. It must be painful. "What happened to you?"

He shrugged, then winced as if that small movement hurt. He undid the top buttons of his jerkin and edged the collar of his shirt aside. A dark bruise shadowed his shoulder.

Lucy gasped again, but not because of the bruise. She'd spotted a hat half hidden in the hedgerow. It had a distinctive black feather tucked into the band. It was the same hat worn by the stranger she'd met after leaving Stoneleigh. On closer inspection, he also wore the same jerkin, and had a chest and shoulders equal in size to the man she'd met. His mouth, however, confirmed her suspicion. It was curved like a bow, the lower lip full.

"Oh," she said, "it's you."

He blinked at her, fanning the longest, blackest lashes she'd ever seen. Such a waste on a man. "We've met? My apologies, madam, but I don't recall the encounter."

"Perhaps if you'd removed your hat and looked at me, you would recognize me now."

"My hat? Where is it?"

She pointed at the hedgerow. "It must have fallen off."

"That's not mine."

She sat back on her haunches and stared at him. He was handsome, even with blood matting his dark hair and crusting the side of his face. "You don't recall our meeting earlier, do you?"

He shook his head then, groaning, went quite pale.

She touched the back of his neck. "Draw your knees up and rest your forehead on them for a moment. Do you feel ill?"

"A little." He did as he was told and sucked in a deep breath, but that merely produced another groan. His ribs must be sore too.

She fetched his hat and pack. The latter appeared untouched, suggesting no thieves had set upon him. "You didn't tell me what happened to you," she said, inspecting the gash again. She had salves and bandages back at the farm. The sooner she could tend it, the better.

"I can't remember," he said, lifting his head. His eyes fluttered closed, and she worried he'd faint. Fortunately, he seemed to rally and opened them again. They were clearer, their dark brown depths warm as he focused on her face for a very long time, particularly her nose where her freckles were more prominent.

He pressed his lips together, and his gaze connected with hers, briefly, before he turned away as if embarrassed to be caught looking. Lucy's face heated. She wasn't used to having such a handsome man study her with intensity.

It was important to not let his handsomeness blind her, however. He'd been rude on their first meeting. She shouldn't soften toward him just because he'd received a blow to the head.

"What do you mean you can't remember what happened? Did you fall?"

"I don't know. I… " He rubbed his temples and looked around at the hedgerow, the trees. "Where am I? This place doesn't look familiar."

"You're on my brother's land. Actually, it's my father's, but Henry manages it and will inherit one day." She snapped her mouth shut. There was no need to tell him anything. Indeed, it was probably best if she didn't. But something about him unsettled her and when she felt nervous, she tended to talk overmuch.

"Oh," he said, frowning. "Are you related to the Whitcombs?"

"No."

His frown deepened. "I must have wandered further than I thought. Father will be furious. You won't tell him, will you?"

Why would this big, strong man be worried what his father thought? Odder and odder.

"We'd better take you home," she said. "Is it far?"

"I told you, I don't recognize this land."

She crossed her arms, studied him. "What's your name?"

"Nicholas Coleclough. What's yours?"

"Lucy Cowdrey. Where are you from, Mr. Coleclough?"

One corner of his mouth lifted in the most impish smile. "Cole-clough Hall."

"I don't know it, and I know all the manors hereabouts. Is it in this part of Hampshire?"

He screwed up his nose. "Kent. Why do you mention Hampshire?"

Lucy waited, but he didn't laugh, and the small smile he'd sported vanished altogether. He wasn't jesting. "Because that's where we are," she said quietly.

Confusion flickered in his eyes. "No, this is Kent." But even as he said it, he looked around again with a mystified frown. "I live in Kent," he muttered. "Coleclough Hall. It's been in my family for generations." He turned back to her, and she was shocked to see him stripped of all cockiness. There wasn't a shred of the man she'd met earlier. He'd been bold and rude then, oozing confidence and power. The fellow sitting before her, bloodied and bruised, was confused, humble. It did not make sense.

"What am I doing in Hampshire?" he asked.

"That must have been quite a bump on your head. I'll take you to the farm for now until we can sort out the mystery of how you came to be so far from home. Perhaps someone in the village knows where you're from. I'll ask tomorrow. In the meantime, you can recuperate in our spare bedchamber."

"That's very kind of you, madam, but please, I don't want to be a burden."

"You're not. I'm glad to help." It suddenly struck her that he might be lying. This could all be a ruse with the aim of robbing her, or worse.

But who would beat themselves almost to death, lie in a meadow hoping to be stumbled upon, then put on an elaborate act, all for the chance to rob someone? Not even the comedies performed by the traveling players were as ridiculous.

"Can you stand?"

"Of course." He tried to get up but had to sit again and rest his forehead on his knees. A few moments later, breathing shallowly, he tried once more and managed to stand. He took one fumbling step and would have fallen, but Lucy slipped in beside him and circled an arm around his waist. He sucked air between his teeth but did not ask her to let go. She tried to hold him gingerly so as not to put more pressure on his bruises.

"All right?" she asked.

"I think so."

She picked up his pack and slung it over one shoulder, then carried both his hat and hers in the same hand. "Put your arm around me," she said.

He hesitated.

"Go on. I don't mind."

"I don't want to hurt you. You're very small and delicate."

She chuckled. "Actually, it is you who are large. If you're going to fall, just do it in the other direction."

He laughed but stopped abruptly with a hiss of pain. "I'll accept your offer after all." He reached across her back and rested his hand on her shoulder.

Something long and hard inside his sleeve pressed into her. A knife, she supposed. It wasn't unusual for a traveler to have an extra weapon tucked away to protect himself.

They walked off, slowly because he limped heavily. He felt tense against her, every muscle taut. And there was a lot of muscle.

"Thank you, Mistress Cowdrey," he said. "This is very kind of you. My father will compensate you for your troubles."

"It's no trouble, and I don't want compensation. Some answers to my questions will do."

"I don't understand what happened. Who would do this to me? Why? My pack appears to be full, so it wasn't thieves."

So he'd noticed that too. "Your memory of the event must have been destroyed," she said. "I've heard of that happening when there is an injury to the head."

She concentrated on where they set each foot and not looking up at him, but she could feel his gaze upon her nevertheless. His fingers relaxed on her shoulder but didn't let go. His thumb stroked her through her layers of clothing. She glanced up and despite his brown skin, she saw him blush.

He let go. "I'm sorry."

She caught his hand and put it around her waist. "We can't have you stumbling, can we?"

"I'm sorry," he said again.

"Stop apologizing."

"I'm s—" They both laughed, but his was short lived. "Ah, that hurts."

"Your ribs?"

"Yes. My stomach too. And my voice…"

"Your throat hurts?"

"No, my voice sounds different. Rougher."

"Not to me. That first time I met you, it was just like it is now. Although…"

"What?"

"Your accent has changed." *And your demeanor.*

"My accent?"

"It's more refined now. You described your voice as rough, but your accent was rougher before too. Very odd."

"Yes," he said, mystified. "There seems to be quite a few odd things about me."

They hobbled back through the fields and paddocks, along uneven tracks trodden by hooves, until the farmhouse finally came into sight. Lucy felt a rush of relief. Despite her continued assurances that he wasn't too heavy, she had begun to feel the strain some time ago. He was a solid man, but he could not have walked on his own all that way, not with his injuries. As it was, his face was as pale as the moon and glistened with sweat.

He made it as far as the henhouse before he collapsed, sending the pecking hens into a flutter. Lucy called out, and two stable boys came running, Brutus too, his ears flopping with each bound.

"Are you able to carry him inside?" she asked.

The scrawny lads exchanged looks. "He's too big. I'll fetch the master," one of them said and ran off.

 Lucy asked the remaining groom to tell the maids to make up the guest bedchamber, and he too departed. Brutus sniffed Coleclough and licked his face, but still the stranger didn't wake. The hound cocked his head to the side and sat on his haunches. Lucy knelt beside him and swept a lock of hair off Coleclough's forehead. With his eyes closed and his face stark against the black hair, he didn't seem as formidable as when she'd first met him. He was so different. That the change had resulted from the beating didn't bear thinking about. She abhorred brutality of any kind, even against men as big and arrogant as this fellow.

 He was very handsome though. Not beautiful like Orlando Holt with his boyish face, but stronger, coarser, like he'd been hewn from hard rock that resisted polishing. A slender white scar cut through his right eyebrow, and another followed the line of his jaw. It looked smooth against the stubble, and without thinking, she touched her fingertip to it to see just how smooth.

 He opened his eyes and looked directly at her. She pulled her hand back. "You fainted."

 He pushed himself up on his elbows, groaned, and slumped down again.

 "Lucy?" Henry ran toward her, and Brutus jumped up to greet him. "Are you all right? Who have you got there?"

 Coleclough struggled to sit again, and Lucy helped him. He was extremely pale, but he met Henry's gaze with a steady one of his own. "My name is Nicholas Coleclough," he said. "From Coleclough Hall. In Kent."

 "Kent? Then you're a long way from home." Henry indicated the wound on the side of Coleclough's head. "What happened?"

 " I–I don't know."

 "I found him in the low meadow like this," Lucy said. "He needs to rest and have his wound cleaned and bandaged. We'll put him in the guest bedchamber."

 Henry squatted beside him and studied the wound. "Aye. He's in no condition to go anywhere further than that today."

 "For quite a few days," she said.

Henry's gaze slid to her. "Appointed yourself as his physician, have you?"

"Do you see anyone else here?"

Henry sighed and beckoned the tallest groom. "Take his other side." They helped Coleclough to stand. Then, between them, they half supported, half carried him inside.

The guest bedchamber was upstairs, and by the time they reached it, Coleclough was looking deathly pale again. They made it to the bed, but as soon as he lay on it, he fell into unconsciousness. His breathing became heavy, fitful, and a sheen of sweat covered his brow.

"Fetch water and linen, Matilda," Lucy said to the maid. The grooms left with her.

"It seems you've found yourself another mission," Henry said.

"Mission? Whatever do you mean?" Lucy sat on the edge of the bed and undid the buttons on Coleclough's jerkin.

"An assignment. Somebody to fuss over. I'm sure Mistress Holt will be pleased."

She shot him a withering look. "This isn't a jest, Henry. This man has been severely hurt. Some parts of his memory appear to be missing as well. He can't recall the event, or indeed how he got to be in Hampshire. He thought he was in Kent when I found him."

"It must have been quite a shock to find himself so far away from home with a freckly red-head leaning over him."

She finished undoing the buttons on his jerkin and started on the laces of his shirt. "Very amusing. And my hair is not red. Remove his boots, will you."

"I think you should remove his boots, and I or one of the men should remove the rest of his clothes while you are out of the room."

"You're not going to go all prudish on me, are you? If I am to treat him properly, I'll have to see parts of his body."

"Not *all* parts, my inquisitive little sister."

"Henry." She was about to remind him that she'd seen Edmund Mallam rolling naked in the grass but thought better of it. There were some things she couldn't discuss with him, no matter how dear he was to her. Nor did she want to think about Edmund, naked or otherwise.

"Don't force me to get all big brotherly and forbid you," he said.

"Just take his boots off. I promise I'll only tend to those wounds from his waist up. Anything below that he can tend himself."

"And you can only come in here if you're accompanied by one of the maids," Henry said, tugging off the left boot. "Good lord!" Strapped to Coleclough's ankle was a small knife about the length of a middle finger.

Lucy parted the edges of his shirt, revealing fine black hair and more scars on his chest.

"Do you accept my conditions?" Henry asked. "If you cannot, we'll have him transported to Stoneleigh."

"Oh. Yes. Of course." She couldn't take her eyes off that scarred patch of skin. What did the rest of him look like? Did he have hair everywhere?

Coleclough's eyelids fluttered open. "Mistress Cowdrey." He swallowed heavily. "Sir," he said to Henry. " I–I 'm sorry… "

"Shhh," she whispered, resting her hand on his brow. It was hot and damp. "Rest. There's no need to talk and certainly no need to apologize."

He gave her a weak smile and settled into the pillow.

Matilda entered carrying a basin and ewer. Linens hung over her arm. Jane the scullery maid followed, carrying a tray with jug, cups, bread and cheese.

"Cook thought ye both might be thirsty after yer ordeal, mistress," Jane said.

"Thank you, and thank Cook for me. Matilda, get bandages and see if we have any Solomon's Seal ointment." Both maids left. Henry remained. "Help Mr. Coleclough to sit up," she told her brother.

She gathered the other cushions and propped them behind him, then poured ale into the cup and handed it to her patient. He took it in both hands and drained it. She filled it again, but he didn't drink.

"Hungry?" she asked.

"No, thank you." He seemed surprised by that. "I'm almost always hungry. The maids tell me I eat more than anyone they've ever known. Perhaps I ate just before… " He looked down at the cup then set it on the table near the bed.

"Perhaps you did," she said quietly. She dipped the linen in the basin she'd filled with water from the ewer and cleaned around the head wound. He grunted but said nothing. "Tell me if it hurts too much, and I'll stop."

He didn't speak as she gently washed away the blood, but he did wince often, and once she heard his teeth grinding. By the time she'd finished, the water in the basin was red. Matilda returned with the bandages and a small jar then left again. Lucy dabbed some of the ointment on a clean square of linen and gently applied it to the wound.

Coleclough tensed and hissed through his teeth.

"I know it stings," she said, "but it'll help seal the wound." She folded a small cloth and placed it against the wound and directed him to hold it as she wrapped a bandage around his head.

"Thank you," he said, when she stood back to admire her handiwork.

He was certainly a polite man. She'd give him that. Not at all ill-mannered like he'd been on their first meeting. "Mr. Coleclough, do you mind if we, uh, remove your jerkin and shirt. I need to see your other injuries."

He glanced at Henry who had sat down on the chair near the table, his elbows on his knees, watching. "I don't know if you ought to…"

"I need to see," she said.

He blushed. Surely he couldn't be embarrassed? Such a man would have revealed much more than his bare chest to a woman before.

"Better do as she says," Henry said. "She may look meek, but she likes to get her own way."

"Henry," she snapped.

Her brother laughed. Coleclough's blush deepened. She helped him out of his jerkin and when it came to his shirt, she wished she'd got him to remove it before she'd put the bandage on his head, but they managed to get it off without too much difficulty.

"Oh," she murmured, his shirt bunched up in her hands. "Oh my." She didn't know where to look. He was covered in bruises. No cuts, thankfully, but the purple blemishes were everywhere—on his chest, shoulders, stomach. "You poor man," she whispered.

Henry swore softly, shook his head.

Coleclough seemed surprised too. He looked down and studied himself.

"Are your, er, legs sore? Do you think they're bruised?"

"They feel fine." He spoke absently, as if his mind were elsewhere. He was gingerly inspecting the bruises on his chest, or so Lucy thought until he said, "Where did all these scars come from?"

Lucy peered closer. So did Henry. "They look old to me," Henry said, sitting back in the chair again. "I'd say they've been there for years."

"Years?" Coleclough shook his head. "Impossible. The only scars I have are on my back from… " He cleared his throat but didn't finish the sentence. He glanced up at Lucy through his thick lashes and pressed his lips together.

"From what, Mr. Coleclough?" She laid a hand on his arm. "I think you'd better tell us. It may shed some light on the mystery of what happened to you."

"I doubt it." He sighed and sat forward. "Take a look on my back. There should be four scars there from when my father's man beat me once." He frowned. "It was my fault," he added quickly. "I disobeyed him."

Lucy moved to where she could see his back. She gasped then covered her mouth with her hand. Her stomach rolled and bile rose to her throat. She caught hold of the bedpost and turned away, closed her eyes, only to open them when she felt Henry move up beside her. He rubbed his hand through his hair and his gaze locked with hers. He looked as sick as she felt.

Beneath the fresh bruises was a web of scars, all a similar length and width, as if the same long, narrow object had inflicted them, and the same hand. They were white and smooth and must have been there a long time.

"Your father's servant did that to you?" Lucy whispered. How could a parent be so cruel as to order such a thing?

"There's only four." Coleclough spoke as if it were nothing… and as if there were really only four. There must have been ten times that many.

Henry put a hand on Lucy's arm and shook his head. "When did you say you got these?" he asked Coleclough.

"About a month ago."

Lucy blinked at Henry. There was no way he'd gotten those scars a mere month ago.

Henry frowned and chewed his bottom lip. Lucy was about to tell her patient that he must have been mistaken, when Henry said, "How old are you, Mr. Coleclough?"

"Call me Nicholas, or Nick. My father is called Mr. Coleclough. I'm eighteen, sir."

CHAPTER 4

*E*ighteen! There was no way the muscular man with the hard, stubbly jaw was a youth of eighteen. Lucy judged him to be five and twenty at the youngest, but likely older.

"Why are you both looking at me like that?" Coleclough asked. His wide-eyed gaze flicked between Lucy and Henry, growing wider with each passing moment. "Is there something wrong?"

"Mr. Coleclough," Henry began. He did not go on but cast a pleading look at Lucy.

She sat on the edge of the bed and clasped the man's hand in her own to reassure him. His long fingers wrapped around hers. He looked vulnerable all of a sudden, and very worried. It was completely at odds with the masculinity.

"Mr. Coleclough," she said gently, "the blow to your head must have wiped away more than your recent memory. I think it has made you forget several years."

"*Years?*" His abrupt laughter fell flat when neither Lucy nor Henry joined in.

"There is nothing of the youth about you." She indicated his face, his chest. "I'd place your age in the late twenties."

"What year is it?"

"The year of our lord, fifteen hundred and ninety-nine."

He gaped at them. "It cannot be. You jest."

"I'm afraid not. What year were you born?"

"Seventy."

"Then you're nine-and-twenty."

His hand fluttered lightly over the hairs on his bruised chest. "That explains this." He flexed both upper arms, and the muscles bulged. "And these. My deeper voice too."

It was a calmer response than she expected, particularly for an eighteen year-old, which, in a strange way, he was.

"That's not all," Henry said. "There are a lot more than four scars on your back."

Coleclough leaned forward and reached around, but it must have hurt because he grunted and stopped trying. "How many?"

"Too many to count."

"Never mind that," Lucy said quickly. She gave Henry a glare, but her brother merely shrugged. Sometimes he could be so thick-headed. "I'm sure you'll get your memory back after a few days of rest, Mr. Coleclough. We'll be happy to accommodate you here while you recuperate."

"Call me Nick," he said. "And thank you for your offer, Mistress Cowdrey. Sir?"

Henry nodded. "If my sister thinks you'll be better off resting here, then I won't go against her wishes." He looked out the window where the sun hung low in the sky. "I have to go. Lucy, a word."

She followed Henry out to the landing and shut the door. "Most odd," she said. "At least he seems to be taking the news of his lost years rather well."

"Do you think it will take him long to regain his memory?"

"Henry, your faith in my skills is flattering, but I'm no physician. I really don't know what to expect. All we can do is patch him up and send him on his way back to Kent."

"Hmmm."

"Why the frown?"

"You're not to be alone with him."

"You've already said that. Don't worry. I'll have Matilda with me the entire time, although I don't think he's in any state to seduce me. Besides, he seems rather shy and sweet. I'd wager seducing older women isn't in his nature." She laughed. It seemed rather absurd to have a grown man with the mind of a youth in her guest bedchamber.

"It's no laughing matter. We know nothing about him."

"You think he could be a danger? Henry, you saw him in there. He's as well-mannered as any young gentleman." Yet mere hours beforehand, he had not been. The blow had not only wiped out his memory, it had changed his nature. She had to remember that it might reverse at any time.

He crossed his arms. "Of all people, you should know that good manners are no indication of a gentleman's worth."

Her face heated and she looked away. He had a very good point. The son of the neighboring gentleman had been her friend as a child and her betrothed later. But after a six-month sojourn with an aunt in Surrey, Edmund had returned home to announce that he'd found the daughter of the local nobleman more to his liking and promptly stated that he'd never promised to wed Lucy. Not in front of witnesses anyway. It was true that the discussion had occurred behind the big oak tree with no one within earshot, and only after she'd refused to give Edmund her maidenhead. A moment later, she'd found her skirts pushed up around her hips and herself betrothed.

Or so she'd thought. Upon his return from Surrey, not only had she found her intended betrothed to another, but her reputation in ruins.

"My apologies, Lucy, I didn't mean… I'm sorry." Henry sighed.

"It's all right. But Nick thinks he's eighteen. Do you remember what you were like at eighteen around gentlewomen a few years older than yourself?"

"Yes, and that's what worries me."

She rolled her eyes. "This conversation is pointless anyway, because I'll have Matilda with me the entire time."

"I hope that will be enough," he muttered.

"Henry!"

"Lucy," he said sternly, "you seem to be forgetting some important facts. The man is traveling alone, far from home. He was beaten half to death, but not by thieves. To me that means someone has a grievance against him. Until we know more about Nicholas Coleclough, we tread cautiously. Understand?"

"You are not telling me anything that hasn't already occurred to me." Her own reservations stemmed more from the man she'd met before the attack, not the boy sitting propped up in her guest bed. They were two completely different people. "I promise I'll be on my guard."

Henry wrinkled one side of his nose. "I'm being the irritating big brother again, aren't I?"

"A little."

"It's difficult. I'm trying to see you as a woman of one and twenty, but I really only know you as a girl. I feel like we're almost strangers."

Henry had been away in London for the last three years, returning only between terms. Usually he spent those brief holidays helping their father and brother on the farm, not talking to his little sister.

"I'll fetch Matilda," he said. "Wait out here until she arrives."

Lucy waited, but only until he was down the stairs and out of earshot. Then she opened the door to the guest bedchamber, but did not shut it behind her. She wasn't a complete fool.

Nick sat as still as a statue on the bed, hands in his lap, and a startled look on a very red face.

"Is everything all right?" she asked.

He nodded quickly. "Of course. Why wouldn't it be? You and your brother have been very kind to me, madam."

So why did he look so guilty? "If I am to call you Nick, you should call me Lucy."

"Lucy. It comes from the Latin for light."

"Yes, I know."

"You understand Latin?"

"My father insisted I learn with my brothers, although I must admit I found it a dull subject. I preferred to be out of doors than in the schoolroom."

"Me too. Father says that's why I'm always getting into trouble."

Trouble that necessitated all those marks on his back? Lucy shuddered.

Matilda came in, and Lucy indicated she should sit in the chair by the door. "What sort of things did you do to get into trouble, Nick?"

"I'm not sure I should reveal all my secrets." He smirked, but it quickly faded and he looked down at the hands in his lap. "I wonder what I did to deserve this?" he said quietly.

"Perhaps you did nothing." But she didn't think he believed it any more than she did. Not with the full pack sitting on the floor beside the bed.

"Open it," he said, indicating the pack as if he'd read her mind. "Perhaps it'll provide a clue as to why I'm so far from home."

She picked up the pack and tipped the contents over the bed covers, near his legs. There was a wooden cup, trencher, clean shirt, provisions wrapped in linen, and—good lord!—another three knives of different sizes plus a club. Together with the two knives strapped to his ankle and arm, that made six weapons. "What do you need so many for?"

He said nothing but stared down at the objects.

"And what's this?" She picked up a long piece of polished wood with a strip of metal slotted into a narrow slit carved into the side.

"Careful." He caught her hand so fast she didn't have time to pull back. His hands were warm, his touch gentle as he cradled her for a moment before taking the object. "That's a knife too." He pulled the metal blade out of the slit to show her then slid it back.

"I've never seen a knife like that before."

Nick weighed it in his palm. "Neither have I."

"Yet you knew how it worked. That's a good sign. You're recalling things from your lost years already."

He lifted one shoulder but didn't look convinced.

Lucy followed his gaze to all the weapons arrayed across the bed covers and felt a chill creep down her spine. No simple traveler required so many.

Nick returned the knives and provisions to his pack. "What's this?" He held up a block of wood the size of a fist. Part of it had been carved away so that a pair of what appeared to be floppy ears protruded from the top at one end.

"The beginnings of an animal perhaps?"

He turned it over and ran his thumb over a smooth ear.

"Can you whittle?" she asked.

"No. At least, not that I know of."

"It appears to be a skill you acquired in recent years. I wonder what you were going to make."

He placed the block of wood back into his pack. She sighed. She had hoped he'd pick up one of the small knives and try to see if the skill returned to him, but he didn't seem interested.

"We should put some Solomon's Seal ointment on the rest of your bruises," she said. "Sit forward a little, so I may reach your back."

She picked up the jar of ointment and asked Matilda to fetch her a clean strip of linen from the trunk under the window, but Matilda's only response was a gentle snore, so Lucy fetched it herself.

"I won't rub hard," she said, perching on the edge of the bed. She dipped the cloth into the jar and gently dabbed the bruises on his back. He sucked air between his teeth and tensed, but after a moment he seemed to relax again. "Am I hurting you?"

"No." He tipped his head forward as she rubbed a particularly nasty bruise on his shoulder. "The cloth is a little rough, though."

She set the linen on the table and continued to rub the ointment over his back with her hands. "Better?"

"Mmmm."

She was careful and intended to be fast, but the sight of his damaged back with its old scars and new bruises made her feel sick, yet fascinated at the same time. She traced the longest and deepest scar from shoulder blade to the middle of his back.

Nick groaned, a deep, low sound that vibrated through him. His bandaged head hung forward, and he arched his back against her hand. She pressed her other hand to his skin, slick and warm from the ointment, and lightly stroked every inch of that broad back. She followed the line of other scars, circled some bruises, massaged his neck where the skin was unmarked. He groaned again, louder, and she shot a glance at Matilda. The maid still slept in the chair by the door, her chin on her chest, her breathing heavy and even.

Lucy concentrated on her task, tried to focus on the bruises alone, but she was fascinated by the beautiful yet damaged skin, and the strong, muscular back with its gruesome branding.

Tears pricked her eyes, and she quickly removed her hands. After all, she hardly knew this man. His injuries, past and present, should not disturb her the way they did. She was too soft for her own good. That's what her eldest brother Simon had told her after Edmund Mallam broke their betrothal. Perhaps he was right. Beatings happened all the time. There was no point letting it upset her.

Nick tilted his head and looked at her through heavy-lidded eyes. "Something wrong?" he asked thickly.

"I'll do the bruises on your chest now."

He sighed and straightened. She shuffled down the bed and dipped her fingers in the jar, but paused before rubbing it on. It was highly inappropriate to touch his chest. Perhaps she shouldn't do it, and he could tend the bruises himself.

But he made no move take over. Indeed, he smiled crookedly as if he sensed her unease—and enjoyed it. The man had a wicked, impish streak.

"Something wrong?" he asked. "Too much hair?"

She laughed. "No." She gently rubbed the ointment on his upper chest. The tiny, springy hairs glistened, and his skin warmed as she worked her way over the undulations of muscle and ribs, down toward his stomach where most of the bruising centered.

His breathing suddenly quickened the further down her hand went. She gently rubbed ointment into the purplish bruises, some of them so large they joined up with others. She followed the path of fine hair, tending to each bruise as she went. She forced herself to focus on his injuries and not the hardness of his body or the smoothness of his skin.

Or what lay beneath the covers, only inches from her fingers.

"Lucy." He whispered her name, barely audible over his heavy breathing. He closed his hand over hers, stilling it.

She glanced up at his face and was struck by the burning heat in his gaze, the tightness of his mouth. She knew that look. He was warring with himself. Desire versus propriety. A gentleman's war. It seemed propriety had won, but only just.

His hand slipped slowly off hers, freeing her again. Free to go under the covers, if she chose to.

"I should leave," she said.

"No!" He cleared his throat. "Stay. I... I enjoy your company. I don't want to be alone. Not yet." The desire disappeared, replaced by naked longing that was childlike by comparison.

She wiped her hands on the dry end of the cloth and placed it beside the jar on the table. She felt his gaze on her, drinking in her every move, and her skin tingled in response.

She should not like the attention, and certainly should know better than to welcome it.

"Of course." She hoped he didn't detect the slight quiver in her voice, the tremble of her hands as she clasped them in her lap. "Shall we talk? It might help you remember some details of your lost years."

"A good idea. What do you want to know?"

"Start with your family. You've already mentioned a father. What about other members?"

She sat on the chair beside the bed and blew out a breath. That had been close. She'd almost kissed him, almost lifted the bedcovers to see if he was big *everywhere*. Lucy covered her smile with her fingers, but he wasn't watching her anymore. He scratched his chin, his gaze unfocused, distant.

"I have a brother, Thomas. He's two years older and lets me know it. He used to wrestle me and throw me in the duck pond." He chuckled. "That's how I learned to swim. But last spring I grew bigger than him, and he took a turn in the pond. I'd wager I'm even bigger again now."

It sounded like the sort of rivalry Simon and Henry had growing up. "Let me guess. Thomas used his position as oldest brother to lord it over you, reminding you that he would inherit and would one day be head of the family."

"Spoken like a woman with brothers."

She laughed. "My brothers are best of friends, but fierce rivals too."

"Aye, it's the same with Thomas and me. It's just the two of us, and Father of course, except when he goes to court in London."

"Court?"

"He's a baron."

"Oh." A baron's son at Cowdrey Farm! Well, well. "Do you ever go with him?"

"Not me. He took Thomas last time."

"Why not you?"

"I… got into trouble. My punishment was to stay home with no one but the servants for company."

"What about neighbors or nearby villagers?"

"I was forbidden to leave the estate." He smirked and leaned forward. "That didn't stop me." He spoke low and glanced at the door as if he were watching for his father. "I snuck into the village and met some lads my own age."

Met? "Did you not know these lads beforehand?"

He shook his head. "Going to the village was banned unless Father accompanied us."

"Banned?"

"By Father."

She gaped at him. He seemed to not think that odd. "You do not mention your mother."

"She died when I was very young."

"I'm so sorry."

"Thank you."

"So it was just your father, Thomas, and you at Coleclough Hall?"

"And the servants. We had tutors too. Father hires only the best."

"Would you consider them your friends then?"

He lifted his shoulders. "My brother is my only true friend. We do everything together, although sometimes against his wishes. I think he only agrees to join in because he hates to be shown up as a coward by his younger brother." He laughed, but it died rapidly.

"What is it, Nick?"

He frowned and plucked the blanket over his lap. "It's nothing."

"Go on," she said gently. "Any information you can offer may help us piece together the puzzle of your lost years."

"It's not so much information as... a question." He lifted his gaze to hers. His brown eyes were huge. "Do you think they know where I am? Thomas and Father?"

Her heart ached. Nick must have felt so alone without his family. She did, and she still had Henry for company, plus she knew what had led her to Cowdrey Farm. Nick did not.

"I'm sure they do. It sounds like you cared for them, and I'd wager they care just as much for you. You must have written to them."

"With what? There are no writing materials in the pack."

"Perhaps you were traveling together when you wandered off and got lost. They could be looking for you now. I'll send someone to ask in the village tomorrow."

He shook his head slowly. "That may be true if I were indeed only eighteen. But I'm a grown man. What grown man travels with his father and brother?"

"A wife then."

He laughed and shook his head. "I doubt it."

"Why? Men your age are almost always married. Particularly gentlemen's sons."

"Speaking from experience?"

"My oldest brother has just married, and my parents are hoping to have Henry betrothed by Christmas. There are few families of our acquaintance that Father wants to be linked to, otherwise he'd be wed by now."

"And you?" Nick said quietly. "Are you betrothed, Lucy?"

"I…" Her face heated. Damnation and curses. Her complexion was the worst!

"I'm sorry," he said. "I didn't want to make you uncomfortable. Forget I said anything." Before she could decide how much she wanted to tell him, he said, "As far as I know, at the age of eighteen, Father has yet to arrange a bride for me."

She crossed her arms and sat back in the chair. "Perhaps we've just struck upon the reason you are in Hampshire and not Kent."

"I don't understand."

"You're married."

"I am?"

"You married a Hampshire girl and moved here. Since your brother will inherit Coleclough, there's nothing to keep you in Kent, so your father must have found you a suitable girl here."

"Then why I am I traveling without my wife, and on foot? I should be on horseback."

He should also be dressed like a gentleman and not like a journeyman. Perhaps he'd somehow lost his money and wound up a pauper who needed to travel from village to village to earn a few coins. Lucy hoped he didn't have a wife if that were the case. It would be a hard life for her.

He sighed. "Unless I can remember, I will never know what happened, or where I'm supposed to be. Lucy, what if my memory never returns?"

She touched his hand and he curled his fingers around hers, as if he needed to hold onto another human being. "We'll take you home to Kent and find Coleclough Hall. All will be well when you see your family again."

She wasn't sure when she'd shifted from letting Nick find his own way home to driving him, but she knew that it was right. As soon as his head had mended enough to travel, she would have some of the servants accompany her if her brother couldn't free himself from the farm.

"Now, tell me more about your childhood in Kent," she said. "It may jog more recent memories. If it's not too hard for you, may I ask how your mother died?"

"Of course you may. I was only a babe, and I don't remember her at all. She died from a weak heart, Father said."

"Was her likeness ever painted?"

"No, unfortunately. I would have liked to have seen her. Our housekeeper is the only servant still at Coleclough Hall from my mother's time, and she says I look very much like her. Thomas is fair like our father, but I'm dark. Mother was the daughter of a merchant from Florence."

"How interesting. That certainly explains your complexion and black hair. I've never seen hair so… " Beautiful. "… dark." She coughed and looked away, but the more she tried to hide her warm cheeks, the hotter they got.

Nick chuckled. "Your freckles become brighter when you blush."

So bright they felt like they would combust. "I, uh, tell me about… " *What?* Brutus wandered in and sat at Lucy's feet, tongue out, tail wagging, waiting for a pat. "Dogs. Do you have dogs at Coleclough Hall?" Good lord—dogs? She concentrated on stroking Brutus and hoped Nick didn't think her question quite as pathetic as she did. Brutus certainly didn't. His tail thumped the rush matting in a rhythmic beat.

"Several." He put his hand down, and Brutus got up to lick the fingers. Nick smiled. "What's his name?"

"Brutus."

"Is he a good hunter?"

"Not in the least. That's why Father gave him to me. Brutus shows no inclination to chase other creatures. He'd rather play with them. He's much too gentle for his own good."

He smiled. "There's no such thing. I never liked hunting myself, but Father insisted we both participate." He scratched Brutus's ears, and the dog rested his chin on the bed and stared adoringly at Nick.

"Supper's ready, mistress," said a maid from the doorway, balancing a tray on one hand.

Matilda woke up with a start, blinked at Lucy and Nick, then wiped the drool from the corner of her mouth. "I was just, er, finking."

"Thinking, Matilda, not finking." Lucy had been trying to teach the maid her letters since their arrival at Cowdrey Farm, in addition to helping her to speak properly too. The previous mistress had not cared a whit for that sort of thing. Indeed, she'd been neglectful at best, and cruel at worst. Henry had decided to keep all the staff to ensure a smooth transition between owners, and Lucy was rather glad. According to the senior servants, the previous mistress used to beat the maids, and the master would pretend not to notice. None of the staff had been sorry to see them go, particularly once they realized Henry and Lucy were not like their cousins.

"I brought up Mr. Coleclough's supper," said the maid. "Yours is in the small parlor, mistress, as usual. Mr. Cowdrey says he'll join you soon."

Lucy cleared the table near the bed, and the maid set the tray on it. "Will there be anything else, mistress?"

"No, that's all for now. Mr. Coleclough?"

Nick stifled a yawn with his hand. "I have everything I need, thank you. You've been most kind."

"Then I'll bid you goodnight. You need your rest, and Matilda will be wanting her supper too. I'll see you in the morning."

"Goodnight."

* * *

Lucy awoke with a start. Her bedchamber was dark. The crescent moon cast little light through the window, just enough to illuminate the shapes of the furniture but none of the detail. She sat up. Listened.

There it was again. A sound coming from somewhere in the house nearby. Low voices? It was difficult to tell.

She slipped out of bed and crept to the door. The rush mat was rough against the soles of her bare feet and the night air warm enough that she didn't need slippers or a housecoat over her nightshift.

She put her ear to the door and heard the same sound that had woken her. A voice, too muffled to make out the words. Then, "No. NO!"

Nick!

CHAPTER 5

"*H*enry! Wake up!" Lucy banged on his door. He was a heavy sleeper, but he couldn't fail to be woken by her knocking.

The door opened almost immediately, and Henry, dressed in a shirt that reached to his knees, blinked sleepily back at her. "What is it?"

"It's Nick. I think someone might be in his bedchamber." She ran back through the rooms, Henry at her heels. "I should have gone straight there. Something's wrong."

"You did the right thing," he said. "If someone is in there, you won't be able to match them."

They reached Nick's door and for some reason, Henry hesitated.

Nick's voice came clear through the heavy wood. "Stop! Please."

"Bloody hell." Henry barged in, but stopped suddenly in the entrance. Lucy slammed into his back.

"What is it?" She pushed Henry aside. "Nick?"

It was difficult to make out much in the dull light, but it was clear that Nick was sitting up on the bed, staring at them. Alone.

"I, uh… " He rubbed both hands down his face. "Is something wrong?"

"I heard shouting," Lucy said, approaching the bed slowly. "I thought someone was in here… "

"Shouting?" he echoed.

"Are you all right?" Henry strode around the room, checking the shadows.

"Yes," Nick said.

"There doesn't appear to be anyone else in here."

"There isn't. I–I was having a vivid dream."

Two of the male servants appeared at the door, feet bare and daggers in hand. Henry sent them away with assurances that nothing was amiss.

Lucy sat on his bed. Now that she was closer, she could see Nick's hand shaking and the sheen on his brow. He gave her a weak smile that did nothing to ease her mind.

"I'm sorry I woke you," he said.

"It's all right." She took his hand and squeezed. "I'm just relived you're unharmed. It sounded… well, it sounded awful. Do you often have nightmares?" He shrugged and she realized her mistake. "Oh, of course. You don't remember."

"No."

"What was it about?"

"Nothing."

"Nothing? How can it be nothing?"

"I mean I don't remember."

"Lucy," Henry growled, "it's none of your business. Leave him be."

She bit her tongue to stop herself arguing with him. She could do that later. For now, she needed to care for her patient. "Can I get you anything to help settle you back to sleep?" she asked Nick.

"No, thank you. You've already done enough."

"Come, Lucy," Henry said. "Let's go."

"Are you sure I can't get you anything, Nick? Does your head pain you? Do you need a tonic?"

"I'm fine. Don't worry about me." He squeezed her hands as she had done his, then let go and folded them over his naked chest.

"Just let the man rest," Henry said.

She joined him outside on the landing and shut the door. "Did you have to be so ill-mannered in there? The poor man had a nightmare, the least we could do is offer him comfort."

He drew her away toward the door leading to her own rooms. "Lucy, I'm tired. I don't like to be dragged from my bed in the middle of the night to offer a grown man comfort."

"You need to remember that he thinks he's eighteen, barely a man."

"Eighteen is certainly man enough."

"Ordinarily, yes, but he's wide-eyed and innocent in many ways, not at all like any youth I've met of that age."

"He is not a child, Lucy."

"But he *is* my patient until he recovers. And don't worry, I am *very* aware that he's not a child."

Henry must have been exhausted because ordinarily such sarcasm would trigger a lecture on not putting herself in a position to be taken advantage of by men. It was something she'd endured more and more after the sorry affair with Edmund Mallam came to light. Indeed, her brothers had been worse than her parents in that regard. Simon had even told her she shouldn't be allowed to be alone with a man ever again, but fortunately her father hadn't been quite so draconian. Lucy suspected her mother's influence there.

"What do you suppose he was dreaming about?" she said. "Something quite awful if all that shouting is anything to go by."

Henry sighed. "Right now, I don't care. I'm going back to bed. If it happens again, just ignore him. He'll stop eventually."

She rolled her eyes, but it was too dark for him to have seen.

* * *

HENRY WAS JUST AS ILL-TEMPERED the following morning before he headed out to the barn. Lucy hailed him from the henhouse and trotted over to meet him.

"I wanted to talk to you about Nick," she said, holding an egg in each hand.

"What now?"

"Do you think you could pretend to be in a jovial mood? Your behavior is becoming more boorish every day."

He blew out a breath and looked Heavenward. "I apologize. I'm tired, and it looks like it'll be another hot day, which means we'll probably achieve less than we should."

"Oh, Henry, I'm sorry. Go."

He put an arm around her shoulder and kissed the cap on the top of her head. "I apologize. Tell me what troubles you."

"It can wait until later."

"Are you sure?"

She gave him a gentle shove. "Go. The men are waiting." She nodded in the direction of a cluster of farm hands chatting to the grooms near the barn as they prepared the horses and cart.

"I won't be back until the end of the day, but we can talk then." He began to walk off, but stopped. "You'll keep Matilda with you at all times when you're with Coleclough."

"I will." *If possible*.

She watched him join his men at the barn then placed the eggs in the basket near the henhouse and searched for more. By the time her basket was full, she was starving.

She decided to wait until after breakfast to see Nick, but he surprised her by being in the kitchen when she brought in the basket of eggs.

"Good morning," he said. There was no sign on his handsome, smiling face that he'd had a poor night's sleep, or indeed that he'd had a nightmare at all.

"You shouldn't be out of bed yet," she said, handing the basket to one of the kitchen maids.

"I feel better, and I can't stay in bed all day." He gazed longingly at the eggs that the cook was systematically cracking and emptying into a large pan.

"Hungry?" the cook asked.

"Starving."

"Shall I serve your breakfasts in the small parlor today, mistress?" Matilda asked.

"An excellent idea," Lucy said.

She led Nick into the smaller of the two parlors at the front of the house. He stopped just inside the doorway, and she thought his gaze had fixed on the table near the window, but on closer inspection, he was actually taking in his surroundings. His gaze, half-hidden beneath those thick lashes, flicked around the room.

"It's all right," she said. "You can look around as much as you want."

"Pardon?"

"You're trying not to let me see you looking. It doesn't embarrass me. This room is my favorite in the whole house. Or it is now, after I changed the furniture and hung the tapestries on the walls."

"My apologies, I didn't realize I was doing it so furtively." He pulled out the chair for her at the table and she sat. "I like this room too."

Her cousins had divided the old great hall into a series of rooms in the modern style, each with its own fireplace and chimney. The smaller of the two new parlors was the coziest in the mornings and had the best outlook with views over the front garden, the orchard, and the woods in the distance. Lucy liked to eat her breakfast alone there and plan what needed doing. This part of Hampshire was extraordinarily pretty, and now that the roses were in bloom, the garden didn't look quite as sparse as it had when she first arrived. It still needed a lot of attention, but with some of the male servants to do the digging and heavy work, it would be done in no time. She'd mapped out an entire year's worth of planting from that small parlor, not to mention drawn up the plan for the new front entrance to the house.

"How is your head today?" she asked.

"It feels enormous with this bandage."

"You have to keep wearing it for now. At least until Widow Dawson can inspect it."

"Widow Dawson?"

"The wise woman of Sutton Grange."

He pulled a face. "I've never held much stock with wise women."

"Never? Is this coming from Nicholas Coleclough the youth or the man?"

One side of his mouth kicked up. "Youth."

"Ah."

"Ah? Does that have another meaning in Hampshire, or does it mean the same as it does in Kent? You don't believe me."

"I believe you. But I think your view is colored by your father's, since he appears to be the biggest influence in your eighteen-year-old life."

He lifted one shoulder and winced. "I suppose you're right. If you say your Widow Dawson is good, then I'll believe it."

"Does the bruise on your shoulder still hurt? You cringed just now."

"I hoped you hadn't seen that."

"You are my patient, Nick. Now is not the time to be all manly and brave."

He chuckled. "Yes, madam."

"What about the other bruises?"

"Those hurt too, although less than yesterday. That ointment must be working." He was wearing the clean shirt that had been in his pack, the old one having gone to one of the maids to wash. He hadn't limped into the parlor, so it seemed he was unharmed from the waist down after all. That was a relief, perhaps more so for him than her.

"Why are you smiling?" he asked, folding his arms on the table and leaning closer.

"I'm not!"

"You were. Now you're blushing too."

"And you are incorrigible."

His smile turned wicked. "I've been called worse."

Was he flirting with her? She wasn't sure whether to be alarmed, flattered or disturbed.

Matilda entered with a tray laden with bread, butter, poached and boiled eggs, and cheese. Another maid followed behind with a jug and two cups, trenchers and knives.

"Shall I stay, mistress?" asked Matilda, setting the trenchers of food on the table.

"Have you eaten?" Lucy asked.

"Aye."

"Then I'm afraid you have to. Henry's orders."

"I don't mind. I'll just sit over there and close me eyes while I fink. Think."

Perhaps Lucy should set some writing tasks for Matilda to practice while she chaperoned. If Nick was going to be with them for a while, it seemed a shame to waste valuable time. Like all of the servants, Matilda worked hard, and the time she had left for learning was limited, but she was quite determined to succeed. It's why Lucy was happy to persist.

"You're very good to let her sleep," Nick said when it was clear from Matilda's snoring that she'd nodded off.

"I don't mind. She's a good worker when she's not chaperoning me."

"You're not worried I'll do something… ungentlemanly while she sleeps?"

She grinned. "No. One shout from me, and she'll wake up and other servants will come running."

"Henry is worried."

"Henry is my only male relative here. He thinks it his duty to protect me from strange men who get beaten up in his meadow and lose their memories."

He stabbed a piece of bacon with his knife. "Happen a lot, does it?"

"Enough to make him anxious."

"You seem very close. As close as Thomas and me, without the wrestling and tossing each other in the duck pond part."

"We used to wrestle when we were younger. I was quite good until he began to grow and decided Simon was more interesting to play with."

He chewed, thoughtful, then swallowed and said, "So what did you do after Henry stopped playing with you? Who did you spend time with? Your mother?"

"Only when she was teaching me to stitch or play the virginals. Sometimes we paid calls on our neighbors or the village women who had daughters my age. Actually, we did that a lot. It was great fun, and I made some lovely friends. I miss them now, but we write often."

He paused with a chunk of bread halfway to his mouth. "You had friends outside your own family?"

"Of course. Family aren't friends, they're… family."

"I suppose so," he muttered and bit into the bread.

She said nothing, just let the silence stretch in the hope he would say more, but he didn't. Odder and odder. Did he not have friends other than his own brother? What sort of father would deny his son the friendship of other boys his own age?

"What else did you do when you were my age?" he asked.

She pressed her hand to her breast. "I am deeply wounded! I am quite a few years younger than you yet."

He laughed. "I mean when you were eighteen."

She smiled. "I studied two mornings and three afternoons a week with my tutors. I'd write letters, draw, and sometimes help the gardeners or the kitchen staff for a bit of company. I liked to make the bread. Kneading dough calms the mind."

"The staff here say you like to help them too." There was no derision in his tone, which she expected from a lord's son.

"You spoke to them about me?"

He nodded. "Just now in the kitchen. They couldn't say enough nice things about you."

"The previous mistress of Cowdrey Farm wasn't so kind, you see," she said, keeping her voice low lest Matilda wasn't really asleep. "Some of the maids told me how she used to beat them, and their master would… well, some of the things he did don't bear repeating. My brother and I are cut from different cloth."

"The previous owners were your cousins, is that right?"

"Yes."

"But you never met them?"

"No."

"The cook said they came to a tragic end at your neighbor's house."

"Stoneleigh. Susanna and Orlando Holt live there now."

"Orlando Holt?" He frowned and his mouth twisted to the side.

She sat forward. "Does the name mean something to you?"

He pressed his fingers to his forehead. "No. It's an unusual name, that's all." His fingers rubbed his temples in a slow circular motion.

Lucy rose and squatted beside him. "You have a headache?"

He nodded.

"Why didn't you tell me?"

"I didn't want to bother you."

"It's no bother. I want to know what hurts and where. I *need* to know." She clasped his arm. "Come on. Back to bed. You need to take a tonic and lie down."

He sighed and allowed himself to be led. "Do I have to?"

"Yes."

"I don't usually lie around in bed all day."

"You don't usually have your skull cracked open either. Matilda," she said as they passed the sleeping maid.

The maid's eyes flew open and she shot up off the chair as if it were as hot as coals. "Something wrong, mistress?"

"I'm taking Mr. Coleclough upstairs. Fetch the headache tonic for him."

The maid gave Nick a sympathetic look. "Poor pet. Let the mistress take care o' you, and you'll feel right again soon enough."

Nick followed Lucy upstairs. When she got to the second floor landing, she turned round to say something and caught him staring at her behind. His eyes widened, and she was sure he blushed, although it was difficult to tell.

She hurried into the guest bedchamber and tried to remember what she'd wanted to say but failed.

He removed his boots, the same ones he'd been wearing when she found him because he owned no others, and placed them neatly under the bed, then climbed in. He settled against the pillows and began unlacing his shirt.

"What are you doing?" She cringed at the hysterical pitch of her voice. Could her embarrassment be any more obvious? Apparently it could because her face heated. It must be the same color as the crimson valance.

Nick's mouth did that little quirk at the corners that she was beginning to realize meant he was trying not to show his amusement. It was rather adorable on an otherwise rough-looking man. "Removing my shirt," he said. "Aren't you going to rub more of that ointment on my bruises?"

"You do it."

"But I can't reach the ones on my back."

"Matilda will then."

"I'd wager your hands are smoother."

Lucy was quickly running out of excuses. "I'm not sure it would be appropriate."

"You did it yesterday, and your brother didn't think it inappropriate then."

True. Indeed, he was right on all counts. When he added "please" and peered up at her with those warm brown eyes and fluttered his long lashes, she surrendered completely. He was the sort of man who could easily talk a girl out of her skirts if he chose. If he was like this at eighteen, she could imagine what he must have been like when he'd learned a thing or two about women.

Lucy hadn't forgotten how he'd been when she'd first met him, but the more she thought about it, the more she suspected his gruff behavior that time had been unusual. He *had* come to her aid when he thought she needed it after all.

Matilda entered with the tonic and the jar of Solomon's Seal ointment. "Thought you might need this again today," she said, holding up the jar.

Nick lifted an eyebrow at Lucy, an impish smile on his lips.

"Thank you," she said, trying to ignore him. "We were just discussing whether to apply more or not."

"I think ye should, but you'd know best, mistress. Can I help?"

"Not here, but there's something you can do. Go find one of the lads from the barn and ask him to take the cart into the village. Tell him to speak to Milner at The Plough Inn and find out if anyone by the name of Nicholas Coleclough stayed there or passed through. If the name doesn't mean anything to Milner, the lad should give a description. With Mr. Coleclough's distinctive appearance, he would have been noticed if he'd been to Sutton Grange. Milner would know. That man is the Argus of the village," she said to Nick. "He sees everything. Oh and Matilda," Lucy said as the maid walked off, "one more thing. Tell the lad to fetch Widow Dawson. He's to offer her a goodly sum to make it worth her while."

"Yes, mistress. I'll send the Greene boy. He's the only one who could remember all that."

She left, and a heavy silence filled the room. Lucy felt Nick's gaze on her, but when she looked at him out of the corner of her eye, his lashes were half-lowered like a protective shield, and it was difficult to tell what he was looking at. The man was quite an expert at furtive glances.

She measured out a small amount of the headache tonic in a spoon then handed it to him. Once he'd swallowed, she picked up the ointment jar.

"Ready?"

"Are you sure?" he asked. "We're all alone in here. Your brother won't be happy."

"If you'd rather we waited for Matilda's return, then I'll—"

"No! If you want to start now, then so do I." He leaned forward off the pillows so that she could reach his back.

She sat beside him and dripped a few drops of ointment onto her palm then splayed her hand across his back just below his right shoulder. He drew in a breath, and let it out slowly as he arched into her. His skin was warm, smooth despite the markings, and she stroked gently, careful not to press too hard lest she hit a sore spot.

Her gaze followed the path of her hands, up to one shoulder then across to the other, down either side of his spine to where it disappeared into his breeches. The map of scars and bruises fascinated and appalled her at the same time. The pain he must have endured…

It was the old scars that bothered her more than the new bruises. They would always be with him. Someone had made sure to strike him hard enough to leave permanent marks.

She wanted to ask him questions, try to tap into his buried memories, but that just seemed unnecessarily cruel. Perhaps it was best if he never remembered—except in his nightmares. She wondered if the previous night's dream had given him more pieces to his puzzle. If it had, he didn't show it and didn't seem to want to discuss it.

He groaned and tipped his head forward, and she pulled back. "Am I hurting you?"

"No," he murmured. "Don't stop."

She rubbed the ointment into the ribs at his side then moved back up to his shoulders. The right seemed to have taken the brunt of whatever had hit him, but the left bore the most scars. She touched the longest one that stretched diagonally across half his back, circled the end of it with her thumb, and traced it back up to his shoulder.

He had magnificent shoulders. So wide and powerful, the gentle undulations of muscle, sinew, and bone a pleasure to explore. The sweet scent of the Solomon's Seal filled her nose and head, making her feel like she'd drunk too much strong wine. She had to taste it, taste those shoulders, press her lips to the soft skin there.

She leaned closer until her chest touched his back. He tensed against her but didn't move away, didn't tell her to stop. She couldn't stop, not now. It was like being in a fast-flowing river, and all she could do was keep her head above water and see where the current took her.

She rested her hands on each shoulder and pressed her lips to the end of that long, horrid scar. The spot deserved some kind attention, and she wished to God that her kiss really could make it vanish.

Nick's breathing quickened, and she felt his heart beating through him, drumming out a rhythm that matched her own erratic one. She slipped her arms around his waist, careful not to hold too tight, and lightly teased the hairs on his chest. He sucked in a breath and half turned so she could see his face and he hers. His eyes turned smoky as he studied the freckles across her nose.

"Beautiful," he murmured. He touched her cheek with his fingertips as if to see if the freckles would rub off, then stroked slowly, so achingly slowly, down to her chin. His thumb caressed her bottom lip from corner to corner, his hooded gaze following it as if he'd never seen anything so fascinating. "May I?"

"Yes," she managed to whisper, although goodness knows how he heard it above their pounding heartbeats. "Kiss me."

CHAPTER 6

*N*ick's lips were soft, the kiss tentative, teasing, yet more powerful than any kiss Lucy had ever had. It melted her insides, broke through her reservations and drove all thoughts from her head.

Except one. She wanted him. She wanted to taste this man, explore him, hold him and be held by him.

A deep, resounding throb pulsed through her, and her heart changed its beat to a rhythm that seemed to be drumming out *this man, this man, this man* over and over. Dear God, she was utterly drunk on him.

Without breaking the kiss, she got up on her knees and took his face in her hands. He circled one arm around her waist and laid the other on her ribs just beneath her breast. Too sweet, too hesitant. She placed her hand over his and guided it higher.

His breath hitched. He half moaned, half whimpered against her lips. "I shouldn't."

"Hush."

"But I've never—"

The door opened and Lucy sprang off the bed, fortunately landing on her feet.

"The Greene boy's on his way now," Matilda said, settling into her chair by the door. "He's a good lad and is pleased as pleased you trust him with this errand, mistress."

Lucy made a sound of acknowledgement that came out a strangled gurgle. Her knees felt weak. Her lips still tingled. They tasted of Nick.

"Don't mind me," Matilda said, closing her eyes. "I'll just do my finking in peace over here until you need me again."

Lucy's voice seemed to have fled. She tried to tell Matilda she should use the time to practice her reading or writing, but she did not.

She glanced at Nick. He rubbed the back of his neck and shrugged as if to apologize. She shook her head and gave him a reassuring smile. That kiss had been nobody's fault, and she didn't want his apology for something that had been so beautiful.

Beautiful yet wrong. It wasn't the fact that she was unwed that troubled her—she'd been guilty of more than kissing with Edmund before they were betrothed—it was that Nick might very well be married. A gentleman his age would surely have a wife.

She must not let it happen again. Not until she'd learned more about this mystery man. But when he gave her that quirk of a smile again, she knew avoiding him was going to be difficult.

"What about my chest?" he said, facing her fully.

Your chest is as magnificent as the rest of you. "I haven't forgotten." She tipped more ointment on her palm, rubbed her hands together, and positioned herself on the bed again. Much, much too close.

She kept her gaze focused on her hands, not on his skin or the muscles, and certainly not on his face. Nevertheless, she could feel him watching her, hear his breathing become more and more ragged.

It didn't take long for her to cover his entire chest in the ointment, but she repeated the process again. By the time she'd finished, Matilda's head had tipped back against the wall and her mouth flopped open, breathing the soft, even breaths of someone in deep sleep.

Nick cupped Lucy's cheek, but she drew away.

"You mustn't," she whispered, not looking at him. "*We* mustn't."

"I know." He sighed and slumped back into the pillows. "I can't help it. It's just that… "

She knew she'd regret asking but did anyway. "What?"

"I like you." He shook his head, rubbed his chin. "No, like isn't the right word. When I'm around you I feel a little light in the head."

"That could be your injury."

He chuckled. "My heart beats furiously too. That's not part of my injury." She shrugged, not sure what to say, not wanting to say that he made her feel that way too. Speaking it would be much too dangerous. "It's not just because you're so beautiful either."

She laughed. "Where did you learn to flatter like that? I'm sure it's not something you knew how to do as an isolated eighteen year-old."

"Actually I did have some interest from the girls from the village. That one time I snuck away, I didn't only meet lads, I met girls too. One of them even kissed me."

"Ah, so that's how you learned to be so good at it."

"I doubt it. I felt like a complete fool and when she stuck her tongue in I bit it accidentally."

Lucy smothered a giggle. "You didn't."

He nodded. "It took me by surprise."

"You've obviously kissed a few more women since then because you knew what you were doing just now." She felt the familiar heat creep up her throat, her face, to the roots of her hair.

"Just my luck I can't remember." Nick pressed his knuckles to her cheek as if to cool it. "Or maybe it's the best of luck. Your kisses are the only ones I want to remember." He looped his hand behind the back of her head, entwined his fingers in her hair and gently tugged her closer.

"No," she whispered, pulling away. "Not until your memory returns." And she could be sure there was no other woman. She didn't want to be any man's plaything, someone to fill in the time and amuse him until he returned to his other life, or in the case of Edmund Mallam, a better wife. "We should get to know each other more anyway."

He frowned. "Oh." He glanced down at her breasts then away.

Her hand fluttered to the large collar at her throat. The breast he'd briefly cupped tingled. "Yes, well, that's before I was thinking clearly. As I recall, you were the one who suggested we shouldn't."

"A moment of stupidity on my part," he said and smiled.

But I've never— The words he'd spoken just before Matilda entered didn't seem like a protest but an excuse, or a warning perhaps—he'd never lain with a woman. At least, not that he could remember.

He sighed again, his smile gone. "You're right, of course. I know it." He tapped his temple. "At least, I know it up here."

But not down there?

She climbed off the bed and rinsed her hands in the basin. "I think Matilda should rub the ointment into your back from now on. Either her or Henry."

"I'll take Matilda."

She wiped her hands on the dry strip of linen, her heart in her throat, her mouth parched. "How do you feel?"

"Frustrated."

Despite everything, a bubble of laughter escaped. She stifled it with a hand over her mouth. Nick suddenly grinned, and she could almost see the eighteen year-old beneath that hard, stubbly jaw and strong cheekbones.

She picked up the jars and slung the linen over her shoulder. "We'll leave you so you can sleep. That headache tonic won't work otherwise."

"I'm not tired."

"Rest then."

"I can rest with you here."

"I have chores to do. Wake up, Matilda," she said loudly and before Nick could convince her to stay. It wouldn't take much. Just a flutter of his eyelashes and a heartfelt "please" would have done it.

"Ready already, mistress?" Matilda asked, stretching.

"Nick needs to rest." She followed the maid out but turned in the doorway because she couldn't resist one last look.

He blew her a kiss then bestowed one of his maddeningly beautiful smiles on her. She raced off before she could change her mind.

LUCY DIDN'T WANT to venture far from the house in case Nick needed her. Widow Dawson wouldn't arrive for some time, so she walked through the garden, if the weed-infested scraggly collection of bushes could be called that. Brutus kept apace beside her, nudging her hand whenever he wanted a pat. She deadheaded the roses and mentally plotted out garden beds. Susanna Holt was also in the process of restoring the formal garden at Stoneleigh, and it might be timely to share ideas and cuttings.

Brutus brought her a stick, and they played a game of throw and fetch until her arm grew sore and the sun too hot. She'd not worn her hat, and she didn't want any more freckles. She touched her cheek the way Nick had done, but it didn't feel the same. His touch had been so gentle for such a big man, and tentative too. She supposed that was the innocent youth coming to the fore. For all his bravado, he had led a sheltered life before the age of eighteen. Imagine being denied the opportunity to make friends… What parent would do that to his child, particularly a young man as amiable as Nick?

She knelt to rub Brutus behind the ears, but he ran off in the direction of the house. Lucy looked up to see the hound bounding up to Nick as he approached. Brutus turned circles of excitement in front of him until Nick stopped to pat him with his free hand. He held Lucy's hat in his other.

"Matilda said you'd want this." He handed her the hat. "She said you'd hate to get more freckles. I don't know why."

"Spoken like someone who's never had a blemish in his life."

"Freckles aren't blemishes." He lifted a hand but she stepped back out of his reach.

"Where is Matilda?" she asked.

"On her way. I told her to meet us in the orchard."

"The orchard?"

"It's a pleasant day to sit outside, but the orchard looks to be the shadiest spot."

"A lovely idea, but I should be helping make the bread."

"Cook said she can do without you today."

"Oh. Very well. But you should be resting. I seem to recall giving orders for you to stay abed."

"I'm not very good at taking orders."

As evidenced by the whipping marks on his back. He'd admitted that four had come from his father because he'd disobeyed him, but had his father inflicted the others when his youngest son rebelled again? She was quite certain now that Nick was the rebellious sort, at least if he thought a rule unnecessary. Like staying in bed.

If he followed her thoughts, he didn't show it. He crooked his elbow but she did not take it. "Come now," he said with a wink. "I promise not to try to kiss you."

She took his arm, and they walked side by side among the rows of apple, cherry and pear trees. Brutus ran ahead, ears flopping, turning often to see if they still followed.

"Will you answer some more questions for me?" she asked.

"If I can."

"What did you dream about last night? And I want the truth this time."

His arm tensed beneath her hand. "It was nothing, Lucy, just a dream."

"It might be a memory from your missing years trying to get out."

"I doubt it."

"Why?"

He shrugged one shoulder.

"You can tell me," she said, quietly. "It'll go no further."

"I know."

"Then tell me."

He let go of her and strode ahead. "I don't want to talk about it. I don't even want to think about it." He did not speak harshly, although he had every right to. She'd pushed him too far, thrust her nose into business that wasn't hers. Yet he didn't even raise his voice.

She trotted to catch up then had to walk fast to keep apace. "I'm sorry. I won't ask again."

He slowed then stopped. "I'm sorry too." His fingertips touched hers. "Perhaps one day I can tell you, but not yet."

"I'll be here when you're ready."

They sat in the shade of an old apple tree, a little apart. Brutus wedged himself between them and rested his chin on his paws as he watched the house. Matilda emerged carrying something, but she was too far away for Lucy to see what it was.

"Tell me about your parents," she said. "How did they meet?"

"My father traveled to Florence when he was eighteen. He says he fell in love with her on first sight. They corresponded for two years before he convinced his father to let them marry."

"How romantic." And not at all like the image she'd built up of his father. How could a man who'd whip his son for a small disobedience know anything about love?

"They had an even more difficult time convincing her father, but the two families must have come to an agreement because they were wed in sixty-eight and my brother was born a year later."

"It must have been difficult for her."

"I'm sure she missed her family."

"Not to mention the other obstacles," Lucy said. "Language,

religion, and the stubborn English pride. England is very different than Florence, after all."

He plucked at the grass. "I never considered it like that."

Matilda was closer now and Lucy could see that she carried a basin, linen, and a small blade. "What are those for?"

Nick rubbed his chin. "I asked her to shave me. It's so itchy."

Lucy laughed. "You're not used to it?"

"As far as I'm concerned, two days ago I could only grow sparse tufts of fine hair. Now it's coarse and growing like weeds."

"You don't want to try doing it yourself with a mirror?"

"I'm not used to doing it myself. I'd probably cut my chin to ribbons."

"He is a baron's son," Matilda said, puffing out her chest. "He would have had a servant do it for him."

Lucy bit back her smile. "Yes, of course."

"I've lived a pampered life," he said with mock seriousness.

"Your clothing states otherwise." And those scars. "Indeed, you didn't look like a gentleman at all when I first met you. You still don't."

"What should a gentleman look like?"

She thought about Lord Lynden up at Sutton Hall. He was away at court, but she'd met him a few times before he left, and even dined with him once. "Colorful. Soft."

"Not so the Colecloughs. Perhaps Father dresses like a peacock at court but not at home." He tilted his chin to give Matilda better access. "What about your parents?" he asked before the maid began. "Tell me more about them."

Lucy's family wasn't nearly as exotic as Nick's, but he appeared to be listening closely while Matilda shaved him. She told him about their home, farm, and her childhood, how growing up with two older brothers could be a blessing as well as a curse, how she missed her parents and friends but enjoyed her new life at Cowdrey Farm too. She told him everything, or almost. There was a gaping hole where Edmund Mallam was concerned. Some things were better left unspoken.

"There you are, sir," Matilda said, sitting back on her haunches and admiring her handiwork. "All smooth."

Nick rubbed his chin. "Thank you. I don't now how I put up with it being so scratchy. How does it look?"

"Much better," the maid said.

'Much better' didn't even begin to describe his new appearance. If he walked into a crowded room, all the women would be swooning within moments, and that was without employing that devastating smile of his.

His brows rose. "Lucy?"

"Mmmm?"

"Are you all right?"

Oh lord, he'd caught her staring. "Yes, of course. Why do you ask?"

"Because you didn't answer my question."

He'd spoken? It seemed her wits had completely failed her.

"I understand if you don't want to tell me." He huffed out a breath and watched Matilda as she emptied the basin of water against a tree trunk. She was out of earshot. "Indeed, don't answer it. I shouldn't have asked."

"No, you can ask me anything. I… I just didn't hear you. Ask me again."

He plucked at the grass some more. "A woman of your age from a good family is usually wed by now. I merely wondered if you were… waiting for someone. Someone in particular, that is."

Matilda slowly and methodically wiped out the basin with a strip of linen. She didn't seem to be in any hurry to return to her chaperoning duties.

"I was betrothed once," Lucy said without taking her gaze off Matilda. "At least, I thought I was. He seemed to think otherwise."

"He didn't honor the agreement?"

She shook her head. Her throat tightened. She didn't want to speak of it. Not with this man. A man who would surely have women lined up to be his wife if the position were open. It was utterly humiliating.

"The cur." He'd stopped picking at the grass and shifted closer to her. For a heart-stopping moment, she thought he'd try to comfort her with an arm around her shoulders, but he did not. "I may not know much about the ways of the world," he said, "but I do know a man ought to honor a commitment made to a woman."

"When the man believes there is no commitment… " She shrugged.

"So he claims you lied too?" He muttered something under his breath. "I hope your kinsmen thrashed him."

She recoiled, but his harsh tone hit her like a blow to the stomach. "My father isn't the thrashing kind. Nor are my brothers."

A look of horror crossed his face, and she suspected it matched her own, but for entirely different reasons. "He should have been punished! Didn't your father want to defend your honor?"

"I didn't say Father sat idly by and did nothing. He spoke to Edmund's father and ceased to trade with him when he supported his son. It was fortunate that most of the village believed me, although I'm sorry to say that Edmund's new wife has not had an easy time of it since she arrived. My friends have shunned her. When the opportunity to come here with Henry presented itself, I begged Father to let me go. He thought it was because I couldn't continue to face Edmund and his new wife, but that was only part of it. I hoped that with me gone, the villagers would forget faster."

He shook his head. "Your kindness to someone who has wronged you astounds me."

"She didn't wrong me. She had no knowledge of me until she arrived."

"And your father simply cut off the cur's father? How is that going to change anything?"

"I didn't want the situation changed. Not once it happened. Why would I want Edmund back when he has wronged me so? I was well rid of him."

"Yes, but your honor should have been defended more vehemently."

"By thrashing Edmund? What would that achieve?"

He blinked at her as if he didn't understand her at all, or her father. He spread his hand on the grass, splaying the fingers so that they almost touched hers lying idle at her side. "If you were mine... if someone hurt you..."

A lump clogged her throat, and she tried to swallow past it. She must remember that he thought like an impetuous youth, not a grown man, and a youth brought up by a father who punished with whippings. With no better mentor than that, why would Nick think any differently?

At eighteen he was still fresh and innocent, relatively unscathed by a brutal father because he'd only just begun to rebel. But what about later? What happened when Nick questioned other rules he thought unfair, or outright disobeyed them?

A severe thrashing, that's what. The sort that left dozens of permanent scars. It must have changed him. How could it not? Changed him from this happy youth into the gruff man she'd first met. She closed her eyes.

"Lucy?" he murmured. "You're angry at me. I'm sorry."

She laid her hand over his on the grass, and he wrapped his thumb around her fingers. She fought back tears. "I'm not angry with you."

"Disappointed?"

"No." She drew in a ragged breath. How could she undo years of cruel control with only a few words? "The thing you must understand is that I *know* my father loves me. I don't need him to prove it by meting out violent punishment upon Edmund."

"How do you know?"

"He never once doubted me. Most fathers would blame their daughter in private, if not in public, for her part in the saga. My father didn't. He has always given my word equal weight as any man's. How could I ever doubt the love of someone who treated me with so much respect?"

He swallowed heavily, making his Adam's apple jerk up and down. Their gazes connected briefly, and she saw the shine in his eyes before he shifted his focus to the ground. "I'm glad your father never hurt you," he said, his voice barely above a whisper. "You deserve every kindness."

She rolled his hand over so that it was palm up and linked her fingers through his. There were so many difficult questions she wanted to ask him about his own family, but Matilda was fast approaching, and Lucy doubted he would have told her more than he already had.

He pulled his hand away when Matilda sat beside them. Lucy fussed with her skirts and didn't meet her maid's gaze.

"There'll be no grass left if you keep picking it out," Matilda said, nodding at Nick's fingers busily plucking the grass again.

His hand curled into a fist.

Matilda untied the pouch attached to the rope girdle at her waist and pulled out a piece of linen she always kept in it, hairpins, and finally a small knife. She handed it to Nick then fished out something else and passed that over. It was the lump of wood with the two ears emerging from it.

"I was tidying your room and thought you might like this to pass the time awhile," Matilda said. "Looks like you might need it now."

Nick turned it over and smoothed his thumb along the grain. "I can't remember how." He held it out but she pushed his hand away.

"Try."

"Go on," Lucy added.

He shook his head and placed it on the grass, the little knife too. Why wouldn't he even try?

"Someone approaches," he said a moment before Brutus jumped up and ran off barking.

Lucy squinted at the long drive leading to the house, but she neither saw nor heard anything. "I can't— Oh, you're right. I hear it now." His senses must be incredibly sharp to have picked up the distant sound of wheels on the road.

Matilda got to her feet. "It must be the Greene lad back with Widow Dawson."

She gathered up her things, including the wood and knife, and headed off. Nick held out his hand to help Lucy up. He did not let go once she was standing.

"I'm sorry," he said quickly.

"There's nothing to forgive."

He rubbed his thumbs across her knuckles and looked down, shook his head. "Lucy, I didn't mean to scare you before when I spoke about thrashing anyone who'd hurt you."

"Nick—"

"You can trust me."

"I know."

"I'd never harm you and or anyone you cared about."

She laid her palm against his newly smooth jaw and gently lifted his face to see it better. His eyes had turned darker, almost black, their depths endless. The urge to kiss him was overwhelming. It was like a compulsion, an addiction, and it took every piece of her strength to resist. She did, however, touch her thumb to the corner of his sad, beautiful mouth.

"I know that, Nick." She had barely known him a full day, and yet it was a truth that she felt deep within her. There were mysteries surrounding him, not the least of which was why he'd been set upon and why he'd been carrying so many weapons, but she didn't need to know the answers to believe him a good man. She knew his essence, his soul. He wouldn't harm her.

He turned his head a little and managed to plant a kiss on her wrist before she removed her hand.

"We'd better meet Widow Dawson," she said, walking off.

Behind her, he sighed deeply.

* * *

Widow Dawson inspected the bruises on Nick's body then the wound on his head. "It must be bandaged for a few more days." She gently applied a salve before wrapping the clean linen around his head again. "Pass me that pin, Bel."

Her young daughter handed over a pin and positioned herself

nearby, so she could watch how her mother secured the bandage. The wise woman had already taught her child a great many things, Lucy knew, and the girl was quite capable with the tasks set her. Bel loved to talk about all she'd learned whenever Lucy visited them in the village. The girl would make an excellent wise woman one day.

Matilda entered the bedchamber and sat on her chair by the door. "No luck," she said, heaving a sigh. "The Greene lad said he asked Milner and some others and no one knows of anyone called Coleclough, and no one went through Sutton Grange who looked like our man here."

"Did he describe Nick?"

"Aye. Says he told them Mr. Coleclough's got tanned skin, black hair, and is as tall and solid as an oak. If he were in the village, they would have noticed him."

Lucy leaned against the bedpost. "We could widen our search to Larkham and the other villages further away."

"I don't want to cause trouble," Nick said.

"Nonsense. It's no trouble. You must have gone through one of the villages."

"You could write to his family," Widow Dawson said. "From Kent, is he? Shouldn't take more than three or four days to get word to the border, perhaps less if the weather stays fair."

"Or I could travel there instead of a letter," Nick said.

"No!" both Widow Dawson and Lucy cried. "The road'll rattle loose the broken bones in yer head," the wise woman said. "There'll be no traveling by horse or cart for you for some weeks."

"Will it heal?" Lucy asked. She stood out of the way on the other side of the bed yet near enough that she could watch.

"Given time and rest, aye. He's a strong lad. Nay, hardly a lad." She chuckled and nodded at his chest, still bare from when she'd inspected it. "Just look at 'im, Lucy! Have you ever seen such a fine one?"

Nick crossed his arms over his chest and arched a brow at

Lucy. Unfair! She hadn't made the comment, why should he tease *her*?

She smiled because she was incredibly pleased that he'd returned to his amiable self again, their earlier conversation apparently forgotten. That vulnerable, melancholy side of him worried her, made her want to forget propriety and just hold him, comfort him.

"What about my memory?" he asked Widow Dawson. "Will it come back?"

She pushed aside the hair that had fallen across her forehead. Never a neat person, she looked even messier after her ride in the cart. "I've only known one other like this, years ago. I was a child meself, and me Ma was the wise woman of Sutton Grange then. He was a man older than yerself, Mr. Coleclough. Fell off a barn roof, he did. Broke his leg and hit his head. Was out cold for a while, and when he woke up, he couldn't remember the accident. He couldn't remember nothin' after his weddin' day, as it turns out."

"His wedding day?" Lucy said. "How odd."

"What happened?" Nick sat forward, his unblinking gaze on the wise woman. "Did he regain his memory?"

"Aye, he did some three days later."

Lucy's heart kicked inside her chest. "What a relief. Only three days."

Nick drew his knees up and wrapped his arms around them. "Do you think three days is the normal length of time?"

She shrugged. "You're only the second one I've seen like this, and I've never heard of no other." Widow Dawson crooked her finger at Lucy. "Come show me the ointment you used on his bruises."

"Why?" Lucy asked.

"I just want to see it, is all."

Lucy followed her out, leaving Bel with Matilda and Nick. Widow Dawson shut the door behind them and caught Lucy's arm to halt her. "I don't want to see the ointment," she said. "I wanted to speak to you away from him."

Dread washed over Lucy. Oh God. "You told us he'd be all right," she said weakly.

"He will be. He will be." Widow Dawson glanced at the door. "He'll recover full well, don't you worry. This is about his memories."

"Oh? He won't get them back?"

"I expect he will. That's the problem."

"I don't follow."

Widow Dawson's golden eyes flared like bright lamps. She drew a breath. "The other patient I told you 'bout, the one who lost his memory too."

"Yes? What about him? Did he not make a full recovery after all?"

"Aye, he did. He's dead now, course, but from old age, not the injury."

"So what is it?"

"I told you he lost his memory and couldn't remember anything that happened before his wedding day."

"Yes."

"His wife died on their weddin' day."

Lucy gasped. "How awful."

"Aye, me Ma said it was a very sad time. The girl was picking flowers down beside Cold Stream out Larkham way to put in her hair, see, but there'd been a lot of rain and the creek ran swift and deep. She fell in and drowned."

"The poor girl. Poor man. He must have been devastated."

"He was. That's why he couldn't remember it, nor nothin' after it."

"I don't follow."

Widow Dawson glanced at the door again and chewed her lip. "He only remembered the good things, not the bad times and not the thing that started the bad times. It was like that day was a wall in his mind, blocking the memories that came after it so they couldn't get through. I think the same thing is happening with Mr. Coleclough."

Lucy leaned against the paneled wall for balance. The world had suddenly tilted, and she was losing her grip. "You think he only remembers up until the age of eighteen because something bad happened then?"

"Aye. I'd wager he recalls up to a partic'lar day. And I'd wager it's got something to do with them scars on his back."

CHAPTER 7

"*T*hose scars could have happened around that time," Lucy said. "Nick says his father's man gave him four lashings just a month ago. Or a month before his last memory, that is."

"He don't remember the other ones?" Widow Dawson asked.

Lucy shook her head. "Do you think he's started to remember already?"

"Aye. Did you see his reaction when I told him the other man remembered everything after three days?"

Lucy frowned, shrugged. "I don't think he said anything."

"He didn't. You was happy when I said he'd remember in a few days. He weren't so pleased. You'd think he'd be happy too—unless he *knew* those memories weren't ones he wanted to remember."

Lucy rubbed her aching forehead. "I don't know. He's given me no sign that his memories have returned. Do you think I should I push him to recall the day he's trying to forget?"

"That depends now."

"On what?"

"On whether you want him to keep on liking you. B'cause I expect he's not goin' to want to remember, and if you're the one makin' him… " She grimaced. "Best to let it happen naturally."

She opened the door, and they both walked back into the bedchamber. Nick was sitting cross-legged on the bed, his shirt once more covering his chest. Bel sat opposite, holding a stack of playing cards, a grin splitting her face.

"I beat him twice, Ma," she said.

"Next time you suggest a game of Primero, I'm going to be busy." Nick handed his cards to Bel then tugged on a lock of her hair. "If I want to gain any respect here, I can't afford to lose to a child."

"I'm ten," Bel said with a withering glare. "Not a child."

"You weren't playin' for coin now, were you?" Widow Dawson asked. "B'cause that wouldn't be fair what with poor Mr. Cole-clough's achin' head."

"You have a headache?" Lucy asked.

He shrugged one shoulder, but it was the wise woman who answered. "Course he does. The crack in his head wouldn't tickle now, would it?"

"Nick? Why didn't you tell me? I could have made up some more of that tonic for you."

"It's not so bad."

She stamped a hand on her hip and gave him a glare she hoped would rival Bel's. The effect was lost, however, because one of the maids entered and announced dinner.

Matilda joined the other servants in the kitchen, but Lucy insisted Widow Dawson and Bel dine with her and Nick. They sat at the large table in the hall and the servants brought in trenchers of ham, roasted lamb, bread, cheese, fruit tarts, and a bowl of pea pottage.

"Master Cowdrey not joinin' us?" Widow Dawson asked, heaping peas onto her trencher.

"He's very busy," Lucy said. "There's so much work to do. I don't know how the previous farmer managed it all. Henry is no lay-about, but he's gone from dawn till dusk most days."

"He worked his men into the ground, that's how." The wise woman shook her head and spooned peas onto her daughter's trencher. "He worked 'em so hard, they got sick. He and his sister never gave their ill staff a moment's care, as was their duty, not even givin' the poor families some bread from their bakery. And I couldn't do nothin' for 'em b'cause they never called me until it was too late. That Walter Cowdrey seemed nice enough when you talked to him in church or at the market, but when you scratched the surface, you'd see the real man, and he weren't one you'd want to cross. His sister too." She waved her knife in the air. "You've heard the stories by now, I expect."

Lucy bowed her head, nodded. She could feel Nick watching her and could sense his burning questions about the previous Cowdreys of Cowdrey Farm, but he didn't ask any. Instead, he said, "Perhaps I can help your brother—"

"No!" Lucy and Widow Dawson said.

"Don't be such a fool," Lucy added.

"You need to rest that head, or you won't be leavin' here at all," the wise woman said.

"I hate doing nothing," Nick muttered. "And what precisely does rest mean anyway? I won't remain in bed."

"I can see that," Widow Dawson said. "Yer not to ride or travel by cart. Too bumpy. Anythin' that'll rattle yer head is bad, 'specially workin' in the fields. You can walk about the house and such, but nothin' more vig'rous. Understand?"

He pulled a face. "You'll have to keep me company, Lucy, or I'll go mad."

Lucy regarded him over her spoonful of peas. "You should take up whittling again to keep yourself occupied."

"You whittle?" Bel picked up a pea and popped it into her mouth. "Make me something, Mr. Cole." She swallowed the pea. "Pleeease."

"Cole*clough*," her mother corrected her.

Nick's knife clattered onto the trencher. His jaw swung open, and he stared at the girl. Bel put her hands together as if in prayer and turned her big golden eyes onto him, pleading. She was oblivious to his shock, but Lucy was not.

"Are you all right?" she asked him. She glanced at Widow Dawson who'd half-risen from the chair.

He shook his head, either dismissing their concerns or shaking loose a memory. Perhaps both. "I don't know how to whittle." He pushed his trencher away and rubbed the bridge of his nose.

"What is it?" Lucy asked. "What have you remembered?"

He waved a hand. "It's nothing. Bel called me Cole just now, and it seemed very familiar, that's all."

"You weren't called that before?"

"No. I'm just Nick to my family." And he'd already told her he had no friends to speak of.

"I wonder who called you Cole then."

"It don't sound like something a wife would call her husband," Widow Dawson said.

"We call Johnny Turtledove 'Turtle,'" Bel said. "Suits him 'cause he's as slow as a turtle. You're not black as coal though, but yer a little bit brown."

"Well," Lucy said cheerfully, "another piece of the puzzle falls into place. It would appear you now have friends who are comfortable enough with you to call you Cole."

He nodded slowly. "I wonder if I was visiting any of them near here."

"Sutton Hall's only a few miles away. Perhaps you was visiting Lord Lynden, what with you being a lord's son too and—"

"You're a lord!" Bel almost bounced out of her chair. "I beat a lord at Primero? I should've played for coin."

Nick chuckled. "I don't have any coin. And I'm not a lord, my father is. My brother will inherit the title and estate, not me."

"Wait till I tell Biddy Yarrow I bet a lord at Primero."

"Beat not bet," Widow Dawson said. She winked at Lucy. "And wait till I tell everyone in the village there's a lord's son with a cracked skull stayin' at Cowdrey Farm. You'll have all the eligible girls and their Ma's stoppin' by."

"We don't know if Mr. Coleclough is already married," Lucy said. She picked up a hunk of bread even though she didn't feel like

79

eating it and proceeded to tear it into smaller chunks. "It might be a good idea to mention that. A very good idea." She dropped the last piece of bread onto the trencher, scattering crumbs.

"Can a village girl marry a lord?" Bel asked.

"I'm not a lord," Nick said. "I'm the second son of a lord, and I will marry whomever I want, no matter what Father thinks." He said it with far more vehemence than necessary, and Lucy glanced up from her trencher. He was looking directly at her, not Bel, a hard gleam in his eye that she'd never seen before. "If he disagrees, I need only remind him that he married a Catholic girl from Florence. Hardly a suitable prospect for the future Lord Coleclough."

The throb of blood through her veins was very loud, drowning out whatever Bel said. Unfortunately, or perhaps it was fortunate, Lucy heard Widow Dawson's words as clear as day:

"If I were to guess, I'd say you was wed already. Men yer age always are. Always, b'cause none wants to live alone."

Lucy rubbed breadcrumbs between her fingers and watched them fall back onto her trencher like little brown snowflakes.

Nick cleared his throat. "You mentioned a Lord Lynden just now," he said. "Perhaps I should meet him. If we're friends, it might trigger my memories."

Lucy's heart lifted and she forked a brow at Widow Dawson. *See?* She wanted to say. *He does want to remember.*

The wise woman gave a slight nod as if to concede the point.

"Unfortunately, he's away," Lucy said. "He attends court on occasion, so it's likely he does know you. Or your father at least."

"Her Majesty's court will be on procession now that it's summer." Nick frowned. "Is Queen Elizabeth still alive? She must be very old."

"She's in her sixties, but well enough by all accounts."

"Do you know when Lynden is expected to return home?"

"Soon," Widow Dawson said. "He wrote to his house steward with instructions to set up two of the bedchambers for ladies."

"Ladies?" Lucy echoed. "Is he bringing home visitors or

someone more permanent?" She didn't know Lord Lynden well, but she did know he was unwed and not in a hurry to change that state if his lack of interest in females was any indication. According to Susanna Holt, he'd never shown the slightest inkling in the fairer sex, and she ought to know being his cousin's widow. On the other hand, he was a nobleman, and noblemen had to marry. Perhaps he'd found himself a wife in need of a titled gentleman, albeit a pompous prig of one. Lucy felt sorry for her already.

"Lord Lynden don't share his plans with me, Lucy," Widow Dawson said with a wink.

Lucy laughed. "I'm sure you're told much more than most in the village, what with your tendency to wield sharp implements when your patient is at their most vulnerable."

Bel giggled. "What about the Holts?" she asked. "Mr. Cole might know them too."

"Aye," her mother said. "Orlando and Susanna Holt at Stoneleigh. I'm going there after I leave here. Susanna's as big as a sow, poor pet, and what with her losing two babies a few years back, I like to keep me eye on her."

"I saw her yesterday morning," Lucy said. "She was— Nick, are you all right?"

"That name… " He rubbed his temple. "Orlando."

"It's an unusual name. You said so yourself yesterday."

"It's more than that." He sighed. "I don't know."

"It's all right. It'll come to you." She reached across the table and touched his hand. "Perhaps you do know him. When I first met you, you were heading in the direction of Stoneleigh."

"We'd already met before…this?"

"Yes. In the meadow that borders Stoneleigh land."

If he found it curious that she'd not mentioned the meeting before, he didn't show it. Indeed, she'd said 'saw' not 'met,' so he might think there was nothing to add.

"I'll tell Mr. Holt about you," Widow Dawson said. "If he knows you he can come out here."

"That's if he'll leave his wife long enough," Lucy said. "He won't go further than the edges of the Stoneleigh estate most days. He's that worried about the baby coming while he's not there."

"He's adores her, he does." Widow Dawson rose and signaled Bel to get up too. "I'll stay with her if he comes here. Won't take 'im long to see you, Mr. Coleclough, and get back to Stoneleigh. There'll be time enough for your man to drive me to the village and be back here before nightfall."

"Mistress Dawson," Nick said, pushing out his chair. "I wonder if you could do something for me when you return to the village. Would you take a letter and see that it gets into the hands of someone traveling to Kent?"

"Aye, I can do that."

"You're going to write to your father?" Lucy asked.

"I can think of no better way to discover more about the events and people I've forgotten."

She wasn't so sure about that. His father seemed like someone best avoided, at least until Nick's memory fully returned, and he knew all the facts.

It was ironic that Widow Dawson had warned Lucy that Nick may not want to remember, but now that he seemed determined, Lucy wasn't so sure it was a good idea. After all, he didn't know that a particular horrible event was responsible for blocking his memories. It might be best if he never remembered it after all.

Widow Dawson took her daughter's hand. "Come, Bel. We'll gather our things." She mouthed 'Tell him' to Lucy as she ushered Bel out.

Lucy stood and took both of Nick's hands in her own. "There's something you ought to know."

He kissed her. The light brush of his lips on hers sent tingles whispering across her skin, and warmed her from head to toe.

"I've been wanting to do that all day." He smiled against her mouth then pulled away. "So what is it Widow Dawson wanted you to tell me?"

"You saw that?"

"I've lost my memory not my eyes."

"Yes, well, of course. I, uh…"

He grinned. "You seem a little distracted, my little light."

"Light? Oh, Lucy, yes." She stepped away because being so near him was indeed distracting, and she needed to say her piece. "Widow Dawson said there may be something blocking your memories. Something that happened when you were eighteen. Something… unfortunate that has troubled you ever since."

His only response was a pulse of the muscle in his jaw.

"Are you sure you want to find out what it was from your father?" A shiver made the hairs on the back of her neck stand on end. She crossed her arms and held herself tightly together.

Nick stepped closer and folded his big hands around her arms. "He seems like the best person to tell me the truth." His voice was a low rumble that hung in the air between them.

He didn't understand. She had to explain it better, blunter. "If he gave you four scars on your back, he may have… given you the others."

He tucked her hair behind her ear and slowly caressed his knuckles down her throat to her small ruff. "It seems likely."

"You agree?"

"I suspected as much, after last night."

The nightmare. "Oh. So what—?"

He put a finger to her lips. "Not yet. It's not all clear to me and I don't want to… " He closed his eyes and tipped his head back. "I don't want to discuss it until I know for certain what happened."

"Perhaps it's best that you don't know, Nick. Not before you're ready."

"Lucy, I can't run away from the past. I must face it, no matter what happened to me. No matter what I did. Otherwise the nightmares will continue to plague me."

"What *you* did? What about what has been done *to* you?"

"That too, perhaps." One side of his mouth kicked up. "We can't make assumptions until we know the full story. Don't worry." He kissed the top of her head. "I think I can face anything with you on my side."

Her heart beat in her throat, choking all the words she wanted to say. She wanted to cry and hold him. She wanted to tell him that she'd never felt like this, not with Edmund, not with anyone.

But she did not. What lay between them was much too strong, too intense, and too new. She should not feel this way about a man she'd known for only a day, a man who didn't even know himself.

So why did it feel so right?

He bent to kiss her again, but she put a hand to his chest, staying him. His heart thumped against her palm. "If you are wed, I could not forgive myself."

He went to rub a hand through his hair, but it met with the bandage. He sighed and scrubbed his face instead. "You're a cruel wench. Too much common sense, that's your problem." He smiled his crooked smile. "Or rather, your common sense is my problem."

She turned away because that smile held too much power over her for her own good. "Come. We'd better write that letter before Widow Dawson leaves."

* * *

THE ONLY WAY Lucy could get Nick to rest was if she remained with him in his bedchamber. That meant Matilda had to stay too. Lucy gave the maid one of her herbals to read, and she seemed quite engrossed in it. Hopefully she wouldn't fall asleep—Lucy didn't want to be left alone with Nick anymore. She couldn't trust herself around him.

"They adore you," Nick said when he was settled on the bed. He refused to lie down and get under the covers, but at least he was sitting still. It was as much rest as he was going to get.

"Who?"

"Widow Dawson and her daughter."

"She's been very kind to me. I worried that she wouldn't like me visiting her patients and offering them comfort, but she has encouraged me from the first day. It's difficult for her to get to the sick outside the village and since I have a cart and horse, I can deliver medicines or supplies for her."

"I'm sure it's more than that." His eyes turned velvety soft, warm.

"Why are you looking at me like that?"

"How am I looking at you?"

"Like you want to… " *Kiss me.* "Nothing. I don't know."

A chuckle rumbled in his chest. "You're flustered."

"I am not."

"And you're blushing again."

She glanced at Matilda, but the maid didn't look up from the book. "Stop it," Lucy whispered. "We agreed not to flirt."

"I didn't agree to anything."

"I think I should go. This isn't restful at all." Not for him and certainly not for her.

He caught her elbow as she rose from the chair. "I apologize. Please stay." When he spoke with such seriousness and looked at her with those big eyes framed by the thick lashes, she felt her principles melting away like butter left in the sun.

It made denying him so very difficult, but she managed it. She shook her head.

He sighed. "I won't sleep."

"Matilda will leave the book here for you."

"You're a cruel wench to deny me your company."

"Keep speaking, and I'll deny you the book too." She looked back at him from the doorway. "Try to rest, Nick."

* * *

ORLANDO HOLT DISMOUNTED and handed the reins to the lad who'd emerged from the barn at the sound of hooves on the gravel drive. Lucy met him at the entrance to the kitchen garden and smiled a greeting. Orlando didn't return it.

"Is everything all right?" she asked. She'd never seen him so anxious. "Susanna?"

"She's well." He looked over her head toward the door. "Widow Dawson said there was a man here without a memory. I thought I'd come see him for myself."

"You think you know him? Thank goodness! I'm so relieved." It would be far better for Orlando to help Nick remember than his father.

He looked at her for the first time since his arrival. "No-o. That is, I can't be sure. I want to see him for myself."

"Surely Widow Dawson described him to you. He's very distinctive. Tanned coloring, tall, strongly built. Does that remind you of anyone? Anyone you were expecting to call on you?"

Something flickered in his eyes, but he blinked and it vanished. He smiled broadly. It was the sort of smile that could make a woman weak at the knees and lose her focus on the conversation. That's what usually happened to Lucy anyway, but not this time. She had come to realize something about Orlando Holt and that smile—he used it when he wanted to dazzle a woman and get the upper hand in a conversation.

How odd that he would use it on her now, and how odd that she did not fall for it.

"Are you going to answer me, Orlando, or should I ride out to Susanna and ask her instead?"

His smiled slipped off. "It does sound like someone I know, but I want to be sure. Widow Dawson said his name is Nicholas Cole-clough, and he's from Kent."

"Yes." When he went to walk past her, she stepped in front of him. "Is the name familiar? Does your acquaintance hail from Kent?"

He narrowed his gaze at her, clearly annoyed that she was asking so many questions and not letting him pass. So be it. She didn't like the way he couldn't give solid answers. It was too strange. What did Orlando Holt have to hide? What was his connection to Nick?

Oh. Oh no. Surely not. He couldn't possibly be responsible for

Nick's injuries. Orlando had a kind heart and soul, his wife too. Susanna would not be in love with a thug.

Yet at that moment, Lucy didn't trust a single thing he said.

"Lucy, come now. Why so many questions? I simply want to see him and get his measure for my own peace of mind. I don't like mysteries, and you have to admit that his story sounds absurd. I've never known anyone to lose their memory after a mere bump on the head."

"It is not a *mere* bump, and it is not entirely absurd. Widow Dawson knew of one other case. What are you implying, Orlando? That he's lying? I would hope you know me well enough by now to realize I am not the most gullible woman." Not anymore at least. If the experience with Edmund had taught her anything, it was that.

"Widow Dawson did say he was handsome and that you seemed to have developed a, uh, an attachment to him."

Lucy crossed her arms and silently cursed her fair complexion as her face heated. "That is neither here nor there. He is telling the truth. Otherwise he is the best actor in the world and should be on stage."

His only response was a grunt as he strode past her.

"I'll fetch him," she called after him, but he walked very fast and was inside the house before she reached the doorway. Orlando stopped. Beyond him, in the narrow entrance between the scullery and the larder, stood Nick.

"You're here," she said, rather stupidly.

Nick and Orlando eyed each other like bulls sizing each other up. Nick was broader in the chest and across the shoulders, but was only a little taller than Orlando. The latter took a step closer and nodded a greeting. Nick nodded back and attempted a smile. Orlando didn't return it. His face had gone blank. Lucy had never seen him lack expression before. Orlando was the sort of man whose eyes always sparkled or whose mouth revealed his inner thoughts. The blandness was new.

"This is Orlando Holt," she said to Nick. "Do you recognize him?

"No. Do you recognize me, sir?"

Orlando hesitated then said, "Yes."

"You do?" Lucy caught Orlando's arm and hugged it in her excitement. "That's wonderful!"

Nick narrowed his gaze. "How do I know you?"

"Before you answer that, let's move into the parlor." Lucy ushered Orlando forward. "This is no place to stand about chatting."

But Orlando refused to move. "I'll speak to him alone."

"I want to be there."

"Lucy, you know he'll be safe with me."

"He doesn't remember you. I'm sure he'll feel happier with me in the room."

"Happier?" Orlando started to laugh, but pressed his lips together when she glared at him.

"He's in a vulnerable state," she said, one hand on her hip.

"Vulnerable? Him?"

"Don't mock her," Nick growled.

Orlando's gaze shifted between them and slowly, he smiled. "Well, well. I'm glad I'm here to witness this."

"What does that mean?" she asked.

Orlando waved a hand. "Never mind. Come, Cole, let's talk in the parlor." He walked off, and Lucy followed. He stopped again. "Just Cole and me."

She had not expected to meet with such opposition, not from Orlando. What was he hiding? "I already told you, no."

He sighed. "Help me, Cole."

Nick crossed his arms and squared up to Orlando, using every bit of his extra size to his advantage. Orlando, however, did not back away. "I'd like her to hear what you have to say to me. And don't call me Cole. It's either Nick or Coleclough. I think only my friends called me Cole, and I'm beginning to doubt that you and I were ever that."

Orlando did a most unexpected thing. He laughed, a loud, raucous, belly aching laugh. "I think that's the longest speech I've ever heard you make." He slapped Nick on the shoulder, right where Lucy knew a bruise to be. Nick did not wince or give any sign that it hurt. "Come then, Lucy. If *Coleclough* desires your presence, you'd better join us. I'll refrain from giving any particularly sensitive information about our friend in deference to your feminine sensibilities."

Damnation. It was the sensitive information she wanted to hear most.

CHAPTER 8

*L*ucy led the way through the house to the larger of the two parlors. She moved her embroidery frame to the corner out of the way, and sat on the chair nearest the unlit fireplace. Neither man sat down on the other chairs arranged nearby. She rolled her eyes, but they were too busy assessing each other to notice. Men! She would expect such childish behavior from Nick since he had the mind of an eighteen year-old, and he clearly didn't remember Orlando, but it surprised her that Orlando seemed equally wary.

Were they friends as he claimed?

"You look ridiculous with that bandage on your head," Orlando said. He laughed as he sat.

She took it back. Only a close friend would dare tease a man the size of Nick.

The sudden change in Orlando's mood seemed to catch Nick by surprise. He touched the bandage and gave a sheepish smile. "Lucy made me wear it."

"Lucy?" Orlando mimicked. Clearly he thought it odd they were using first names already.

"It was not only I who made you wear it," she said in an attempt to keep the conversation away from awkward subjects. "Widow Dawson wants you to keep it on a while longer too."

"Does it hurt?" Orlando asked.

"A little." Nick sat on the chair beside Lucy and stretched out his long legs.

"How did it happen?"

"I don't know."

"Surely you must have some inkling. Did you fall out of a tree or were you set upon?"

"What would he be doing up a tree?" Lucy asked.

Orlando raised his hands, palm up. "Cole… clough gets up to all sorts of things when he's… traveling."

"Why would I be traveling in these parts at all?" Nick said, leaning forward.

"One question at a time."

Nick glanced at Lucy. She shrugged. Let Orlando satisfy his own curiosity first. Their questions could wait.

Matilda entered with ale in pewter cups and a trencher laden with gingerbreads. She set them on a table nearby then left. Lucy handed the cups to her guests.

"We think I was set upon," Nick said, setting his cup down on the table. "Lucy found me covered in blood in one of her brother's meadows."

"He was dazed," she added. "He didn't know where he was. I brought him home and patched him up as best as I could. Did Widow Dawson explain about his memory loss and that he thinks he's eighteen?"

"She did," Orlando said, holding Nick's gaze. "So you really can't recall anything of the last eleven years?"

Nick rested his elbows on his knees and shook his head. "How did we meet, Mr. Holt?"

Orlando gave a wry smile. "That's the first time you've ever addressed me as Mr. It's always been just Holt or Orlando." He paused, but neither Nick nor Lucy filled the silence. Did he expect them to? "We worked together," he said. "That's how we met."

"We worked?"

"Ye-es. Why do you say it as if I'd just told you your hair was green?"

"What did we work at?"

Orlando's brow furrowed. "We were retained by a man named Lord Oxley. Do you remember him?"

Nick rubbed a finger over his lips and gave a single nod. "It sounds familiar. What sort of things did we do for this Oxley?"

Orlando's hesitation was fleeting, but Lucy noticed it. "Errands."

Nick frowned. "I'm an errand boy?"

"Hardly a boy."

"Quite," said Lucy. "But it does seem odd that the son of Lord Coleclough would—"

"Son of a lord!" Orlando stood and set his cup very deliberately and carefully on the mantelpiece. "Bloody hell."

"Don't use that language in front of a lady," Nick said.

"You don't know who his father is?" Lucy asked. "Yet you claim to be his friend."

"We are friends." Orlando ran a hand through his blond hair then down his face. He looked tired, haggard. Susanna's pregnancy must have been worrying him more than Lucy thought. "We're recent friends, comparatively anyway. I've known him only four years. Cole… clough never told me about his life before that." He spoke to Lucy but looked at Nick. "He never told anyone. Except perhaps Lord Oxley." He rested a hand on the mantelpiece and stared into the fireplace. "He'll want to know you're here."

"I can't see myself running errands for anyone, lord or not," Nick said.

"Nor can I," Lucy said. "Or you for that matter, Orlando."

"What sort of errands?" Nick asked.

"You'll have to ask Hughe that. I don't work for him anymore."

Nick brightened. "Hughe! That name sounds much more familiar. Is that what we called this Lord Oxley? We must have been good friends then."

"We were. Are. He was at my wedding."

"Was I?"

"No. You usually don't involve yourself in our personal matters."

"Then why was I in this area at all? Did I visit you?"

Orlando nodded. "Just after Lucy left yesterday morning, you arrived unannounced. You gave us a baby's rattle."

"A rattle? Ah yes, your wife is with child. So my sole purpose for being in this part of Hampshire was to deliver a baby's rattle?" Nick shook his head. "We must have been very good friends indeed."

It didn't quite make sense. The pieces didn't fit together to make a whole. "Yet you didn't attend Orlando and Susanna's wedding," Lucy said. "How odd."

Orlando merely shrugged. "The workings of Cole's mind are a mystery to me. Always have been. I assure you we are friends, good ones. Before Susanna came along, I'd have given my life for him, and I know he'd do the same for me." His gaze briefly met Nick's before he looked away. "But I never really *knew* him. How could I when he never spoke about his past? I didn't even know he was the son of a lord. What rank?"

"Baron," Nick said.

"Oxley's an earl. I wonder if he knows your father. Is he still alive?"

"He was when I was eighteen. He may be dead now." He lowered his head and blew out a breath. Lucy touched his knee, and he gave her a reassuring smile that didn't reach his eyes.

"So you know nothing of Nick's life before four years ago," she said to Orlando. All questions about the scars on his back would be futile then. "What about his other friends or acquaintances? Did you meet any of them?"

"Only our mutual colleagues. There are others who work for Hughe."

Lucy cleared her throat. "Are they all men?"

"Yes." The familiar sparkle was back in Orlando's eye. "Are you trying to ask me if he's married?"

She lifted one shoulder and concentrated on meeting his gaze without blinking or blushing. She didn't dare look at Nick.

"He's not, as far as I know," Orlando said.

Lucy's heart plunged and rose, making her feel a little nauseous and giddy.

"What sort of answer is that?" Nick asked, echoing Lucy's thoughts. "Either I am or I'm not."

"You may have been married before I knew you," said Orlando with barely strained patience. "I already told you, you're secretive. I knew nothing of your life before four years ago. You hid the fact that your father is a baron, perhaps you hid the fact you had a wife too."

"Are you implying I abandoned my wife to work for this Lord Oxley?"

"It happens. Wives are abandoned all the time."

Nick shot to his feet. "What sort of cur do you take me for?"

Orlando held up his hands. "Or she may have died. If you cared deeply for her, it would explain why you brood so."

"I don't think we were friends. It must be a lie. If you knew me at all, you'd know I'd never abandon a wife or keep the existence of my marriage a secret from those I call friend."

Did Orlando hear the slight waver when he said 'friend'? Did he notice the way Nick didn't quite meet his gaze? Lucy did, but that could be because she knew Nick had no friends before the age of eighteen. He couldn't possibly know how he'd treat one.

Orlando's mouth twisted in thought. "I agree, in a way. The Cole I knew wouldn't avoid his responsibilities where a wife was concerned, but I disagree on the rest of your claim. If it were an unhappy marriage, it's precisely the sort of thing you would keep from us."

"It's Coleclough to you," Nick growled.

Lucy's hands ached, and she realized she'd been holding the chair arms too hard. She let go and clasped her fingers in her lap.

Nick couldn't be married. He was right. He would never abandon a wife. The man she knew was honorable, and Lucy was utterly convinced that the Nicholas Coleclough she'd spent almost every waking moment with since yesterday was the *right* one. The secretive, brooding one that Orlando described was not *her* Nick. It was a mask. It had to be. But why did he need to wear one?

"You called him brooding just now," she said to Orlando. It was a description that matched the man she'd first met in the meadow, but it did not fit the Nick who had kissed her so tenderly and smiled so readily. "Yet Nick is not like that. He's amiable and sweet. Quite charming in fact."

"Charming? Sweet? At eighteen perhaps, but not at nine-and-twenty." He chuckled. "Believe me, when he's back to his usual self, you'll find him as aggravating and broody as I do."

"Perhaps…"

"Just wait and see."

"I am right here," Nick snapped. "And with respect, sir, it's likely that *you* find me aggravating because *you* aggravate *me*. I doubt I treat anyone else with less respect than they deserve."

Orlando's response was a good-natured shrug. Lucy wanted to leap to Nick's defense but held herself in check. Orlando wouldn't exaggerate such a thing, and besides, Nick had been no charmer on their first meeting.

"Where is this Lord Oxley now? Perhaps we should write to him too," she said.

"Too?" Orlando picked up his cup and sipped.

"We wrote to Nick's father at Coleclough Hall. Widow Dawson has the letter now."

"I see. I'll notify Hughe for you. No need to trouble yourself."

"That's not necessary," Nick said. "We don't want to inconvenience you, what with your wife being so close to her time."

"I'll send a man in my stead."

"Where does he live?"

"Oxley House, only a day's ride away. But he's probably not there."

"How could you possibly know that?"

Orlando sipped slowly, a delaying tactic if Lucy ever saw one. "He rarely is," he said, setting his cup down on the mantelpiece again. "He travels a lot."

"Then how will you know where to find him?"

"I know places he frequents."

It was like watching two bulls butting heads in the paddock. Neither was prepared to back away, yet they didn't move forward either. Were they this aggressive toward each other all the time?

Orlando sat down again and fixed Lucy with an alarmingly serious gaze. "How many people know he's here aside from Widow Dawson and Bel?"

She glanced at Nick, but he was studying Orlando, his eyes narrowed. It would seem he had heard the tightness in Orlando's voice too.

"Everyone in Sutton Grange would have heard by now," she said. "I sent a lad to ask Milner if anyone matching Nick's description had been through. Milner said none had, but you know what he's like. He would have told half the village."

"More than half." Orlando dragged his hand through his hair again. "You need to come home to Stoneleigh with me, Cole."

"What?" Nick blurted out.

"Absolutely not," Lucy said. "Susanna is in no state to care for him, and she shouldn't be burdened with a guest at the moment." She picked up the trencher of sweetmeats and thrust them under Orlando's nose. "I would have thought you'd have more care for your wife's condition."

Orlando took a sweetmeat and popped it into his mouth.

"Why?" Nick's lips were white from pressing them together. "What does it matter if the whole county knows I'm here?"

"It was simply a friendly gesture." Orlando shrugged and rose.

Lucy didn't believe him for a moment. He'd been genuinely worried when she told him Milner knew about Nick staying at the farm.

"I have to go," he said, glancing out the window. "It's growing late. Lucy, would you be so kind as to inform the lad to bring my horse around?"

"Of course." She left but not before glancing back at the two men standing on either side of the fireplace like two sentinels. Orlando smiled at her. Nick did not. He was watching the other man with deep distrust.

She couldn't blame him. Orlando had not only avoided answering important questions, but he'd just sent Lucy out of the room. Cold dread settled in her belly where it formed a knot.

When she met the men out the front again, they hadn't changed, except perhaps Nick looked even more troubled. His dark gaze bored into Orlando's as if he could dig out some answers from him.

Orlando kissed the back of Lucy's hand. "Come and see me if you need anything."

"Give Susanna my love."

He held his hand out to Nick. Nick regarded it for a long time then clasped Orlando's forearm. They nodded once and sported the most curious expressions that Lucy suspected she'd just witnessed a silent conversation between them. Unfortunately she couldn't interpret it.

Orlando mounted and rode fast down the drive. Gravel flicked out from under the hooves as he urged the horse onward. Was he in a hurry to get back to Susanna or to send his man to find Lord Oxley?

"What did he say to you after he sent me out of the parlor?" she asked Nick.

"Nothing." He turned to go inside. "Nothing that I believe anyway."

* * *

Eleven years earlier

THEY SAID the witch lived deep in Bowen Wood at the edge of

Coleclough land. They said she was old and bent with a hawk's beak for a nose and hands like a raven's claws. Her long, gray hair tumbled down past her waist in a matted tangle, and her eyes were as black as a moonless night. So they said.

Nick didn't believe them. "There are no witches in the wood," he told the two village lads. "My father would have told me if there was."

Billy and Sidney were the sons of the blacksmith and tanner, respectively. Nick had met them the first time he'd been to the village a month earlier but hadn't seen them since. He'd not been able to sneak away from the house again, not with his father home.

But now, with his father gone for two nights to check on his tenant farms, Nick was left alone with the servants. It was easier to escape them than his father because they were too busy to keep an eye on him. Carter the house steward was the only one Nick needed to avoid. He was loyal to Nick's father and followed orders precisely. He also had fists like cannonballs and, at his master's orders, would wield them against Nick and Thomas if they disobeyed the baron.

And the baron's orders were to make sure Nick stayed in the house and immediate grounds.

"He can't be trusted not to go into the village again," Nick heard his father tell Carter before he left. "I don't want him anywhere near that place."

When he was younger, Nick used to think the village was where bad things happened to children. He imagined giants scooping small boys up off the street and taking them to their lairs. His imagination never got beyond that point because he couldn't imagine what giants would want with weak children. Nevertheless, he was sure that the village should be avoided. His father had told him so.

As he grew older, he began to doubt the existence of giants. None of his books spoke of them. He and Thomas asked their tutors about the world beyond Coleclough Hall and were told about village and city life. It didn't sound frightening at all. Indeed, it sounded interesting and Nick *needed* to experience something interesting. Coleclough Hall had become achingly dull.

So when their father went away to court, Nick took the opportunity to go into the village and see for himself. Thomas refused to join him, but that was to be expected. Thomas never disobeyed their father, never questioned his word. Nick on the other hand was beginning to think their father was lying to them, and he wanted to know why.

The village turned out to be quite safe. There were no giants, and no one tried to take him away or hurt him. The adults stared and whispered behind their hands when they saw him walking down the main street. The young children ran away and most of the youths gave him challenging glares. Only two lads, Billy and Sidney, hailed him.

Nick soon discovered they were both apprenticed to their fathers but had the afternoon off along with some other village youths, including two girls who giggled more than they talked. The tanner's son reeked from his work, but he was the more amiable of the two. It was he who first mentioned the witch in Bowen Wood. He'd heard stories about a wild woman living in a crooked cottage and he asked Nick if he'd seen her since the wood was on his father's property and not too distant from the house. Nick scoffed and told them no one could live in the wood and not come out for supplies. Someone would have seen her.

The others insisted she lived there, but the discussion was never finished because Carter found Nick and hauled him back to the house. He gave Nick four lashings for disobedience.

Nick's back had felt like it was on fire for days. He had to lie on his stomach in bed, and even the touch of his linen shirt stung. Now, a month later, the skin had healed enough that he sometimes forgot the scars altogether.

He was reminded of them, however, when he met up with Billy and Sidney in the village again. With his father away at the outlying farms, it was the first chance he'd had to sneak off. All he had to do was to keep one step ahead of Carter. That shouldn't be too difficult. Thomas had agreed, albeit reluctantly, to tell Carter that Nick was staying abed because he felt unwell. That gave Nick all day to find the lads and prove to them that nobody lived in Bowen Wood.

"I asked my Pa about her again," Billy said. He carried a small knife in his hand, and his eyes darted from tree to tree. He spoke softly, but his voice sounded loud in the still air of the densely wooded forest. Of the two lads, he seemed the most frightened. Sidney didn't seem the least bit scared. He was treating the outing as an adventure and a chance to tease his friend. He made Billy jump more than once by tapping his shoulder.

"Pa said the witch put a spell on him that made him get lost in this wood," Billy said. "He couldn't find his way out after getting too close to her cottage and if he hadn't been a good tracker, he'd have been lost in here forever."

"What was your Pa doing in here anyways?" Sidney asked. "This is Coleclough land. Hmmm?"

"Shut it," Billy hissed with a quick glance at Nick.

Nick ignored them both. He suspected Billy's father had been poaching, but he wasn't going to say so. He wouldn't jeopardize their fledgling friendship over a few birds.

"Did he say in which part of the wood he saw the cottage?" Nick asked. "We can't wander around all day." He doubted Thomas could fool Carter for more than a few hours, and Nick didn't want to get his brother in any trouble.

"There's only one path in and out," Billy said. "This must be it." Leaves rustled off to their right and he stopped dead. His wild eyes scanned the trees and undergrowth.

"It's just a bird or fox," Sidney said. "God's blood, but you're more skittish than a little girl."

"Shut yer mouth, or I'll shut it for you." But Billy didn't look in the least like he would thump anyone. He might stab them, however. His hand gripped the knife so tight his knuckles were white. A drip of sweat slipped out from beneath his cap down past his ear. "We must be in the middle of the wood by now. It's dark enough."

The canopy was so thick overhead that little light got through. Creatures scuttled about in the fallen leaves that covered the path and deadened their footsteps. If they stopped talking, no one would hear their approach, but getting Sidney to stay quiet wouldn't be easy.

"They say she lives with her familiar," the tanner's son said.

"What's a familiar?" Nick asked.

"A cat. You don't know much about witches, do you?"

"I couldn't find any books on them in our library, and my tutors didn't want to talk about the subject."

"Then what does yer Pa pay 'em for?" Sidney scoffed. "Waste of money if you ask me."

"Nobody's asking you, Sid. Now shut it or she'll hear us coming." Billy forged on, knife poised to strike.

The path was no longer straight as it had been in the outer part of the wood. It twisted to avoid larger trees and fallen logs, and cut through small clearings littered with the fat heads of mushrooms only to turn suddenly to left or right without reason.

The air was cool and damp on Nick's skin, despite the dry summer day. Leaves and twigs clawed at his clothes as if trying to stop him going further. He glanced at Sidney, expecting to see a sparkle of humor in the mischievous eyes, but there was none. He walked beside his friend, vigilant, tense.

The path suddenly narrowed, and they had to follow it in single file. Neither Sidney nor Billy seemed to want to go first so Nick took the lead. With the trees all around them, above them, it was like entering a tunnel to another world, a forgotten place.

The path wound past a large oak tree and Nick sucked in a breath. Stopped.

"What is it?" Sidney hissed behind him. "Let me see." He pushed Nick aside. "God's blood," he muttered.

The path led to a clearing in the middle of which stood a house. It was small but not crooked as the boys had claimed. In fact it appeared to be well cared for. The plaster between the wooden frame was free of gaps, and the windows had glass panes in them, which not even all of the village houses could claim. There were no outbuildings that Nick could see and only a small herb garden. The woods came up close on all sides as if it were about to swallow the cottage whole. If left untended, it probably would.

Behind Nick, one of the lads began to whimper. Billy, if he had to guess.

"Told you," Sidney said, a slight tremor in his voice. "We seen it. Now, let's go."

"Wait." Nick wasn't going to let the opportunity pass. He may not have another chance to come back. "I was wrong and you were right. Somebody does live in here. Don't you want to see who?"

"No!" Billy whispered.

"You're mad," Sidney said. "Let's go before she comes out."

"She?"

"Witches are always women. Christ, don't you know anything?"

"I know there's someone living in there. See the smoke coming out of the chimney? And I know whoever lives here must get their supplies somehow. They're not growing anything except a few herbs, and I don't see a single goat, pig or even a hen." The entire scene was like a painting, very still except for the slow drift of smoke from the chimney. "Come on."

Billy grabbed his arm and pulled back hard. "You *are* mad! I'm leaving. I don't want no witch to put a spell on me. Might never find me way out of here. Come on, Sid."

But Sidney didn't seem to hear him. He stared at the cottage. His breaths came short and fast and he made a noise in the back of his throat like he was choking. "Someone's watching."

Nick squinted at the cottage and his stomach flipped. A face stared back at them from the window, framed by gray, wavy hair.

"We should speak to her," he said. But neither lad heard him. Sidney and Billy had fled back along the path.

The woman in the cottage pressed her palms to the window-panes. She stared back at him, her lips slightly apart, her dark eyes unblinking. She was no beauty but nor was she a wrinkled crone with a beak nose and talons for fingers. She was just an ordinary old woman.

He lifted a hand and waved. She jerked back from the window.

Nick took a step toward the house but stopped. Something crashed along the path behind him. Twigs snapped, and the swat of leaves meant the creature was big and close. Nick felt for the knife tucked into his belt, but he was too late. Carter emerged from the trees, his massive frame like an ancient trunk itself. He grabbed Nick's arm and hauled him back the way he'd come. He didn't speak, just growled and grunted like a wild animal.

"Stop!" Nick shouted. "There's someone living in there! Let me go!"

But Carter stormed back along the path to where it widened, and his horse was tethered to a tree. "Get up," he ordered.

When Nick didn't move, Carter slammed his fist into Nick's jaw. He stumbled, but Carter caught him by the front of his jerkin and lifted him onto the horse.

"No!" Nick shouted, struggling to right himself. Carter's arm clamped over his back and held him down. The steward mounted and the horse took off. "Let me go! Stop! NO!"

CHAPTER 9

*L*ucy ran across the landing to the guest bedchamber but paused outside the door. She pressed her ear to the wood and heard the bed creak and Nick groan "No." He was having another nightmare. He would be in need of comfort, and she saw no point in waking Henry for that. Her brother must get his sleep, or he'd be unbearable in the morning. Of course he would be angry if he found out she'd been in Nick's bedchamber alone—so she simply wouldn't tell him. She was in no danger from Nick, and she would not let him suffer on his own.

She pushed open the door. The room was dark but she could just make out the shapes of the furniture. "Nick, wake up."

He sat up in the bed. His gasping breaths filled the silence. "Lucy?" His voice was rough, almost concealing the slight tremor, but not quite.

Lucy knelt on the floor beside him and touched his arm. A shudder rippled through him. "Are you all right?"

"Yes," he said and leaned back into the pillows. She could not see his face in the darkness, only his silhouette.

"Let me light a candle," she said.

"No. No light." He wiped the back of his hand across his forehead and drew in another heavy breath. "Stay here. Please."

She entwined her fingers with his and waited until his breathing returned to normal. The rush matting pressed into her knees through the linen of her nightgown, and she shifted her weight from one knee to the other.

"It's more comfortable on the bed," he said, gently tugging her up.

She sat beside him, hip to hip with the covers between them. She could feel the tension crackling through him via their linked hands but his face was still hidden in shadow. Despite the darkness, she could feel his gaze on her, watching, as if he could see her.

"Tell me about the nightmare," she said.

"I'd rather not."

"I understand, but if you want your memory back, it might help to talk about it."

The fingers grasping her hand tightened. "I can't make complete sense of it yet."

"How do you mean?"

"The dream is incomplete, and…"

"And what?"

"It's only a dream, Lucy. It may have been vivid, but until my memory returns, I'll treat it as nothing more than that."

"Then you should have no qualms telling me about it."

He grunted a laugh. "Is that female logic?"

"It's the logic of someone who cares for you and wants to help."

He pressed her knuckles to his lips, and she shifted closer. Her arm brushed his bare chest and her stomach fluttered. A few more inches and her nipples would press against all that hard muscle. It would be so easy to do it, and she desperately wanted to. The fluttering became a somersault.

She felt him smile against her knuckles. "With logic like that, how can I deny you anything?"

She waited for him to begin, but he did not. Every passing moment stretched her nerves tighter until she thought they might snap.

Finally, he lowered her hand to the bed. "Do you remember that I told you I defied my father and went into the village? Well, in my dream, I did it again a month later and met up with two lads. I wanted to prove them wrong about a witch they said lived in Bowen Wood. No one could live there without anyone seeing her. Or so I thought. When Father left for two days, I took the lads into the wood. We came across a cottage. It was small but well kept."

"Someone was living there?"

He nodded. "I saw a face at the window."

Lucy gasped. "Man or woman?"

"Woman. She was old and looked as surprised to see us as we were to see her."

"What did you do?"

"Billy and Sidney fled, but I wanted to speak to her. Only I didn't. Carter, my father's steward, found me and… took me home."

She waited but he said no more. "Took you? What do you mean?" It was impossible to think that anyone could make Nick go where he didn't want to go. He may have been barely a man at eighteen, but he must have been taller than most, even then. "Tell me," she said when he didn't answer. "Tell me what he did."

"I was too slow and distracted by the sight of the woman in the cottage, and he is a big man. I didn't see his fist coming."

"*He* hit you? Not your father?"

"Carter was given free reign when Father was absent. He was allowed to discipline us as he saw fit. Carter's fists belonged to my father."

"Good lord," she said on a breath. "Was he the one who whipped you?"

"That first time, yes. The second time…I don't know. I was dazed after that punch. I think I blacked out because the dream fades and starts again back at the house. Father was there, waiting. He'd returned early because he'd forgotten something." He shook his head and pressed his fingers into his eyes. "The dream is faint at best from that point. All I remember is Father ranting. He was furious. The next thing I recall is being whipped, over and over. I struggled, but… I couldn't get away." He swallowed loudly. "I still wore my shirt. It felt like the linen was being driven into my skin." He leaned forward as if he could feel the sting of the lashes against his back and needed to get away from them.

It brought him into Lucy's arms, open and waiting for him. He buried his face into the hollow where her shoulder met her throat. His hot, ragged breaths warmed her skin. His heart pounded against her breast, and he could not fail to have felt hers beating equally fast. She wiped her cheeks lest her tears drip onto him. He didn't need the burden of her sadness on top of his own.

"Then I woke up and you were here," he said, wrapping his arms around her waist.

"I'll always be here for you." She hadn't meant to say it out loud, but now that she had, her heart swelled to near bursting.

He pulled away, and she could just make out the shine in his eyes as he peered back at her. "Always?"

She took his face in her hands. "Yes," she whispered.

The kiss was gentle but sure at first. There was none of the tentativeness of their first kiss, or the teasing. It was as if he didn't care if he did it wrong, he just let instinct take over. His lips were achingly soft, but his tongue was urgent, exploring, tasting and finally, ravaging. The kiss swamped her, brought every nerve to life and then set them alight.

Nick brushed his hand through her hair and held her head in place. It was unnecessary. She wasn't going anywhere. All she wanted was to be in his arms, in his bed, with his skin against hers and all that hardness…

She reached down, lightly brushing his bruised chest, down his flat stomach, reaching under the covers. She *had* to feel it. Just a feel. Nothing more.

But when she wrapped her fingers around his thick shaft, and he groaned into her mouth, she knew she would do anything to have him. To claim him as her own.

This man, this man, this man.

So right. So perfect.

He broke the kiss and rose onto his knees, drawing her up with him. He helped her remove the nightshift over her head then captured her in his arms once more and kissed her until she was nothing but a loose collection of bones inside hot skin.

His hand rested on her hip and slowly, slowly moved up to her breast. He cupped it and thrummed the nipple with his thumb. She sucked air between her teeth. She may have even whimpered. She was too dazed to know what sounds she made.

"Like that?" he asked.

"Yesssss."

"Tell me what else you like. I... I don't know what to do."

It was almost laughable, but she did not even smile. The man knew more than any closeted eighteen year-old should. "Touch me. Everywhere."

He removed his hand and replaced it with his mouth. His tongue circled her nipple and little sparks shot through her. Heat spread beneath her skin, pooling in her inner thighs where his hand now explored. He found her opening, dipped the tip of one finger in to the first knuckle. She bit her lip to stop herself crying out.

He smiled around her breast. "You like that?"

"Mmmmm."

He pushed the finger in all the way, meeting no resistance. She thought he would be shocked, or perhaps horrified, but he said nothing. Perhaps he'd forgotten what virginal women were supposed to feel like.

Then all thoughts fled when the heel of his palm rubbed her swollen, sensitive nub. She must have made a sound because he paused.

"Don't stop." Her voice was husky, thick.

She reached down between them and found his member once more. He jerked at the touch then groaned deep in his chest. His mouth left her breast, and he kissed her throat, her lips. The kiss turned hungry, devouring, desperate.

A drop of moisture formed on the tip of his shaft. She rubbed it around the smooth head with her thumb. His body tensed against her, as taut as a lute string. "I want to enter you," he rasped.

Somewhere, a kernel of sense remained. She cursed it for appearing now when it had not appeared with Edmund. It seemed cruel, but she couldn't push it away, no matter how hard she tried. "We shouldn't."

He kissed her just beneath her ear. If he was trying to render her senseless, so she couldn't protest, he was going about it the right way. "Orlando didn't think I was wed," he said. "And nor do I."

"It's not that."

"It's all right, my little light. I won't empty into you. I can wait for that, although I might go mad in the meantime." His mouth was on hers again, and she felt his wicked, crooked smile against her lips. "But there are other things we can do together that I think you will enjoy."

"I thought you said you didn't know how." She cupped his face and it may have been dark but she could make out the heat burning in his eyes well enough.

"My memory seems to be returning. Or perhaps it's instinct."

"Just how many lovers have you had?"

"I can't remember." He thrust his finger inside her again and at the same time teased her nub with his thumb.

She cried out and rode his hand, wanting that finger to drive in harder, all the way. His other hand snaked behind her lower back. She arched against it, thrusting her breasts up. He took one in his mouth, and she almost lost the last thread of self-control holding her together. She had never felt this before. Never felt the tightness in her belly and between her thighs, nor the intensity nor the odd sensation of her body winding up like a spring.

She may not have experienced such feelings before, but her body seemed to have deep knowledge that knew what was coming. The anticipation was maddening. Thrilling.

Not yet. Not yet. She wanted to take him over the edge with her.

She reached between them and clasped his manhood. It was

rigid as a pole, the head slippery with moisture. His body jerked as she pumped him.

"Lucy," he murmured around her nipple. "My little light." His soft words shredded her last threads of self-control. The spring that had been steadily winding up inside her finally snapped. She exploded on his hand.

Shocks rocked her. Waves of an intensely satisfying pleasure crashed through her, scattering pieces of her across the bed. And then they all came rushing back and slammed together as Nick pulsed in her hand. He tipped his head back and a low growl began in his throat. It grew louder, louder, and then he gave one final jerk and spurted his seed over her hand, her stomach.

When the last drop fell and his last groan subsided, he sat back on his haunches and regarded her. At least, she suspected he was looking at her, although she couldn't see his expression.

"What are you thinking?" she asked softly.

He reached out and gently teased a strand of her hair. It had come free from its nighttime braid at some point. "I'm thinking how lucky I am to receive such a gift."

"But I didn't give you anything." She had not given her body, not completely. Not the way she wanted to.

"That's not how it felt from here." He climbed off the bed and padded over to the trunk near the window. He returned to the bed and wiped her clean with a cloth. "I hope I deserved that."

What an odd thing to say. "Why wouldn't you?"

He didn't answer immediately but set the cloth on the table. He lay down and lifted the covers for her to join him. She slipped in beside him, skin against skin, one leg resting on top of his. He tucked her into his side and kissed the top of her head. She thought he was thinking of an answer but after a moment, his body relaxed and his breathing became steady and deep. He was asleep.

* * *

"GOOD MORNING, MISTRESS," Matilda said when Lucy passed by the kitchen.

"Hmmmm?" Lucy smiled at her. "Oh yes, good morning. It looks like another lovely day out. How is everybody today?"

The cook looked up from her chopping board and cocked an eyebrow at one of the maids working opposite at the central kitchen table.

Matilda narrowed her eyes. "We're all well, thank the lord. Yer in fine spirits this mornin', mistress. Had a good sleep, did ye?"

"Yes," Lucy said and turned away before the maids could see her blush. "A very sound sleep. I'll be back in a moment with the eggs."

Matilda followed her into the narrow passageway leading outside. "Mr. Coleclough's already up and about," she said. "He's talkin' to the master outside."

"He's supposed to be resting." Lucy collected her egg basket and went out through the kitchen yard to the barn.

Nick and Henry were deep in conversation as the two grooms prepared the horses for the day's work. A cluster of farm hands helped and more would be preparing equipment inside. It promised to be another full day of plowing.

Brutus bounded out of the barn and jumped up and down at her feet until she bent and scratched his ears. He licked her face then returned to the barn where he sat between Nick and Henry, his wagging tail sweeping an arc in the dirt. She followed him and decided she would not look at Nick. Not even once. If she did, she would surely blush, and Henry would guess what they'd done.

"Good morning," Nick said, a smile in his voice.

"Good morning," she said, all politeness.

Henry, leaning against the stable wall, nodded a greeting. She'd not thought it possible, but he looked even more exhausted than the day before.

"Are you all right?" she asked him.

He sighed. "Yes, just tired. I didn't sleep well."

"Oh?" she squeaked. "Any reason for that?"

"I thought I heard a noise, but it must have been the house creaking because I didn't hear it again."

"The house does creak in this weather. A lot."

"And groan too," Nick said. He spoke with such sincerity that not even Lucy could detect any mischief.

She stared at Henry. The harder she stared, the less chance she had of laughing or blushing.

Fie! She blushed.

Beside her, Nick cleared his throat. Henry, fortunately, didn't notice. He watched one of the grooms pull the plow out of the barn.

"So," she said, swinging her basket on her arm, "what were you two talking about?"

"Farming," Henry said. "You wouldn't be interested."

"Yes, I am. It's our livelihood after all. I may not have shown much interest when I was younger, but now that I'm mistress, I want to share ideas and burdens with you."

He grunted and kicked at the dirt with the toe of his boot. "Very well, let me share my day with you. I rose before dawn, ate a hearty breakfast, and I'll spend the rest of the day standing in the sun, helping with the plowing. That's it. No, wait, there is more. After supper I'll try to read a book, but I doubt I'll get further than a page because the light will be poor, and I'll fall asleep anyway. There? Satisfied? Did you find that interesting, Sis?" He pushed off from the barn wall and stalked inside.

Lucy bit her lip and watched him go. If they didn't have an audience, she would have gone after him and demanded he not speak to her so. Not that it would have done him any good, but it would have made her feel better, at least for a little while.

"Don't be angry with him," Nick said.

"He didn't have to snap at me. I really am interested in learning more about farming. If I'm to be mistress of Cowdrey Farm for some time, I want to help."

His arm brushed hers and she looked up into those soothing eyes. "Your presence here alongside him is more than helpful. I think he's glad just to have your company. He didn't say so, but it's as clear as day."

"Oh."

"He was telling me how proud he is that you were accepted into the community of Sutton Grange so quickly and easily. Your brother adores you, Lucy. Of course, you're an easy person to adore."

Her eyes widened, and she quickly checked to make sure no one was within earshot. "Stop it," she hissed.

"Why?"

"Because if Henry hears, he'll send you away." Her chest tightened at the bleak thought.

He bent down to her level. Amusement tugged at the corners of his mouth. "Not if my intentions are honorable."

Her heart came to a grinding halt. Her mouth fell open and she stared at him.

"Breathe," he said, grinning.

She did, but ended up gulping in air and coughing. He rubbed her back. "But… we've only known each other two days," she said weakly.

"It feels much longer." His smile faded and his gaze grew serious. "I *know* you, Lucy Cowdrey, and you know me. Nothing else matters."

"Your memories matter."

He looked away. "Yes." His voice sounded strained through his clenched jaw.

She wanted to touch him, make him look her in the eye, but she could not with so many people wandering about nearby. "Tell me what Orlando said, Nick. What does he know about you that bothers you so much?"

He turned back to her, smiling once more, but she knew it was false. "It's nothing."

"I don't think—"

"Cowdrey!" he called over the top of her head. "Did you speak to your man?"

Henry joined them again. He removed the wide straw hat he always wore in the fields and nodded at Nick. "Aye, and he likes your idea. He said he wanted to speak to the blacksmith for some time about a new coulter for the plow, but he was waiting for me to settle in as master here before he broached the subject. They're costly, so he said."

"True, but pay for themselves in the long run."

So Nick and Henry really had been discussing farming before she arrived. How odd. She'd not pegged Nick as the farming type, although he said his father had tenant farmers working Coleclough land. He must have learned some of the skill through them. Yet he'd implied that his father had kept him prisoner in Coleclough Hall, not letting him venture further than the immediate vicinity. Where had he learned about plows then?

"What will you do today, Sis?" Henry asked her.

"Take care of Nick."

Henry sighed dramatically. "You have my sympathies, Coleclough."

Lucy crossed her arms and glared at her brother. It was nice to see him in a teasing mood, but did he have to do it in front of Nick? It made her feel like a child again.

"I don't need taking care of now," Nick said. "I feel much better. Why not do something for yourself today?"

"Myself?"

"Visit friends, go for a walk. Do whatever it is you like to do."

"Why?" What she'd really wanted to say was '*But I want to spend time with you.*'

"I agree," Henry said. "You should see your friends. I know how important they are to you, especially Susanna Holt." He chucked her under the chin. "Enjoy your day, and I'll speak to you at supper." It was a great change from the angry retort of a few minutes ago, but that was Henry. Quick to flare up and quick to return to his even-tempered self. She supposed the unexpected kindness was his way of apologizing for his outburst.

"I will," she said to Henry. He walked off and she turned on Nick. "You really don't want me here?"

"I didn't say that." Brutus ran out of the barn and planted himself at Nick's booted feet. Nick bent down to pat him. "You deserve to spend some time doing the things you enjoy doing and not thinking about my needs."

There was that word again. Deserve. "I like being with you, you fool."

He smiled up at her. "Good, because I like being with you. Which is why I also want you to live your life as you usually would without worrying about me."

"You think me not being here will stop me worrying about you?"

He stood and Brutus whimpered. "Please, Lucy, I'd feel happier knowing you're not giving anything up to care for me. Go and visit Mistress Holt. I'm sure she must be bored senseless by now."

"She has her husband for company."

"Then she's probably desperate for good company." He took the basket from her and crooked his elbow. "After breakfast, take the cart and have the grooms escort you."

"Escort me?"

"The roads can be dangerous these days. You never know who you might meet."

"I don't need an escort."

He said nothing, but she got the feeling she'd just lost their first disagreement.

* * *

ORLANDO STEPPED through the archway of the walled garden when Lucy's horse and cart rattled up the gravel drive of Stoneleigh. He rubbed the horse's nose as the cart came to a stop.

"Glad to see you've got an escort today," he said to Lucy.

She frowned. He was sounding remarkably like Nick. "Why?"

He shrugged. "The roads can be treacherous."

"So I hear."

He returned to his gardening, and Lucy went inside where the maid led her to the main parlor. Susanna sat with her feet on a stool, rubbing her large belly and staring out the window. A single white cloud hung in the otherwise clear sky. It looked small and lost in the vast blueness.

"I feel like an oliphant," she said, turning and smiling at Lucy.

"Have you ever seen an oliphant?" Lucy asked, sitting on the chair near her friend. Susanna was indeed large, although she'd seen larger.

"No, but Orlando has and he says they're enormous. I made the mistake of telling him I feel like one and now he calls me Ollie." She rubbed her belly again, a wistful smile on her lips. Susanna always appeared so content. It was difficult to imagine that her life had been anything but easy.

"When did Orlando see an oliphant?"

The question seemed to take Susanna by surprise. Her hand stopped its swirling motion and she shrugged. The smile vanished. "He's traveled extensively."

"Do you mean he saw one in the wild or at a fair?" Exotic creatures like monkeys and dancing bears weren't uncommon sights at the grander fairs, why not an oliphant too?

Susanna shrugged. "I don't know."

"But if it were in the wild, he must have traveled very far indeed, and to dangerous places." When Susanna didn't answer, Lucy prompted her with a, "Well?"

The maid re-entered carrying a tray with two glasses. "Cider for you both," she said, handing the glasses to Lucy and Susanna.

Susanna slowly sipped her cider. Very slowly.

"Why are you avoiding the question?" Lucy asked after the maid left.

Susanna lowered the cup. "Why are you so interested in where my husband has been? Not even I know the full extent of his travels."

"I don't mean to pry. Actually, I do mean to pry. You see,

Orlando knows my patient, Nicholas Coleclough, and I would like to know more about him. How did they meet? Where?"

"He didn't tell you?" she asked, taking great interest in the contents of her cup.

Lucy watched Susanna try to avoid answering. She wasn't very good at it, not like her husband. He was an expert. "Susanna." Lucy leaned forward and plucked the cup out of her friend's hands. "I know you know. Orlando tells you everything. Please, I must learn more about him."

"Why? Why must you know what happened in Cole's past?"

Lucy sat back, a little shocked by Susanna's vehemence. "I... I just want to understand what his life has been like up until this point."

"You've become very close very quickly, so Orlando said. Can you not tell what he's like without knowing his past? Is it not enough that he and Orlando are friends? You know my husband is a good man. He wouldn't be friends with a blackguard."

"No-o." Lucy looked to the rafters. How to explain it? "The very first time I met Nick, before the incident that robbed him of his memories, he was quite different to what he is now. He was ill-mannered and evasive. He didn't want me to see his face. Then to be set upon in such a cruel fashion... it's as if someone wanted to hurt him deliberately, perhaps even... " Bile rose to her throat. She swallowed and looked past Susanna's head to the colorful tapestry depicting a blooming garden hanging on the wall. It didn't calm her like it usually did.

Susanna reached out her hand and Lucy took it. "My dear," she said softly, "has it occurred to you that it's better for him if he doesn't remember?"

Lucy closed her eyes. "Yes. Most assuredly yes. But he doesn't want to live half a life, and I don't want that for him either. He needs to remember the good and the bad and come to terms with it so he can move forward."

"What if the bad is something he can't move forward from? What if he *is* the bad?"

"Don't be absurd. Nick is a good man, I know it in my heart, and good men don't do terrible things."

Susanna's fingers trailed across her belly as if she were stroking the babe within. "If Orlando told Nick how they met, and Nick hasn't told you, perhaps he's not ready to. Give him time, Lucy."

Lucy shook her head and rubbed her temple. "Curses."

"I know," Susanna muttered. "If it makes you feel any better, I'm not at all happy with Orlando for the way he's handled this." She smiled grimly. "I'm sorry, Lucy, but it's Orlando's wish that you not be told the details of their friendship. For now. But don't worry, I'll work on him. He's not very good at denying me anything, especially lately."

Despite her melancholy, Lucy laughed. "If you cannot tell me what they spoke about yesterday, then perchance you can tell me what Nick was like before his accident."

"I only met him twice, both times only briefly. Indeed, our first meeting was under very trying circumstances." She looked away, and Lucy winced.

"My cousins?"

Susanna nodded. "He was reticent then and again two days ago when I saw him for the second time."

"In what manner?"

"When he spoke it was with great care, as if he considered every word first. Not only that. He never smiled even when Orlando joked with him. Most odd."

"That's not at all like him now. He laughs all the time. Indeed, his mouth is always curved in some sort of smile. It's very—" She caught Susanna's own not-so secretive smile and blushed to her roots.

"I'm pleased to see you and he have become, er, friends already, no matter what Orlando says."

"What does Orlando say?"

Susanna waved her hand. "Nothing that I take very seriously. I'm beginning to think he didn't know Cole as well as he thought.

He certainly didn't know Cole was the son of a baron until yesterday."

"It's almost as if Nick is two different people."

"Perhaps. Or perhaps not as much as you think." She reached into a sewing basket near her chair. Tucked into the side next to a woolen baby blanket with an unfinished design embroidered into it was a wooden rattle. She handed it to Lucy. "He gave me this."

Lucy caressed the main branch carved into the handle with her thumb. Each leaf springing from it was different in size, shape or the way it bent. They looked so real, right down to the tiny raised veins. "It's beautiful," she said on a breath. She rattled it and the balls tumbled around the hollow larger one. "How did they get inside?" she asked, holding it up to the light.

"It's ingenious, isn't it?"

"It must have cost a considerable sum."

"That's the thing. Cole didn't buy it. He made it."

"Really?" Lucy inspected it anew. She'd never seen carving like it. "He's very skilled."

"When he gave it to me, he let me believe he bought it. It wasn't until after he was gone that Orlando told me Cole made it himself."

"Why did he wait?"

"Because Cole would be embarrassed, he said, but he didn't have an answer as to why." She shrugged and accepted the rattle from Lucy. "It seems Cole is as much a mystery to Orlando as he is to me."

"But they're friends."

"According to my husband, men can be friends without knowing every detail of each other's lives." She rolled her eyes. "I tried to argue that point with him, but I'm afraid I lost. He said he may not know how such a fearsome man as Cole can carve such a beautiful thing for a baby or why he never smiles, but he does know he can trust him not only with his own life, but with mine and this child's as well." She placed the rattle back in the basket. "There was nothing else to say after that."

Lucy's throat hurt, and she blinked rapidly. "No, I suppose not."

CHAPTER 10

 ick found the bloodstained patch of grass easily enough. He'd been dazed when Lucy found him, but he remembered being near a hedgerow in a meadow to the west of the farmhouse.

If only he could remember something about his attacker. Anything would suffice—hair color, voice, size. Or better still, the reason for the attack.

Then again, that part might be easy to explain. If what Orlando Holt said was true—and Nick still wasn't convinced on that score —someone wanted to kill him in revenge.

Except they hadn't.

It was likely his attacker had fled before finishing the task when he saw Lucy approach. If only she'd seen who it was.

No. He took that back. If she'd seen him, she'd have been his next victim.

A wave of nausea gripped his insides and his head swam. He crouched near the bloodstain and squeezed the bridge of his nose until it passed. It was the most violent reaction he'd had in two days. After the initial dizziness subsided sometime during that first night, he'd only had to put up with the headaches. The tonic Lucy had given him helped ease their severity.

Lucy. An apt name for her. She was a beacon of light in a confusing, strange world. If it weren't for her, he'd be completely alone and perhaps even dead. But she was more than merely someone to talk to, she was… she was…

There were no words to describe what being with her felt like. When she was in the room, it brightened. Her smile made his headaches lessen and when she touched him, they faded altogether. She occupied his mind when he was awake, made him hot all over when he lay in bed. He'd never felt like that about anyone, including during the forgotten years. Memory or not, he would just *know* if there'd been a woman who'd roused him as much as Lucy Cowdrey. How could a man not?

Man, youth… what in God's name was he? He felt like an eighteen year-old, but he looked much older. His face was more defined, his chest and chin hairier, and he had bulges in places he didn't know muscles formed. He was bigger *everywhere*.

Lucy had walked in on him as he'd inspected his cock under the covers that first afternoon. He'd almost burned up from embarrassment. She was so beautiful, so lovely and sophisticated, and he was a childish fool by comparison. From that moment on, he'd tried to act like the twenty-nine year-old he apparently was and not the youth he thought himself to be. Not an easy thing. It didn't take long to realize he'd lived a closeted life compared to most his age.

His bloody father. When Nick saw him again, he would find out why in God's name he kept his sons hidden from the world. He'd never doubted his father's authority before, not until those dreams of the beatings. Nick shuddered and part of him wished those memories had never returned, yet the other part knew they were something he needed to accept. If only he could remember what had happened after the second beating and in the following years, it might help complete the muddled picture of his life.

One thing was certain. When he was well enough, he'd travel back to Kent and confront his father. Then he'd get Thomas as far away from Coleclough Hall as possible, if he wasn't already.

Nick scrubbed his hands over his face and stood. Enough reminiscing. He'd come to this spot to see if he remembered more about the attack. He inspected the area. There were no overhanging branches and few hiding spots except for the hedgerow, but the ground was grassy and soft. Footfalls would be near impossible to hear, especially if he'd been sound asleep.

Odd that he should be aware of those things. Observing his surroundings seemed to come naturally to him, as instinctive as breathing. He always knew when someone was near, particularly Lucy, and his hearing seemed as acute as Brutus's. He could wield a knife with skill too, he'd found, and when he'd snuck out of the farmhouse, it had been easy to do so without being seen except by Lucy's dog. All traits of a good assassin. And he'd been good, so Holt claimed.

He rubbed his forehead, but it pounded harder than ever. Too full of wild thoughts, that was the problem. The only time he'd been able to forget Holt's claim was when Lucy had given him his first experience with a woman—or the first that he could recall.

He smiled, closed his eyes and pictured her naked in his bed. It made him hard again. She was perfection. Her skin was soft and her curves fit his body as if she'd been made for him. Just him. He'd not expected her to respond to his touch with such abandon, such pure enjoyment. He didn't think women were supposed to like the act, merely endure it. But then, his brother had told him everything he knew about coupling, and Thomas was probably as naïve as Nick.

Thank God he'd somehow known what to do to make her react like that. It would have been too humiliating to be a bumbling fool. Instincts again, he supposed. Powerful things.

She would be back soon from her visit to Susanna Holt's house. He wanted to be there for her return and since the meadow hadn't shaken loose any memories of the attack, he whistled for Brutus. The hound bounded across the grass and fell into step with Nick as he headed along the track to the farmhouse. He kept vigilant, his senses tuned to any strange noise or movement. Just like an assassin.

It seemed more and more likely that Holt had not lied to him as Nick had first thought. Holt told him they'd been friends, although they saw each other rarely since he'd left the Assassin's Guild. His wife knew about his past, he'd said, but Lucy did not. Nor would she. There was no need to darken her world with such knowledge. No need to change her opinion of either Nick or Holt. They had agreed on that score.

Besides, Nick wasn't going to be an assassin anymore. As soon as he was well enough, he was going home to Coleclough Hall, and he was taking Lucy with him.

* * *

BRUTUS GREETED the cart by barking and circling round and round on the spot. It was his way of showing enthusiasm without getting too close to the horse. The driver brought the cart to a halt near the house and Lucy hopped down. Brutus approached with apparent calmness, but from the *whip whip* of his tail it was obvious it took him a lot of effort to restrain himself around the horse as he'd been trained to do.

"Good boy," Lucy said, bending down to ruffle his ears. He put his paws on her shoulders, almost knocking her over.

"Steady," said Nick, suddenly beside her. He caught her elbow and helped her to stand.

"Where did you spring from?"

"Just over the way," he said.

"Which way?"

His hand slipped down to grasp hers. Their fingers entwined. "I'm glad you're back safe and sound."

"Why wouldn't I be?"

He shrugged and looked down at their linked hands.

It seemed he didn't want to answer any of her questions. Well, that was too bad for him. She'd had quite enough evasiveness for one day. "Where have you been?"

He looked up. "Why do you think I've been out?"

"Your boots are dusty."

"I'm sure they're always dusty."

"Matilda cleaned them this morning. I saw them in the storeroom tucked out of the way."

"You're very observant."

She pulled her hand out and stamped it on her hip. "Answer the question."

He sighed. "I walked over to the meadow where you found me."

"Nick! You shouldn't exert yourself. Widow Dawson said no activity until your head wound has healed."

"There was nothing to do once you were gone."

"I only left because you insisted." She took his elbow and drew him toward the house. Brutus ran ahead, turned once to see if they followed, then took off again. "You shouldn't have gone alone. You're not well enough."

"I wasn't alone. I had Brutus."

"What if you'd collapsed? How would you get back?"

"Brutus would raise the alarm."

"Much good that would do you if you'd opened up the wound and bled to death in the meantime."

He nudged her shoulder. "Worried about me?"

"Yes, you big fool."

He stopped. Stared at her.

"What is it?" she said, frowning.

"You really are worried about me?" The soft wonder in his voice took her by surprise.

"Of course I am."

"Because I'm your patient?"

"No. Is that what you think you are to me? After last night?"

"Forgive me for my bluntness." His gaze turned smoky, warm, and he sported the most curious smile. "I know nothing about the

ways of the heart, or women for that matter. I had to make sure."
He leaned down and kissed her lightly on the lips.

She gasped and pulled away. "Someone might see."

He stepped back as if she'd pushed him. His face paled. " I–I'm
sorry. Forgive me, Lucy. I thought… " He pressed the heel of his
hand into his eye. "I'm a fool."

He turned to go but she caught his arm. "Stay. I'm the one who
should be sorry." What in God's name was she doing? They liked
each other, and a kiss wasn't the same as being ravaged behind the
oak tree. Indeed, she wouldn't mind in the least if Nick took her
behind a tree, or in a bed, or in the barn with straw poking her in
tender places. She'd have him anywhere. There would be no need
for the persuasive tactics Edmund found necessary.

"Don't apologize," he said, looking down at his shuffling feet. "I
thought… " He shook his head. "I'm not used to this. God's blood."

She slipped her hand inside his, and he peered at her through
his long lashes. He was maddeningly adorable when he did that
and she wanted to throw her arms around him and kiss him all
over.

"I don't know why I reacted like that," she said. "It's just that I'm
afraid Henry will send you away if he finds out."

His fingers tightened around hers. "So it's not that you don't
like me?"

"Oh, Nick, you really are a big fool. Of course I like you." And
more, but she didn't think he was ready to hear how much. She
wasn't sure she was ready to tell him. Time. That's what she
needed. Time to get to know him better, and time for him to
remember himself.

"Then why would your brother object? If I tell him my intentions toward you are honorable, wouldn't that keep him happy?"

"My brother is a lawyer, or he almost was. He works with
truths and certainties. He wouldn't believe that two people could
care for each other after such a short time, nor would he like it
that much of your life is shrouded in shadows. He doesn't know

your family or friends, and he has no proof that you are indeed who you say you are. Not even Orlando knows your past."

"When you put it like that, I sound like a mercenary. I'm sorry, Lucy, I didn't think of it from his point of view. If I were responsible for a younger sister, I'm not sure I would have allowed me in the house at all."

She drew in a deep breath. It wasn't fair for him to blame himself. It was time to be honest. Otherwise, it would always stand in the way. "Especially when you know that younger sister's history."

"What do you mean?"

"Do you remember I told you that I was betrothed to another man? Or I thought I was?"

"Ye-es." He trailed a finger down her cheek to her chin, tracking the path of tears she'd once shed by the barrelful over Edmund Mallam. "Does he still claim a piece of your heart?"

"No! Good lord, nothing like that."

His chest rose and fell with his deep breath.

"The thing I didn't tell you, Nick, was that I gave myself to Edmund. He promised to marry me if he could have my maidenhead. Fool that I was, I believed him."

His mouth worked, opening and closing several times as if he wanted to speak but thought better of it. At least he didn't stalk off, but this reaction was little better.

"I should have told you," she muttered. "Before…"

"No. Don't."

"But you're angry with me."

"Angry? Lucy, no. Never." He threw his hands in the air and let them fall on his hips. "I'm not angry at you, don't think that. I just wish I'd known." He shook his head. "Then again, perhaps it's best that I didn't."

"Oh?"

He glanced around as if checking to see they were alone, or perhaps he was simply avoiding her gaze. "I don't know if I like being less experienced than you."

She tried hard not to laugh. She really did, but it just burst out of her like a fountain. "Oh Nick, last night could not have been your first time. You knew exactly what you were doing."

"I'm sure it's something I would remember. It was very, er, interesting. Not the sort of thing I'd forget."

She rolled her eyes. "You'll just have to accept that I'm right, and you're wrong. Not easy for a man, I know, but there you have it." She hooked her arm through his and they walked toward the house. "Perhaps you don't remember because last night was nothing like those other times," she said quietly. "It wasn't for me."

"What do you mean?"

"It's not something I can explain. Perhaps when your memories return, you'll understand the difference."

"Returning to the topic of kissing you, what if—"

"Mistress!" called the lankier of the two grooms, trotting up to them. "Mistress, there's a lad here. Matilda let him wait in the barn for you. He says he's lookin' for work."

"What kind of work?"

"Laboring, mucking out stalls or the milkhouse, whatever he can get." As he spoke, a boy of about fifteen emerged from the barn, blinking in the bright light. He lifted a hand to shield his eyes as he looked at Lucy.

"Henry's in need of help," she said. "The lad's arrival is timely. Give him something to do until my brother returns. He can decide what to do with him then."

He nodded and walked back to the barn, shouting an order at the newcomer.

"Henry's not happy here, is he?" Nick asked.

"He will be once he's used to farming. He just needs time to adjust."

"Perhaps it's not a good idea to let him catch me kissing his sister, then."

She grinned. "He's probably more inclined to challenge you to a duel now than he would have been only a few months ago. His temper has certainly worsened."

"I used to be quite a good swordsman," Nick said. "Thomas too. We had wooden swords as children and used to battle each other in the long gallery. Because he was older and fairer, he got to be the English sea captain, and I was always the Corsair. As we grew up, the level of our playing did too. The wooden swords got replaced for starters."

"You fought your brother with a *real* sword?"

He smirked. "How else were we to learn the art of swordplay?"

"But you could have hurt each other." She clicked her tongue. "I honestly don't understand men at times."

"Yet you have two brothers."

"Gentle creatures, both of them. They own swords, of course, but they've never used them in real combat. Henry doesn't even take his into the village on market day, although other gentlemen do."

"So I have nothing to worry about if he challenges me to a duel?"

They'd reached the kitchen garden. Brutus sat near a rosemary bush, panting, his big eyes watching their every move.

"Is that your way of saying you're going to try and kiss me in public again?" she asked.

He strode ahead along the path that separated the garden into herbs on one side and lettuces on the other. Brutus fell into step beside him. Both paused at the doorway and waited for her. "Only when you're ready, my little light. Only when you're ready."

NICK AND BRUTUS heard the riders before Lucy did. She and Nick were inspecting the day's progress with the front porch as they waited for Henry and his farmhands to return. The builders were almost finished, and she couldn't wait to see it without the network of scaffolding covering the brickwork.

"Wait here," Nick said as the two men rode toward the house. "I'll see what they want."

He strode off before she could remind him that she was the mistress and he the guest. Brutus trotted alongside him, his tail wagging madly. He loved meeting new people.

Nick hailed the riders and the two men dismounted and nodded a greeting.

"Are you the master here?" one asked.

"I'm Mistress Cowdrey," Lucy said before Nick could speak. "This farm belongs to my father and my brother manages it. This is our guest, Mr. Coleclough."

The men removed their hats but neither looked at her. Both boldly kept their gazes locked with Nick's.

"Do I know you?" he asked them.

The older of the two licked his lips as he inspected Nick, taking particular interest in the bandage. The few strands of gray hair clinging to the man's shiny head were matted with sweat, and his face was craggier than a cliff. His companion was a little younger and leaner with a reddish beard that was in need of a trim. He wore a brown linen doublet with brass buttons down the front, the embroidered shirt cuffs poking out of the sleeves for effect. A townsman then, and a well-off one at that.

The lanky groom strode toward them. "Take yer mounts for you, sirs?" The men handed him the reins and he led the horses to the trough near the barn.

"My name is John Sawyer," the younger man said to Nick and Lucy. "And this is Thomas Upfield. We're from Larkham."

Lucy felt rather than saw Nick stiffen.

"You been in Larkham of late?" the older man, Upfield, asked.

"No," she said. "Why? Has something happened?"

"Sir?" Upfield said to Nick. "Have you been to the village of Larkham?"

"Mistress Cowdrey asked you a question," Nick said. "It would be ungentlemanly not to answer her."

Upfield sneered. "Do we look like gen'lemen to you?"

"You look like you need to be taught some manners. I'm available, and I'm an excellent instructor."

Sawyer cleared his throat and bowed to Lucy. "Our apologies, madam. We didn't mean to offend. Upfield and I are weary from riding all day, and our business is unpleasant."

"And the nature of your business?" she pressed.

"Murder."

She gasped and pressed a hand to her stomach. "Good lord, who has been murdered?"

"Alderman Renny."

She'd never met the man, but she'd seen him around the Sutton Grange market. He'd pranced about like a peacock, his large belly almost bursting out of his doublet. His booming voice carried through the crowd, and no one could have failed to hear his derogatory remarks about the produce supplied by all the Sutton Grange villagers and surrounding farms, including Cowdrey. Later, he'd apparently become rolling drunk at the Plough Inn and spoken crudely to a few of the women. He'd been thrown out after he'd tried to lift Milner's daughter's skirts. The only ones who'd gotten angry on his behalf had been a few of his fellow Larkham villagers. Perhaps these two had been among them.

"Who would do such a thing and why?" she asked.

"'Twas a traveler," Upfield said, scratching his balding head. He continued to study Nick, his gaze sweeping up, down, up, down. "Nobody knows why."

Sawyer rubbed the back of his neck and for a moment Lucy thought he'd disagree with his companion, but he did not.

"He was a big man, like you," Upfield said to Nick.

A cold ball of dread settled in Lucy's chest. Her fists closed at her sides. Slowly, slowly, she turned to look at Nick. His Adam's apple bobbed, and he crossed his arms. He did not meet her gaze but stared at Upfield.

"He was fairer, though," said Sawyer. "His hair was brown and reached his shoulders, and he had a full beard.

Lucy's knees weakened, and Nick caught her arm to steady her. He did not let her go, but his hand relaxed and his thumb caressed little circles on her sleeve.

"How long have you been here?" Upfield asked Nick.

"Three days," Lucy said.

The men exchanged glances. "And before that?"

"He can't re—"

"Stoneleigh," Nick cut in. His thumb stopped circling and his fingers tightened their grip. "Do you know it?"

"Aye," said Sawyer. "Old Farley's a good man, his daughter and her new husband too. Holt, isn't it?"

"He's a friend of mine," Nick said. "I was visiting him when I met with an accident that prevented me leaving the area."

"Then why ain't you stayin' at Stoneleigh?" Upfield asked.

Nick touched the bandage on his head. "I'm not supposed to be moved, or the wound will open up. Mistress Cowdrey and her brother were kind enough to offer me a room until I recover."

Upfield grunted but didn't look convinced. Lucy tried very hard to keep her face bland, her gaze unwavering. She even managed a warm smile. "You both look tired and it grows late. Supper will be served as soon as my brother returns, and you're welcome to join us."

"Thank you, madam, that's kind of you," said Sawyer. He jabbed his elbow into Upfield who thanked her too. "Can we trouble you further for a bed for the night? It's a fair ride into Sutton Grange from here, and it'll be dark soon."

"Of course, if you don't mind sharing a small bedchamber with each other."

He gave her a little bow. "Don't mind at all, madam."

"There's a pail of water for washing near the barn. Everyone has to use the kitchen entrance, I'm afraid," she said, indicating the scaffolding. "One of the maids will show you to the room."

They nodded and wandered off toward the barn. Upfield glanced back at Nick, but Sawyer trudged across the gravel, his gaze on his feet.

"Why did you lie?" she said to Nick as they watched them go.

"It wasn't a lie," he said. "I was at Stoneleigh before I came here."

"Yes, but not for any length of time. You could have been in Larkham before that."

"You heard them. The alderman was murdered by a big man. I'm a big man. The alderman's family would be baying for retribution, and it would be too easy to blame me."

"The killer was fairer in coloring, and he had a beard. That's not at all like you."

"I still think it's best not to give them any reason to doubt their witness accounts." He rubbed his forehead and sighed. "I have a headache, Lucy. I don't think I'll be down for supper."

"I'll have it sent to your room." She pressed her hand to his cheek. It was hot. "Can I get you anything?"

He leaned into her palm. "You've done more than enough, little light." He did not smile, and there was no gleam of good humor in his eyes. It was like looking into a different set. Where before they were two velvety soft orbs, now they were deep and black and devoid of spark.

They walked together to the kitchen entrance and went inside. They parted at the main stairs and she headed to the parlor where Matilda was strewing herbs over the rushes. Lucy paused at the door and turned to see him halfway up the staircase, watching her. She waved and he lifted his chin in response then continued on.

It was like looking at a different man. Where had her amiable youth gone? And why did he look like someone beset by demons?

CHAPTER 11

Eleven years earlier

*N*ick hadn't been able to go anywhere for two weeks after the whipping. Even the smallest movement opened up the wounds anew, so he'd stayed in bed until they healed. His only visitors had been the maids and his brother. Thomas took one look at the marks on Nick's back and turned green.

"Carter?" he asked after taking several deep breaths.

"I don't know. I blacked out. Ask Father," Nick spat. "He was there."

Thomas swore and paced the room, shaking his head and muttering to himself. He came to an abrupt stop beside the bed where Nick lay on his side, his head propped up on his hand. "Why? Why would he do this?"

"Because of whom I saw in the cottage."

"Who was it?"

Nick sat up slowly and swung his legs over the edge of the bed. "Our mother."

Thomas dropped into a nearby chair and shoved his hands through his hair. He did not argue or disagree, but sat there like a limp sack. Nick had never seen his brother look so small before. So vulnerable. "Is she all right?" he asked.

"I don't know," Nick said. "You should go and see for yourself."

"You know I can't," he choked out.

Nick knew. Thomas didn't have it in him to disobey their father. "I'm leaving," Nick told him.

Thomas merely nodded, as if he'd known all along it would come to that.

While Nick remained isolated in his bedchamber, waiting for his wounds to heal, Thomas quietly went about gathering supplies and stocking a pack for him. He refused to go with Nick, but he didn't try to convince him to stay either. They talked a lot over the next few days, more than they ever had. About where Nick would go, what he'd do, and about their childhood, which they had begun to realize was unusual. Ever since his first visit to the village, Nick had slowly become aware of how isolated he and Thomas were. His brother seemed to have formed the same conclusion on his own.

"I don't like leaving you behind," Nick said on the night before he was set to leave.

"I'll be all right," Thomas assured him. "Father is aging. He needs me." He spread his hands to indicate the bedchamber that Nick had occupied since he was a child. "This is my home, my birthright. I won't walk away from it. Anyway, I'm twenty now, and he said he'll take me to court next time to find a wife." He offered up a small smile, as if in apology for not having the strength to confront their father.

Nick didn't blame him. Thomas had always been given more leeway, even being allowed to visit the tenant farms with their father on occasion. Perhaps because he was the heir and needed to know how to run the estate, or perhaps because he wasn't the disobedient son.

"There will always be a home here for you, Brother," Thomas said. "When I inherit, things will be different."

It was relatively easy to sneak out of the house without anyone noticing. Nick's father had set some of the grooms at intervals around the perimeter, but only during the day. Apparently no one expected Nick to escape at night.

The vines covering the front of the house held his weight, and he dropped down to the ground with a soft thud that didn't even wake the dogs sleeping inside. With his pack in hand, he raced through the formal gardens and past the outbuildings into Bowen Wood beyond. He wasn't afraid. The woman wasn't a witch. She was most likely his mother, and he didn't believe in fairies or monsters.

He hadn't counted on getting completely lost, however. The moonlight couldn't break through the dense canopy, and in the darkness, he veered off the path. He kept walking but gave up and decided to wait for dawn. The night was crisp but dry, and he must have fallen asleep. He woke up with the strong sense that he was being watched.

It took a moment for his eyes to adjust to the dull early morning light, but then he saw her. She stood amid the trees, staring at him, her face not exactly blank but empty somehow. If she recognized him, she didn't show it. She wore a simple black gown, and her gray hair hung in ropey tangles to her waist.

"Good morrow," he said. He rose slowly so as not to startle her, but needn't have worried. She came at him, very fast, and clamped her hand around his wrist. Her grip was stronger than he'd expected.

"Nicholassss." Her voice was thin and scratchy with a slight accent.

"You know my name?"

"Of course I know my son's name."

So she *was* his mother. Now that he was closer he could see the Mediterranean complexion, the near-black eyes. There were hints of beauty in her high cheekbones and full, curving mouth, but time had ravaged her skin and scored deep wrinkles across her forehead.

"I never liked it," she said before he could make his voice work.

He found that absurd for some reason and laughed. She laughed too, revealing broken and blackened teeth.

"Why are you living out here?" he asked.

"*He* put me here." She screwed up her face and pointed down the path which Nick assumed was in the direction of Coleclough Hall although he was still too disoriented to know for certain.

"Father? But why?"

"Mad."

He wasn't sure if she meant her husband or herself. It could even refer to both.

She pulled his wrist hard. "Come."

"Where are we going?"

"Eat."

He let her lead him along the winding path to her cottage. The inside was just as neat as the outside. There were no rushes on the floor, but the boards were scrubbed clean, and the walls too. What little furniture occupied the small parlor bore not a speck of dust, and the hearth was cleaner than any at Coleclough Hall.

"Do you live here alone?" he asked as she pushed him into a chair near the window. A small fire burned low in the grate, over which hung a cast iron pot. Delicious smells of stewing meat filled the room. His stomach growled, and she smiled as if it were the sweetest sound. "Mother?" he prompted when she didn't answer him.

"Mama. Thomas called me Mama. You were too little to talk, but now you're big… call me Mama."

A piece of his heart that he'd thought long broken, began to tick. His chest swelled. "Mama," he echoed.

She caressed his face. Her fingers were rough and callused, but her touch gentle.

"I've been watching you when you play in the garden. Watching from the trees. I waited for you to come. Waited a long, long time."

"Waited? Here?"

"I could have gone. I could have sailed home to *Firenze*, but I wanted to stay." She stroked his cheek and her broken fingernail scratched him. "I wanted to be near you. My boy. My beautiful baby boy. When you were born I knew everything would be all right, as long as I had you."

Her hand began to shake. Nick clasped it between both of his own. It was stone cold.

"Did Father send you away?

"He did not let me come to you. Not anymore." Her eyes were as dark as a starless night and seemed to stare into nothingness.

"Father? But why? Why has he kept you away from Thomas and me?"

"Because the devil lives in him," she spat.

Nick frowned. "I don't understand. Mama, tell me what happened. Is it because you wanted to leave Father when you found out what he was like? Did you want to take us with you back to Florence? Is that what he's afraid of?"

She grunted a laugh and pulled away. "Herbs. It needs herbs." She walked out of the house, and he could see her through the window in the small garden, picking at the low growing plants. When she came back in, she tipped the leaves into the pot and dusted her hands.

He stood and wanted to grasp her shoulders or take her hand. He did not. He wasn't entirely sure how she would react to his touch. She didn't seem skittish, but she did not appear to be completely aware either. Her attention seemed to be either focused on the pot or some distant sound that only she could hear.

"Mama, we have to get away. Now. We'll go somewhere safe, somewhere far away from Coleclough Hall. Don't worry. I'll take care of you."

She picked up a wooden spoon and stirred the contents of the pot. "I'm your mother," she said, peering into the pot. "I take care of you."

He smiled though his vision blurred. He'd wanted to hear a

mother say that to him for many, many years. As a child, he'd hoped his father would find a new wife, someone homely with kind eyes. Someone who wanted sons as much as he, and Thomas wanted a mother. But hearing his real mother tell him she would take care of him was all his boyhood dreams come true.

"It's ready," she announced. She picked up a bowl from the nearby table and spooned stew into it.

"What about you?" he said when she handed it to him. There didn't appear to be any other bowls in the cottage.

"I ate earlier. This is all for you." She touched his hair and smiled. "Eat now. You're too thin."

"We have to go, Mama. When they realize I've gone, this will be the first place Father will come."

"You eat, I'll gather my things. We'll leave when you're finished."

"There's no time."

But she disappeared into an adjoining room, and he had no choice but to wait. He might as well appease her. He swallowed a few mouthfuls of the stew. His mind was too occupied with plans to really taste it. They needed to move fast but with no means of transport, they would have to walk. They couldn't go into the villages, and he wasn't sure if his mother was up to sleeping outside or in barns. It wasn't going to be easy.

Shouts coming from outside made him jerk his head around. It took him a moment to realize most of the shouting came from his mother. Nick saw her through the window, running at the trees, a knife in her hand. Carter emerged from the forest into the clearing and easily caught her wrist and wrenched the knife from her. She screamed in pain and shouted a torrent of words in her native tongue.

Nick dropped the bowl and ran out of the cottage. He'd left his knife in his pack, but he had his fists. He would have used them to beat Carter to a pulp if it hadn't been for his father and the two servants. They tore out of the wood and tackled Nick to the ground. He fought them off and got in a few good punches before his father slapped him across the face.

"Did you learn nothing from the last time?" he shouted. He sat on Nick's legs, but Nick punched him in the jaw, almost dislodging him. The two servants scrambled to hold his arms, pinning him to the ground.

"You cur!" Nick growled. "You kept her here the whole time! She's our mother, your *wife*, and you kept her prisoner."

He did not see the fist coming until it was too late.

The blow hit him in the side of the head, then another and another rained down on him until his father was foaming at the mouth. With his arms held, Nick couldn't defend himself. He blacked out.

He must have lost consciousness for only a few moments because when he came to, he found he was still on the ground. At least his father had stopped hitting him. Nick's head ached liked the devil and his stomach ached. He was going to throw up.

"You do not question my decisions," his father said. His nostrils flared and a bruise shadowed his jaw. "Understand? Never, ever disobey me again, or you will suffer a worse fate. Fool." This he muttered as he got up. "Always the fool. There's too much of *her* in you, that's the problem."

Nick tried to rise, but his stomach cramped, the pain like a sword ramming through his belly. He rolled over and vomited into the dirt.

"Get up," his father ordered.

But Nick couldn't stand. All he could do was turn his aching head to look at his mother, struggling against Carter. She suddenly stopped fighting and smiled gently. Her eyes filled with what Nick assumed was love. No one had ever looked at him with quite so much depth of feeling.

"My sweet baby boy," she said, her voice soothing. "Do not fear. I *will* take care of you."

Another wave of nausea hit him, and he vomited again, right before he blacked out.

139

NICK AWOKE with a thumping headache but no nausea, thank goodness. That had been entirely in his dream. He sat up and went to rub his head, only to come into contact with the bandage. Sometimes he forgot it was there. The bruises, on the other hand, he rarely forgot about. They made every move hurt, especially around his ribs and stomach. He could swallow the pain to a certain extent, however, especially in Lucy's presence. He didn't want her to see how much it hurt, didn't want her pity. It was the only thing he didn't want from her.

That almost made him smile. The look on her face as his fingers had worked her into a state of bliss... she'd never looked so beautiful. And she was indeed a beauty. He might not remember much of the past eleven years, but he knew deep inside that no woman had hair quite that shade of red, or freckles scattered across her nose and cheeks like flecks of gold. She was unique. She was his.

He wasn't sure how he was going to give her up when the time came.

A keen ache gripped him. The nausea he thought confined to his dreams knotted his gut and weighed down his limbs. How could he ever bring himself to do it? He wanted her, not only in his bed, but his life. The thought of being without her was so alien, so *wrong*, he couldn't stand to even entertain it. It had hovered on the edge of his consciousness ever since Orlando told Nick he was an assassin for Lord Oxley. It had grown worse when the two men from Larkham arrived, and the dream only hammered it home. Now that he knew how furious he'd been with his father, Nick could almost believe that he was a killer. Almost.

But there was still a spark of hope that kept him at Cowdrey Farm and Lucy's side. Orlando Holt could be wrong or lying. Nick may not have killed the alderman from Larkham.

He might not have taken out his anger on his father in the most brutal way imaginable.

He got up and put on his breeches and jerkin, and went out to the landing. Lucy's room was empty, and he realized it wasn't so late, despite the darkness. Voices drifted up the stairs, the lighter one of Lucy's and other masculine ones he recognized as Henry and the two Larkham strangers.

He crept downstairs, not wanting to join them and risk being recognized, but wanting to be nearby in case Lucy needed him. It wasn't fair that she should shoulder the burdens of his recent past without him.

"He wasn't well liked," one of the men said. It sounded like Sawyer, the younger, more sensible visitor.

"He weren't so bad," Upfield said. "And it don't mean he should've been allowed to die like that. Slit his throat clean across, that fellow did. Blood splattered everywhere."

"All right," Henry said. "Not in front of my sister."

"Our apologies," said Sawyer. He sounded like he was talking under strain, perhaps through a tight jaw. "Upfield isn't used to tempering his words around ladies."

"It's not that," snapped Upfield. "Renny was well known. He may not have been well liked by all, but he got things done."

"Aye, that he did," Sawyer said. "If you were his friend."

"His wife and sons don't deserve to be left on their own."

"It's a sad business," Henry said. "I hope you find the man who did it. He was brown-haired, you say?"

"Aye, and his skin was pale as milk," Sawyer said. "Saw him with my own eyes. If it weren't for that, I'd have thought your guest had something to do with it, big as he is and considering he only arrived three days ago."

"It can't have been him," Lucy said. "He's too dark, and he's a good friend of Orlando Holt. A very good friend."

Upfield grunted. "Holt's word means naught to us Larkham folk."

"We'll keep hunting until we've exhausted the immediate area," Sawyer said. "We can't have a man like that walking about. He's too dangerous. The look in his eyes… Dead, they were. Killer's eyes. That man has no soul."

"Lucy, are you all right?" Henry asked. "You've gone quite pale."

There was a silence that seemed to stretch forever. Nick wanted to burst through the door and see if she was indeed all right, but then she spoke. "The thought of someone like that being nearby. It's horrible, Henry, just awful. I don't want that for our friends, not after…"

Nick pressed a palm flat to the oak door. The sorrow in her voice tugged at him. She still felt guilt for what her cousins had done to the Holts. It wasn't fair, but he knew it was a burden she carried with her, even though she rarely let it show.

The rustle of skirts signaled that Lucy had stood. She bid the men good night, and they each bid her a good eve in turn. Nick took the stairs two at a time and returned to his room. He didn't want Lucy to know he'd been eavesdropping, and he especially didn't want the Larkham men to see him again. It wouldn't be long before one of them realized he'd worn a disguise when he slit Renny's throat. After all, they only had to look into his eyes properly, and they'd recognize him again.

Killer's eyes.

The more Nick's dream sank into his consciousness, the more he thought that perhaps Sawyer had described him perfectly. Nick may not have liked the idea of killing when he was young, but after being caught at his mother's cottage, he was quite certain everything had changed.

Including, and perhaps most of all, him.

* * *

NICK OPENED the door upon Lucy's first knock. The light from her candle reflected in his eyes and highlighted his cheeks, making them look as sharp as cut stone.

"Did I wake you?" she asked.

"No."

She waited, but he didn't open the door wider or step aside to let her in. "Is everything all right?"

"Yes."

"Can I come in?"

He paused then opened the door for her.

She pressed her hand to his chest as she moved past him into the room. "Nick, I'm worried about you."

"Why?"

"You seem to only be able to speak in single word sentences."

He chuckled, and the tension that she'd felt in him dissolved. "I'm merely worried that someone will see you enter."

"There's nobody about up here." She stood on her toes and kissed him lightly on the lips. He caught her face in his hands and held her tenderly, as if she were a piece of delicate glass. She could have pulled away, but she didn't want to. The kiss triggered a deep yearning inside her, a longing to be possessed thoroughly and completely by this man who'd captured her heart and soul in only a few short days. It was madness, but she didn't care. All she knew was that she wanted to be with Nick, always and in the most basic, primal sense.

"Take me," she whispered, against his mouth.

A low groan rose from the depths of his chest, and he broke the kiss and spun away. He pressed a hand to the doorframe and bowed his head. "We shouldn't, Lucy." His voice was barely above a whisper, but she heard it as clearly as if he'd shouted.

Her eyes stung, and she bit the inside of her cheek to stop the tears. She wanted to ask him what had happened to change his mind, but she didn't think her voice would work.

It was probably the straining silence that made him turn to look at her. He gently removed the candlestick from her shaking hand and set it down on a nearby table. She'd forgotten she'd been holding it.

"Say something," he muttered. "Rail against me, curse me. Anything but coldness."

She wanted to lift his chin and make him look at her, but she feared his reaction to her touch. One rejection was enough. Instead, she folded her arms over her chest to ward off the chill creeping through her. "What's changed?" she managed to ask. "What have you remembered?"

"Nothing I fully understand yet. There are no other women in my past as far as I know, if that's what you're thinking."

It was a relief to hear, but only partly. "Then what? Tell me."

He shook his head and lowered his gaze.

So he couldn't face her, couldn't even give her a proper excuse. There may not be another woman, but there was certainly *something*. It was like facing Edmund Mallam all over again. "What's wrong?" she pressed. "What's wrong with me?"

His head snapped up. "Nothing's wrong with you! Christ." He gripped her shoulders, and dipped his head to meet her gaze. "Don't think any of this is your fault, Lucy, because it's not. I need to wait until my memories return. There are events in my past that I need to clear up first before we... before I let you into my life. Do you understand?"

God's blood, she did *not*. How could she when he'd told her nothing? "Did you have another nightmare? Did it reveal something bad?"

He let her go. "Don't ask. Not yet." He turned away and rested his hand on the doorknob. "I need to discover the answers on my own. I must find out who I am, so I can be the man you deserve."

She moved to stand before him and placed her hand over his on the doorknob. "Don't shut me out, Nick. We can find the answers together."

"No. It's better for you this way."

"That's absurd!" She pushed him in the chest but he barely moved. "I won't let you do this alone. Let me help you. Let me love you."

She was so close to him she could make out the ripple of shock across his face and the shine in his eyes as he stared at her. "Ah, Lucy," he murmured. "My bright, little light. I can't help myself around you." He pressed both hands against the door on either side of her head and leaned in.

The kiss was achingly gentle. It sucked the air from her chest and made her feel like she was floating away. Her whole body caught fire as if he'd touched her everywhere, but his hands remained on the door, trapping her within his arms, yet not. It was a kiss to set her heart soaring, to chase away the doubts and fears.

Unless...

She crashed back down to earth with a sickening thud.

It wasn't a kiss to reassure her of his affection. It was a goodbye kiss.

CHAPTER 12

*T*he Larkham men left early, thank goodness. For some reason, their presence disturbed Lucy. Perhaps it was all their talk of murder, or perhaps it was simply her melancholic mood, but she was glad to see the dust kicked up by their horses' hooves as they rode off. Let them continue their search for their alderman's killer elsewhere. Cowdrey Farm was well rid of them.

She shivered and hugged herself as she turned to walk back inside. She met Nick near the kitchen entrance.

"Are you all right?" he asked.

She nodded. Her throat was too tight to talk. She hadn't expected to see him this morning, not after their strange liaison the night before. What should she say? *Why did you kiss me as if it were the last one?*

He too seemed suddenly awkward. His gaze didn't quite meet hers, and he scuffed the ground with the toe of his boot. "I'm going to help the lads in the barn," he said.

"You can't! Your injuries."

The corners of his mouth quirked then flattened, as if he'd liked hearing her protest but didn't want to show it. "I'll do light duties only."

"What about the lad who wandered in yesterday? Surely you're not needed as well as him."

"Your brother took him into the fields, and the other two grooms don't know much about the plow. It's not working as well as it should and I told Henry I'd take a look at it." He shrugged. "I seem to have some knowledge of farm equipment, so we'll see how far my instincts extend."

"Will that require you to do anything strenuous?"

"I doubt it."

"Ensure that it doesn't. I won't patch that thick head of yours again if you insist on undoing all my work."

He grinned. "Yes, ma'am."

She narrowed her eyes at him but was relieved his good humor had returned. She couldn't abide the awkwardness. They may not be able to return to the intimacy she so desperately wanted just yet, but at least they could remain friends until then.

"You don't need to do this," she said.

He gazed over her head to the barn. "I have to earn my keep somehow."

"You don't owe us, Nick."

He nodded once. "It's not only that." The smile he gave her was filled with the same melancholy that encased her heart. She understood—he needed to keep himself occupied, somewhere away from her.

She too needed to take her mind off him, or she'd go mad wondering what it was his dream had revealed. It must have been something unpleasant enough that he wanted to protect her from it. She only hoped it could be resolved quickly so that he would return once more to where he belonged—with her.

* * *

NICK KNEW Lucy was in the bakehouse helping to sift the flour. He knew because he'd looked up from the plow he was inspecting just as she'd gone inside the bakehouse. He always knew when she was near. Instincts again. He seemed to have a few well-honed ones.

With the Larkham men gone, Nick could breathe easier. They hadn't recognized him, although there'd been a spark of suspicion thanks to Nick's size and the timing of his arrival at Cowdrey. Hopefully the spark wouldn't ignite into a blaze.

He worked all morning on the plow, directing the older stable lad since he had little experience. It must have been something Nick was used to doing before he lost his memory because, like whittling, he didn't have to think about it, he just knew what to do.

It was almost midday when he heard horses' hooves on the gravel drive. His heart lurched. If the Larkham men were back, it could only mean one thing: they suspected Nick.

He wiped his hands on his leather apron and went to meet them. No more hiding. It was time to learn how deep their suspicions ran.

But it wasn't the Larkham men on the two magnificent stallions prancing restlessly near the stable door. Two gentlemen dismounted and handed the reins to the younger of the grooms who led the horses away. One wore a ludicrous hat with a long peacock feather shooting from the tall crown and a yellow doublet that skimmed his thighs. His fashion was in contrast to his companion who wore all black with a single row of silver buttons down his doublet. Both men stared at Nick as if he had three heads.

"May I help you?" Nick asked.

The gentlemen exchanged brief but worried glances. "Orlando was right," said the one dressed all in black.

Orlando. So these men knew Holt. That meant one of them was likely to be Lord Oxley since Orlando had sent a man to fetch the earl. Nick waited for them to reveal themselves.

"You truly don't recognize us?" the dandy asked.

Which one was the earl? Both wore tailored clothes of silk, yet only the dandy's was an impractical color for the country. It must be he.

"No," Nick said. "Should I?"

The dandy's gaze drifted idly past Nick's shoulder to where one of the grooms brushed the white horse within earshot. He removed his hat and bowed, causing the feather to skim the dirt. He clicked his tongue and flicked dust off it with his fingertips. Nick thought he heard the other man sigh, but his face remained blank. He merely nodded a greeting.

"My name is Monk," the man dressed in black said. "This is Lord Oxley."

"Coleclough," Nick said, extending his arm. Monk gripped it, holding it a little longer than polite. His gray gaze briefly softened, then he too glanced over Nick's shoulder at the groom.

"You truly don't remember us?" Monk asked.

"No."

"Not even me?" Oxley pouted. "I cannot believe I'm that easy to forget. Everyone tells me I'm rather memorable." He turned his face to the left. "What about now? This is my best side."

This was the Hughe that Orlando Holt claimed was the leader of a band of assassins? How could anyone respect such a foppish, ridiculous figure? Nick certainly couldn't and he doubted he ever had. Holt must have been mistaken.

"I don't recognize either of you," he said. "Your name is a little familiar to me, but not your faces."

Oxley huffed out a breath. "Well. I am deeply offended. We've been friends for *years*."

"Then you should be able to tell me a little about myself." He had to be careful. Clearly the men didn't want to say much around the servants. "Let me clean up, and we'll go inside."

"Are the owners of this fine farm at home?" Oxley asked.

"The mistress is in the bakehouse. Her brother is in the fields."

"Another brother and sister Cowdrey?" Oxley wrinkled his nose. "How repetitive."

A burst of red flashed before Nick's eyes. He grabbed the dandy's pretty silk doublet at his throat and shook him. Nick was only an inch or so taller, but he was much broader in the chest and shoulders. Oxley didn't look like he could swat a fly. On the other hand, he didn't look particularly worried about having his nose smashed either. He simply raised a lazy eyebrow as if impatiently waiting for the next act of the show.

"You will keep your thoughts about the previous owners of this farm to yourself," Nick snarled. "Understand?"

Oxley put his hat back on his head, casual as can be. "Well, well. Developed an affection for the little wench, have you?" He spoke so quietly that no one outside their immediate circle would have heard.

Nick's grip tightened. He must have been almost choking Oxley by now, but he didn't care. The rage inside him could not be dampened. It consumed him like a blistering, hot fire. He'd only ever felt such anger once before that he could recall—when his father had found him at his mother's cottage.

"It's good to see you're still with us, Cole," Oxley went on as if this sort of thing happened to him all the time. "Orlando had me worried there. I thought perhaps we'd lost you too. Now, would you mind letting go? Your hands are filthy, and I'd rather not break your fingers."

"I'd like to see you try, *my lord*."

"Don't tempt him," Monk said idly.

Oxley sighed loudly. "I really have missed you, and breaking your fingers wouldn't do either of us any good." He fixed that pale, otherworldly stare on Nick. Nick stared right back, but instead of meeting aloof, cold eyes, he saw warmth and a depth of feeling he couldn't even begin to fathom.

His fingers sprang apart, and he stepped back, rubbed his mouth with the back of his hand. Where had that overpowering anger come from? And how did Lord Oxley dissolve it with a single stare?

"So you know about her family," Oxley said. The silk of his doublet was still creased where Nick's fingers had curled into it. For someone who seemed to care a lot about his appearance, it was odd that he didn't straighten it out.

"Those people were not her family," Nick growled. "Not in the real sense of the word. Have a care in her presence. If either of you utter a single word to upset Lucy, I'll thrash you."

Monk looked to Oxley, but Oxley merely sighed once more. "Let's go inside and see if we can't dig out some of your memories," he said. "Everything might appear different then."

Nick washed up in the pail of water near the stable entrance, then led Oxley and Monk to the house. Brutus bounded up as they approached the kitchen garden, Lucy not far behind. She paused when she saw them, her eyes wide.

"My apologies," she said, quickly removing her apron. "I didn't hear anyone arrive. Brutus usually barks, but for some reason he didn't."

Upon hearing his name, Brutus sat at his mistress's feet and looked up at her through adoring eyes. He gave a small whine, as if he knew she was displeased with him.

Nick performed introductions as he rubbed the dog's back and ears.

"My lord," Lucy said, giving an awkward little curtsey. "I apologize for the state of the house. We must enter through the kitchen for now, until the renovations on the front porch are complete."

Oxley smiled and showed no sign that he found the arrangement distasteful. Nick wasn't sure what he'd expected the earl to say or do. The man was a difficult one to pin down based on what Nick had seen so far.

"You're friends of Nick's, aren't you?" she asked.

"Indeed, although he doesn't seem to remember just how close we are." Oxley rubbed his throat, but his smile didn't waver.

"Orlando mentioned you," she went on. "He and Susanna are good friends and neighbors of ours."

"And Lord Lynden?" Monk asked. "Is he a good neighbor too?"

"I see him but rarely. Are you and he friends, Mr. Monk?"

"Acquaintances."

Oxley cleared his throat and offered his arm to Lucy. She

glanced at Nick before taking it. "We thought we might stay at Sutton Hall while we're in the area," Hughe said.

"Lord Lynden isn't at home. He'll be returning with his ladies shortly, I believe."

Monk's head snapped round. "Ladies? What ladies?"

Lucy shrugged. "I'm not sure. Perhaps you can tell us, since you know him. Does he have sisters or cousins who might come to—? Mr. Monk, are you all right? You've gone quite pale."

Indeed he had. Even his lips were white. "Cousins," he muttered. "He has always been fond of his female cousins."

"It must be they," Lucy said, letting go of Oxley's arm and taking Monk's. "I think you'd better come inside and sit down."

Lucy and Monk walked in together. Nick glared at their backs. She'd hardly even looked at him since the arrival of the two gentlemen, and now she had a new patient to fuss over, it was as if he wasn't there.

It was his fault for pushing her away. He couldn't blame her for being angry with him after he'd rejected her the night before. He may deserve it, and it was definitely for the best, but he didn't like it.

"Bloody hell," Oxley said softly. Nick glanced at him, but the earl was gazing at the doorway through which Lucy and Monk had just walked. With a heavy sigh, he followed them in.

* * *

Lucy found the two gentlemen to be delightful company, yet entirely different from one another. Monk was friendly enough, but there was a reserve to him and steeliness behind his carefully chosen words. She wondered if it was wholly to do with the news that Lord Lynden was bringing home his cousins, or whether it was just his nature.

Lord Oxley, on the other hand, was like an exotic bird, all bright feathers and twittering chatter with very little conversation of any depth passing his lips. Why men as interesting as Orlando and Nick would be friends with him was beyond her imagination. Even Monk seemed not to want to engage in Oxley's conversations and stood quietly by the parlor window, staring into the distance.

"Lord Oxley," she said when he paused in his retelling of their long journey to Cowdrey Farm. "Can you tell Nick anything about his past? There is a significant gap in his memory, and it would be helpful if you could fill some of it in."

It was no less than the third attempt at bringing the conversation back to Nick and his lost memories, and the third failure. Oxley laughed and waved his hand in the air. "There's little to tell. He has poor sense of style, as you can see, and he's decidedly moody."

"Moody?" It was something that Orlando had mentioned in regard to Nick, but she was yet to see any real proof of it. She glanced at him, sitting on her right, but he was as stiff as a statue. No doubt he hated being the object of discussion, but surely the need to learn more about himself would override his feelings. So why didn't he help her and question Lord Oxley instead of acting like a disinterested bystander? "I wouldn't describe him as moody," she said.

Lord Oxley twisted a large sapphire ring on the middle finger of his left hand. "How would you describe him, Mistress Cowdrey?"

"Kind. Amiable." She glanced at Nick again out of the corner of her eye. He swallowed hard and stared down at his feet. "That must have been what he was like when he was eighteen."

"Hmmm. Eighteen, eh?" Oxley chuckled. "I'd wager you got up to all sorts of mischief, as we all did at that age."

"I doubt it," Nick said.

"So it's true then? You can't recall anything that happened to you in the last eleven years? That must have been one nasty blow to the head." He winced and patted the pale hair at his temple. "Do you have to wear that bandage, Cole? It's not the most fetching headgear."

Nick's gaze slid to Oxley's. "The name's Nick or Coleclough."

Oxley made a miffed sound through his nose. "See what I mean? Moody."

Nick wouldn't hit the earl, would he? Surely not. It wasn't in his nature. Lucy didn't think this moroseness was in his nature either, yet there he sat like a grim statue glaring at his so-called friend. "My lord, is there anything you can tell us about the time you two spent together?" she asked. "It might help trigger his memories. How did you meet, for example?"

Oxley twisted his ring again and scrunched up his handsome face in either thought or distaste, it was difficult to tell which. "It was *so* long ago." He pressed his hand to his stomach and apologized for the rumbling. Lucy hadn't heard anything. "It's been hours since we ate."

"It is close to dinnertime," Nick said, rising. "I'll take Monk and Oxley into the hall if you want to see to the servants," he said to her.

She narrowed her eyes at him, but he was already striding away to the door. Well!

"Thank you, Mistress Cowdrey," Monk said, moving away from the window. "We appreciate your hospitality at such short notice."

"You are a kind, dear lady," Lord Oxley said, bowing. "My stomach thanks you, as do I."

She swept past Nick in the doorway. Her arm brushed his. She looked up and saw the same deep sadness in his eyes that had been there that morning. Their fingers touched ever so lightly until he pulled away. His jaw hardened. His eyes darkened.

"Come with me," he said to their visitors.

She left them without being entirely sure she was doing the right thing in leaving Nick alone with those two. She didn't trust them, although she didn't entirely distrust them either. It's just that they were odd, and their connection to Orlando and Nick was shrouded in secrecy. Oxley in particular had avoided answering her questions.

She would leave them alone for a while and let them talk about whatever it was they didn't want her to hear. Hopefully Nick would confide in her later.

* * *

"WE ONLY HAVE a few minutes until she returns," Lord Oxley said, rounding on Nick as soon as the door was shut. "So talk. What in God's name happened to you?" He crossed his arms and set his feet apart. Suddenly, he didn't look like the limp dandy anymore, but an earl in command of an army.

"I told you," Nick snapped. "I don't remember."

Oxley's eyes narrowed. "Truthfully?"

"Yes."

"You thought Orlando was mistaken?" Monk asked the earl.

"I thought his messenger got confused." Oxley blew out a breath. "Bloody hell. Of all the things to go wrong, I didn't plan on this being one of them."

Monk gave a grudging laugh. "Nice to know the mighty Lord Oxley is human after all. I have been wondering."

"Very amusing," Oxley muttered. "Cole—Nick—is there nothing you remember about the attack? A sound or—"

"No. Holt has already grilled me, and my answer to him was the same as my answer to you. I don't remember anything. Not a voice, a footfall, nothing. The last thing I recall was… was being eighteen. Then I woke up in a meadow with my head feeling like it had been cleaved in two."

"It's just a crack," Oxley said.

"Thanks for your sympathy."

"The Cole I know would have shrugged it off."

"The Cole you knew has disappeared. I'm not sure he even existed."

Monk and Oxley exchanged a glance. "He existed well enough," Monk said. "I spent from sunup to sundown for an entire month in his company while he trained me. *You* trained me."

"At what?"

"Killing."

Bile rose to Nick's throat, and the world tilted. He gripped the edge of the large dining table to steady himself.

Monk lifted one shoulder. "We're assassins. What did you think you taught me?"

"It's a little too late to let it bother you now," Oxley said. He pulled out a chair near Nick and gripped his shoulder. With far more strength than Nick thought the wiry man possessed, he forced Nick to sit.

Nick blinked up at the men who were supposed to be his friends. It seemed so unreal, as if they were talking about someone else. Orlando Holt had told Nick they were assassins, but he hadn't really believed him. Yet here were two more saying the same thing.

"Was I... am I good at... killing?" Nick asked.

Oxley sat on the chair beside him and fixed him with that peculiar ice-blue gaze. "Yes." One side of his mouth lifted in a wry smile. "You were—are—bloody good."

"You're an unforgiving, cold-hearted prick," Monk said. "I thought you'd kill me on more than one occasion during my training. Hughe assured me you wouldn't, but I don't think he'd ever looked into your eyes when you wielded a sword."

Killer's eyes.

"Holt told me we only assassinate the deserving." It was the one redeeming quality of those missing years that Nick could hold on to. Perhaps he wasn't all bad. Perhaps he could take something good from those lost years, before he left them behind forever. "Tell me about the Larkham man I... killed."

Oxley sat back in the chair and stretched out his long legs under the table. "He forced two young women to... well, let's just say the acts were despicable. Unforgiveable. They were virgins both. Nice girls from nice families. He disfigured them horribly but not on their faces, not where anyone can see."

Nick's stomach rolled again, and out of the corner of his eye he saw Monk shake his head slowly. Oxley, however, spoke with detached candor. If the horror of Renny's crimes bothered him, he didn't show it.

"Surely the people of Larkham would bring justice down on the man if they found out," Nick said. "Why not let them take care of their own?"

"That would mean the girls would be identified. They and their families don't want that. This way, our way, they keep their anonymity, and justice is done."

Nick closed his eyes, drew a deep breath. He was right. It was the only way. Those girls had to be protected at all costs. A public trial would only have hurt them more and would probably have amounted to nothing if the man held influence.

"So I killed this man Renny in the local tavern," Nick said.

Oxley drew his legs under his chair and sat up straight. "How do you know that? Did Orlando tell you?"

"Two Larkham men were here last night. They're looking for Renny's killer."

Monk swore softly. "You didn't give anything away, did you?"

"Of course not," Nick said.

"And they didn't recognize you?" Oxley asked.

"No. Apparently I wore a disguise. I only know it was me because Holt told me. He said I'd somehow made a mess of it. That I shouldn't have done it in public view."

Oxley looked to Monk. "No, you shouldn't have," he said. "The disguises are always an extra precaution, but we never kill where we can be seen. It's not like you to make such a mistake."

"Maybe it wasn't a mistake," Nick ground out. "But I don't know."

Oxley held up his hands in surrender. "You're probably right. So the Larkham men didn't suspect you? This is important, Cole. Was there any recognition in their eyes? Any doubt as to your innocence?"

Nick nodded slowly. "Some. They found the timing of my arrival in the area too coincidental, and both said I was about the killer's size."

Oxley muttered something under his breath. "Did you give them your full name? Your real name?"

"Yes."

"Fuck."

Nick was beginning to see the problem. If the men knew his name, he couldn't slip quietly away from Cowdrey Farm. Not if they came to realize he was the killer in disguise, and not if he wanted to keep his family out of it, or Lucy for that matter.

"They may never make the connection," Monk offered.

Oxley shook his head. "Someone already has." He indicated the bandage with a single nod.

It did seem the most likely reason behind the attack. "But why didn't they kill me if they knew I was the one who killed Renny?" Nick asked.

Oxley shrugged. "They were disturbed or changed their mind. Perhaps they never intended to kill you, but just wanted to teach you a lesson."

"Why didn't they inform the authorities?" Monk asked.

Oxley lifted his hands and Nick shrugged.

"I need to leave," Nick said. He glanced at the closed door. Lucy would be returning soon.

"You can't," Oxley said. "Not yet. Stay and you appear innocent. Go, and you'll look guilty. If they brand Nicholas Coleclough as a murderer, you can never return home, never speak to your family again or be yourself."

"You don't understand. I have to see my brother. Something happened when I was eighteen, but I can't remember how it turned out. I have to know if… if everyone is all right."

"That was eleven years ago. A few more weeks won't matter."

"Perhaps Oxley can help with that particular memory," Monk offered. "Perhaps you confided in him. Or, knowing him, he probably investigated you."

Oxley fixed that cool glare on Monk. The man lifted a brow in question.

"Well?" Nick prompted. "Did I confide in you?"

A few beats passed before Oxley sighed. "A little but not every-thing. All I know is something happened between you and your family that made you want to leave Coleclough Hall. You never told me what."

"But you investigated me?"

Oxley nodded. "After we met. I already employed Orlando and Rafe Fletcher and wasn't particularly looking for another to join us, but when I met you, I knew I needed you in the Guild."

"Why?"

A few more beats passed. Nick steeled himself for the answer.

"You were—are—the darkest man I've ever met. I'd seen you fight in organized brawls and knife fights, the sort that don't get advertised on handbills but are only whispered about among certain circles. I heard about you after your first fight. They were already saying you were the best ever. So I went along to watch the next time. Four times, as a matter of fact. You beat every opponent, and easily. But your skill meant naught to me if you were a madman or devoid of morals. I don't want thugs working for me. So I followed you."

Nick rubbed his knuckles. There was a scar on his right, and more scars on his face and chest. None of them were like the ones on his back, but he knew with certainty that he'd got them brawling.

"It was after following you one afternoon that I realized I was wrong. I had thought you didn't care about anything or anyone, but I discovered you had a deep sense of justice running through you. It was *yourself* that you didn't care about."

"What happened?" Monk asked.

Nick wiped his forehead. He felt as if he were in a fever, or perhaps a living nightmare. He didn't want to hear anymore, but he knew had to. If he were to have any future with Lucy, or with his family, he needed to know everything about his past.

"You started a riot in a London inn." Oxley gave a short, sharp laugh. "A playwright was having a quiet drink with friends when a big fellow came up to him. He said he'd just come from the Rose

Theatre and seen the latest play by the playwright's company. He claimed that one of the characters was based on himself. It must have been the villain or the fool because he was deeply offended. The playwright said the characters weren't real and that he'd never even met this man. It was clear the big fellow was drunk as a sailor. He took offense to everything about the playwright—his clothes, his manner, and particularly his wit. By this time, the playwright was looking very worried. I was sitting near you at the time, but you didn't take any notice of me. You watched the two men arguing, and when the drunk grabbed the playwright by his ruff, you stood and ordered the drunk to leave, or you'd break his jaw. It was at that point I knew you had no care for yourself."

"Why? One against one isn't so dangerous."

"The drunkard had a group of about twenty others with him. All angry looking beasts."

"Ah. Not such good odds then."

"It was lucky for us that the playwright had some friends capable of wielding swords too."

"Us?"

"It had been a long time since I'd been in an affray, and I was up for some sport."

Sport? The man must be a little mad himself.

"Before long, stools and tankards were flying about the taproom. You fought with great skill, sometimes four at a time, with only a dagger for a weapon. I was impressed. Of course I had to speak to you."

"I decided to join you? Just like that?"

"You took a little convincing. In the end it wasn't the money that won you over."

"I'm not surprised," Monk said with a shake of his head. At Nick's arched brow, he added, "You spend or give away almost every penny Hughe pays you."

"So once I joined the Guild, and we became friends, did I tell you about my past?" Nick asked.

"You told me you'd worked in various counties, mostly as a

farmhand, but just before we met, you'd been working in Newcastle coal mines. Hellish work, fit only for the mad and desperate."

"It pays well," Monk said.

"That's because nobody wants to do it," Oxley said. "Nobody who wants to live, that is."

Nick ignored that. Of course he wanted to live. Oxley couldn't know him at all if he thought that. "But what about before? When did I leave Coleclough Hall and why? Did I tell you that?"

Oxley shook his head. "You were very closed about your upbringing, but I did manage to get your name out of you. I conducted my own investigation, but learned surprisingly little considering you're the son of Lord Coleclough. I see him at court from time to time, although we've never spoken. I keep my distance on purpose. As far as I know, he's a widower with one son, Thomas. There was talk of another son, but no one had met him, and it was generally thought that he was deformed or soft-headed. Your father is considered a good, solid man who dislikes court life and only attends when he needs to. He prefers to farm his land and live quietly."

"You speak of him as if he's still alive. Is he?"

"As far as I know. I saw him at court last autumn. Your brother too."

So Nick hadn't killed him. Then what *had* he done? Why was there a terrible foreboding in his gut that worsened with each nightmare?

CHAPTER 13

Eleven years ago

ick didn't know how long he'd been slipping into and out of consciousness. It could have been days, or perhaps weeks. He would awake only to throw up, even though his stomach was empty. With every grind of his belly, he curled into a ball and prayed it was the last time. But it seemed to go on forever.

Sometimes Thomas was in his room, his forehead scored with worry, his hands clasped as if in prayer. Once, Nick's father stood by the window, silently watching as Nick folded himself in half and waited out the surge of pain. He left soon afterward without saying a word.

When he was well enough to get out of bed, Nick tried to leave, but his bedchamber door was locked from the outside. He banged on it until someone came. That someone was Carter, his father's man. Nick swung at him and landed a punch on the oaf's jaw, albeit a weak one. Carter barely moved. He simply grunted, walked out, and locked the door again.

Later, his father returned.

"Where is she?" Nick snarled. "Where's our mother?"

"Her old apartments," he said. "I'll keep her there until I know what to do with her."

Nick's stomach churned but he didn't throw up. Whatever illness had befallen him was finally subsiding enough that he could function again. "She's not a *thing*, Father, she's our mother, your wife. Does that mean nothing to you?"

His father sighed and signaled for Nick to sit down. He remained standing, but his father sat heavily on the chair beside the bed. He rubbed his hand down his face and when he removed it, he looked older, wearier. "Your mother is mad, Nick. I removed her from this house years ago for… safekeeping."

Nick put a hand to the tester to steady himself, but the world still felt unbalanced. "If she's mad, it's because you drove her to that state."

"I've done my best."

"Your best? You've kept your sons and wife prisoner, you've had me whipped to the bone, or maybe you did it yourself. If that's your best, God help us when you're at your worst."

"You don't understand—"

"No, *you* don't understand."

His father rose slowly, his mouth twisted in anger, his eyes flashing with that glare that Nick knew all too well. But he would be ready for the fist this time. He would not let his father hit him ever again.

"You do *not* speak to me like that. I am your father. Show me some respect."

"Show it to our mother."

His father swung his fist. Nick easily dodged it. The momentum of the missed punch sent the baron careening forward onto the bed. "She's not deserving!" he spat over his shoulder. "She's not deserving of your—"

A scream cut off his words. Nick ran, his father on his heels. Another scream, female and frightened. It came from his mother's apartments.

Then a male shout: "Stop!" Thomas.

Nick streaked ahead of his father and crashed through door after door until he reached the inner chamber of his mother's rooms. A sobbing maid flew past him, blood smeared down her apron. Thomas stood in the middle of the room, facing their mother. She clutched a knife, raised to strike. Thomas turned to see who had entered.

It was the wrong thing to do.

She struck Thomas. He roared in pain and crumpled to the floor. She raised the knife to strike again.

"NO!" Nick slammed into her, shoving her backward. He wrested the knife off her as they fell, but he need not have worried. She lay limply on the rushes, her eyes closed. "Thomas?"

Their father leaned over his oldest son, blocking Nick's view. *Thomas.* No! Nick was going to be sick.

"I'm all right," Thomas said. His voice shook, and he needed help sitting up, but at least he was talking.

Nick knelt at his side and embraced him briefly before tearing off his own shirt sleeve and pressing it to the bleeding wound on Thomas's shoulder, alarmingly close to the base of his throat.

Their father knelt on one knee beside them, his head bowed, his breathing uneven. Nick ignored him and glanced at his mother, still lying on the floor.

"Mama?" he whispered.

No answer.

Thomas gripped his arm, but Nick pulled away. He crouched at her side, and that's when he noticed the blood. So much blood. It soaked into the rushes around her head, darkened her gray hair. He sat on his haunches and stared at her face. She looked so serene, almost beautiful.

Someone came up beside him and checked her pulse. "Dead." His father's voice. "Her head hit the corner of the trunk as she fell."

Thomas gripped Nick's shoulder, no doubt trying to reassure him. "It's not your fault," he said.

Not my fault. Not my fault.

"She was mad," his father said. "She would have killed your brother."

Nick's stomach heaved, and he threw up where he knelt. He could tell himself a million times over that it wasn't his fault, or that she was mad, but the fact remained. His own mother had died by his hand.

* * *

Lucy was alert to any sounds coming from Nick's bedchamber, but she heard none. Perhaps his nightmares had ceased. Perhaps he was asleep. As should she be. She wouldn't succumb to slumber until she knew if he was all right.

She lit a candle and slipped quietly to his room. She was about to knock when she heard a low groan coming from the other side of the door. He sprang off the bed as she entered.

"Lucy!" His ragged breathing filled the room. "Christ." He sat down and bent his head. He was naked.

"Who did you think it was?" She set her candle on the table and touched his shoulder. The muscles rippled with tension. "Did you have another nightmare?"

"Not quite."

"Care to tell me about it?"

He shook his head, but still he didn't look up. She touched his jaw and gently forced him to look at her. It was difficult to make out his expression, but he seemed different somehow. Harder.

Perhaps it was simply the way the candlelight played across his cheekbones.

She was about to prompt him again but decided not to. Something held him back, and the more she asked, the more he would push her away. Instead, she kissed him.

He kissed back and for a brief moment, he seemed to relax.

Then he pulled away and bent his head again.

"Why won't you kiss me?" she said. When he didn't answer, she added, "Am I too forward?"

"No."

She looked down at her hands in her lap, but soon she couldn't even see those through her pooling tears. Why wouldn't he talk to her anymore? Had he begun to change when she'd told him about Edmund? She tried to recall exactly when Nick had first pushed her away, but she couldn't. It seemed to happen so slowly.

"Well." She sniffed. "Good night."

He caught her hand and pinned it to her lap. "Don't cry," he whispered. "Please, don't cry."

His gentle plea only made her feel worse. This wonderful, clever, handsome man cared about her, yet not enough to be with her. "Let me go," she said. "I understand."

He touched her face, as she had done to him only moments ago, and gently made her look at him. His thumb wiped away the tear that had traitorously leaked from her left eye.

"Ah, Lucy. What am I going to do with you?"

She had no idea what to say to that, and it didn't matter anyway because he kissed her. It was soft and slow, so excruciatingly slow. He clasped either side of her face gently, as if he were holding something precious. He groaned low in his chest and tipped her backward onto the bed.

He gave another groan as he freed her breasts from the laces of her nightgown. She wrapped her leg around his waist and drew up her hem to above her thighs. She wanted to feel skin on skin. Feel his heat, his need. Wanted him to enter her.

He pressed himself to her opening, but hesitated. She thrust up her hips, and he slid all the way in. She gasped at the thickness. He froze and broke the kiss.

"Don't stop," she said quickly, not wanting to give him time to have second thoughts.

"Lucy," he muttered on a breath. "This is… "

He ended the sentence with another hot kiss that set her body on fire, made her nipples tingle, and her nether region ache with longing. She was going mad with desire, and something deeper. It surged and swelled inside her chest, filled her heart.

"Nick." There was too much too say and the words wouldn't come, only tears. *Don't leave me. Love me the way I love you.*

She wrapped her other leg around him, her arms too, so that they were as close as they could ever be. As one.

Did he feel it too? Or was she alone on the precipice, looking down into the swirling ocean?

His rhythm quickened, his breathing too. It came in short, sharp bursts and he stopped kissing her to bury his face in her throat. She pressed her ankles in harder at the base of his spine, but he didn't stay inside her. With a deep shudder, he pulled out of her and spurted his seed on the bedcovers.

He rolled off and lay on his back, pulling her with him. She nestled into his side and breathed in the scent of her man. There were so many questions, so many things to say to him, but already his breathing had softened. She didn't want to keep him awake, so she closed her eyes and let sleep take her too. Words could wait until the next day. For now, she would enjoy being in the arms of the man who'd captured her heart and soul.

* * *

COLE WAS A BLOODY FOOL. One suggestive kiss from a girl in a nightgown, and he was throwing his newly made resolution to keep his distance out the window.

Yet it wasn't just any girl in a nightgown. It was his Lucy. From the moment she'd touched him, he'd never stood a chance. He was weak where she was concerned. The iron will he now remembered he possessed in abundance had failed him.

Fuck.

Lucy was light, and he was dark, through and through. He would not dim her brightness, not for anything. He cared too much for her to do that.

Loved her too much.

He would make sure she understood they had no future together. Not now that he remembered who he was, and worse, what he'd become. He was Cole, a cold-blooded killer. Hopefully, one day, she would realize he had done the right thing by leaving and would forgive him.

But that was tomorrow. Tonight, he was going to hold her one last time. No way was he going to fall asleep and miss a moment of her warm breath on his throat, her smooth breast pillowed against his chest. He was going to commit the feel of her to memory. A memory he'd never, ever lose, even though he knew he would one day want to, if only to keep his sanity. Loving her and not having her was going to drive him to madness.

If he wasn't already there.

He kissed the top of her head and drew in her scent. *I love you, Lucy Cowdrey. Forgive me, because I can never forgive myself.*

He squeezed his eyes shut, but it was no good. Sadness welled so deeply inside him he felt like he was drowning.

Yet even through the sound of the blood swirling between his ears he heard it: the click of a door opening. His door.

Henry? Hell, now he had to contend with her brother too.

No, not Henry. Lucy's candle had flickered out, but he could just see the shape of the intruder. It was shorter than Henry but fat. Then, the shadow split into two thinner ones.

Bloody hell. Why couldn't they just let him enjoy these few remaining hours alone with Lucy?

She still slept in his arms. If he remained silent to draw the intruders closer, she would be at risk of getting hurt. But if he let them know he was aware of them, they'd have a head start in getting away.

It was no real choice.

"What do you want?" he whispered. The attackers—for it must be the same ones who'd made a mess of him in the meadow—froze, then turned and ran. One grabbed Cole's pack from where it sat by the door.

Lucy stirred as he slipped out from beneath her. "Get dressed," he ordered as he ran to the door.

"Nick? What's wrong?"

There was no time to answer. He raced out of the bedchamber and down the stairs, treading as lightly as possible so as not to wake anyone, but he felt sluggish compared to the two small men. They were fast. He caught sight of them at the bottom of the stairs where they split up. One headed for the kitchens, the other through the parlors.

Lucy! If he followed one, he risked the other doubling back and going after her. He couldn't be sure they wouldn't take out their anger on her since she'd saved the life of the man who'd killed Renny. Cole had no doubt that this was another attempt at getting revenge for the alderman's death.

Panic seized his limbs, but he pushed on, ran faster, back up the stairs to his bedchamber. Lucy was alone, thank God, standing by the door with a large candlestick clutched in both hands. She lowered it when she saw him.

He suddenly felt giddy and light headed and so fucking relieved. He wanted to take her in his arms and hold her, kiss her all over just to make sure she was unharmed. Instead, he strode past her and picked up his shirt. He couldn't face her interrogation without clothes on. Thankfully she already wore her nightgown again, thin as it was.

Lucy set the candlestick down on the mantelpiece and watched Nick dress as calmly as can be. Her heart thumped wildly although she hadn't been the one who'd chased after an intruder. Two, if her eyes hadn't deceived her. How could Nick be so unaffected?

"Did you see them?" she asked.

"Not their faces."

"Have they gone?"

"Yes."

He padded across the floor in his bare feet, but instead of meeting her, he walked straight past and opened the tinderbox beside the fireplace and removed the flint. She watched as he lit her candle and two others, throwing some light around the bedchamber. He placed the three candlesticks on the mantelpiece, but didn't turn around.

She came up behind him and slipped her arms around his waist. He sucked in air and slowly turned.

"Lucy." He stepped out of her embrace and lowered his head. "We need to talk."

Ominous words, and all too familiar. It was how Edmund had begun his pretty speech that ended their betrothal. She folded her arms against a sudden chill and stepped back.

He glanced up through his long lashes. "Don't."

His whispered plea clenched her heart like a vise. "Don't what?"

"Don't look at me like that. I… " He shook his head. "There's no easy way to say this, but I'll be leaving Cowdrey as soon as possible."

The vise tightened. "When your head is better. Yes, I know." She didn't tell him that she thought they'd be leaving together, had *hoped* they would. It seemed irrelevant now. She bit the inside of her lip but still her eyes welled with tears.

His face seemed to change somehow, and the softness disappeared. The bones re-set into hard, unforgiving angles. "It's for the best."

She would not cry, nor would she beg. Past experience had taught her that hysterics and pleas changed nothing. But she had not given up. Not yet and not without a fight. Something had changed him. Most likely an old memory had returned, a terrible memory, something he needed to face alone, or thought he did. It was up to her to dig it out of him and try to fix it.

"Why? At least answer me that." Her voice sounded remarkably calm considering the turmoil inside her. Perhaps it was the new determination within, holding the pieces of her together. She would not give up.

His gaze drifted to the window where the sky was beginning to lighten. "Those intruders were probably after me."

First the attack in the meadow and now this one. "But why, Nick?"

"My name's Cole. I haven't gone by Nick in a long time."

It was like watching a transformation from tadpole to frog, or calf to bull. Nick was being taken over by a tougher, more detached version of himself. Cole.

"I'll sleep in the barn until I'm ready to leave," he said.

"No! Don't be ridiculous. You'll sleep here. Nick—"

"Cole."

"*Nick*. Don't do this. Don't push me away and pretend nothing ever happened between us."

"I'm not pretending. It happened and now it's over. You're better off forgetting about me, Lucy. Remembering will only bring you heartache." His detachment made her shiver. It would have been better if he'd spoken harshly to her. This coolness was so out of character.

"You're not like this. You're not... Cole."

He grunted a harsh laugh. It was so different from his joyous laughter, and yet looking at him now with those severe cheeks and rigid jaw, she could almost believe that he'd never smiled.

"Does this change upset you?" he said. "Because this is who I am. I'm the man you met in the meadow that very first time. The man who wouldn't lift his hat. Ill-mannered, you called me."

"Yet you came to my aid when I fell. *That's* the man you are, Nick."

"Are you sure? Would you stake your life on it? Your future?"

His words stung like a slap across the face. "Nick," she whispered. But it was hopeless. He was already turning away and heading for the door.

"You'd better leave now," he said, opening it.

She strode straight past him and did not look back. She didn't want him to see the tears streaming down her face. Later, when she felt more composed, she would speak to him again. Nick must be in there somewhere. Surely Cole hadn't completely smothered him.

* * *

COLE SAT on the bed and felt under the mattress for the piece of wood and whittling knife he'd thrust there before Lucy had entered his room. He'd not wanted her to see it, although he didn't know why. It was quite good, considering he'd carved it purely on instinct.

He ran his thumb over the sleek back, down the nose. The little statue, whittling knife, and clothes were the only possessions he had left. Everything else had been in his pack, now stolen. All his weapons.

He closed his fist around the wood and stood to go down for breakfast. He thought about slipping away, telling no one, but decided against such foolish timing. He needed food, both in his belly and for the journey, or he'd have to stop again before long and beg for charity. Too risky. Straight after breakfast then, he'd have a maid bundle up some food.

There would be no avoiding Lucy, so he steeled himself for their first meeting. It came in the kitchen where he chose to eat. She wouldn't confront him in front of the servants.

He was wrong.

"You cannot leave," she said, stabbing a finger into the bundle sitting on the table beside him. She set her empty basket down. "I don't know which of the maids you charmed, but this is all going back in the larder." She handed the bundle to the young scullery maid who scurried away with it.

"It's better if I leave." Once it became known that Cole had left, the attackers wouldn't strike again. It was impossible to tell her that with so many onlookers, however. He didn't want to alarm them. It was better if no one else knew about the intruders.

"Don't be such a pig-headed fool."

The cook snickered, but stopped upon Lucy's glare, as sharp as any of the kitchen knives.

"You may think I care more about my feelings than your health," Lucy said, "but I assure you, I do not. You can't leave until you're fully recovered." And with that, she spun on her heel and stalked out of the kitchen, almost smacking into her brother.

"What's wrong with her?" Henry asked, watching her go. When nobody answered him, he fixed Cole with a glare. "Well?"

"I'm leaving."

Henry blinked. "Today? Are you healed?"

"Almost."

Henry pressed his lips together and half shook his head. "Walk to the barn with me."

"I can't. I have to go."

"You've stayed in my house for four nights and upset my sister. The least you can do is walk with me to the barn."

It was a fair point. No favors, that was Cole's adage. He paid for everything. Cole owed Cowdrey, but he had no money. Payment would need to come some other way.

Fuck.

They crossed the yard, bypassing the henhouse where Lucy collected eggs, and walked to the barn. "You can't leave yet," Henry said. "I need help in the fields, and if you're well enough to leave, then you're well enough to do light duties."

Cole had to tell him. There was no other choice. "Someone tried to attack me last night."

Henry suddenly stopped. "What! Were you hurt?"

"I chased them away, but they may try again. The only way I can keep you and your sister safe is if I leave."

Henry removed his hat and raked a hand through his hair. "God's blood! Do you know why? Have you remembered something?"

Cole shook his head. Lie upon lie upon lie. "I'll send you money as thanks for your kindness."

"Money? We don't want money from you." His eyes narrowed and he stepped up to Cole. "My sister doesn't want money from you."

"It's all I can offer."

"It's not. Here's what you can do. Come work in the fields with me today, and let me think on the next course of action. I'll write to my father and ask him to approach your father about a union. I know you're a baron's son, but it's love after all."

The speed of his mind would have been laughable if it weren't so tragic.

"You don't understand," Cole said. "My presence here will bring danger. That won't change. There's no need to write to anyone. Lucy will forget me soon enough."

But he would never forget her. Not in this life or beyond.

Henry sighed and glanced past Cole to the henhouse. "She comes." He shook his head and swore again. "She'll hate me for a long time for saying this, but if you believe your presence brings her danger, then you're right. You have to go." He clapped Cole on the shoulder. "I know you wouldn't leave her if the situation wasn't dire. The bloody curs had better not come back here, or I'll flay them. Just return when you can, but do not leave it too long."

Such naiveté. Henry believed Cole was in the right, and the attackers in the wrong. He also believed Cole would return.

"Help me in the fields this morning, and you can leave directly from there," Henry said. "You won't need to face her at all. I'll tell her later." He squeezed Cole's shoulder then walked off just as Lucy approached.

"Have you told him about the intruders?" she asked.

He nodded. "I'm going with him to work in the fields. We agreed—"

"You can't! Nick, you can no more do farming work than you can leave. You're not ready." She sniffed, and her lower lip wobbled ever so slightly.

He couldn't do this with her teetering on the edge. He'd always been able to close his heart, but no matter how much he tried this time, a small opening remained and she had her foot placed firmly in it.

He turned away, partly so he didn't have to look into those sad eyes, but mostly so she couldn't look into his. "It isn't up for discussion," he said and strode off.

"You are a stubborn, infuriating *fool!*"

She wasn't going to give in lightly, not to him and not to her emotions. Good for her. It was just one of the reasons why he adored her.

And the main reason why he had to slip away without telling her.

Goodbye, my little light.

He breathed deeply, but not steadily. Breathed again. Better. Another breath and there was no sign of the raggedness.

"I haven't given up on you yet, Nicholas Coleclough." She didn't shout, but he heard her clear enough. Her voice was clogged with her tears, but a quiet determination underpinned her words. He clenched his fists at his sides and kept walking, kept looking straight ahead, although he couldn't see a bloody thing anymore. "You are *not* this man, no matter what you think," she said.

Cole couldn't agree more. The man whose heart was trying to punch a hole through his chest was as foreign to him as the youth who'd killed his own mother. The sooner he came to accept that, the sooner he could conquer this affliction and return to his normal life of working for Hughe.

CHAPTER 14

*I*t was fortunate that Lord Oxley and Mr. Monk were still at Stoneleigh. Lucy wanted to confront all of Nick's friends together. Perhaps his lordship had some insights into Nick's past that Orlando didn't.

Susanna herded all her guests plus her husband into the parlor upon Lucy's arrival, and her maid followed with a bowl filled with orange succades that Lord Oxley began to devour piece by piece. Monk sat a little apart, more an observer than a participator, with an air of expectation in his shrewd gray eyes.

"Succade, Lucy?" Susanna asked.

"No, thank you. This isn't a social visit. I'm worried about Nick. He's changed quite dramatically this past day or two, and I thought his friends might know why."

"What makes you think we can help?" Orlando asked.

"You know him best. I'm convinced he has remembered something that worries him. If I know what it is, I may be able to help him."

"Perhaps he doesn't need help," Monk said.

Lucy regarded him levelly. He was a quiet man in both manner and appearance when compared to the golden beauty of Orlando and the vibrant personality of Oxley. There was a steadiness in those eyes, and his face seemed to become more handsome the longer one stared at him. She had liked him instantly when they first met, so this challenge was unexpected.

"Of course he needs help," she said. "He just won't admit it."

He held up his hands. "The Nicholas Coleclough you're seeing now may be the real twenty-nine year-old one, not the one who thought he was eighteen. A lot can happen to change a man in a decade."

"True enough," Orlando said.

"I believe a person does not change this dramatically in one decade or five. Superficially, yes. He can put on airs or become disenchanted with his lot. He can even become a gentleman if he has enough money." This produced a snort from Lord Oxley. Lucy ignored him. Monk, she noticed, no longer looked at her. "But I don't believe anyone can alter their soul. An honest man remains honest. A liar will always be a liar. Someone with a happy countenance will always look forward to a better day. Nick's soul is—was —a bright, gentle one. He just needs to find it again."

"Perhaps he doesn't want to find it," Monk said quietly.

She straightened, but she wasn't angry with him. It had become clear that he, like the rest of them, didn't know Nick the way she did. "Mr. Monk, have you ever cared for someone so deeply that you felt compelled to help them, no matter what they said or how hard they pushed you away?"

Those gray eyes penetrated through her to her bones. "Yes. That's why I can tell you that you can't change a person. They are what they are, and will never be what others want them to be." He stood and bowed to Lucy and Susanna. "Forgive me, ladies, but I don't think I'm needed in this conversation."

Lucy watched him go, her heart a little sorer than before she'd sat down.

"He seems so sad," Susanna said. "Do you know why that is?" she asked her husband.

"I hardly know him," he said. "You'd have to ask Hughe, but you probably won't receive an answer that'll satisfy you, eh, Hughe? Men don't sit around talking about souls and love the way you ladies do."

Susanna rolled her eyes. "It's quite acceptable to speak of love these days. All the poets do it."

Lucy tuned out their banter and watched Lord Oxley through half lowered lashes. He'd gone very quiet and a single deep frown line marked the bridge of his nose. His frivolousness was nowhere to be seen.

"Tell me what it is you know about Nick," she said to him.

Susanna and Orlando stopped talking. She rubbed her swollen belly, and he cleared his throat. Both looked to Oxley.

The earl picked a succade out of the bowl and popped it into his mouth. His eyes lit up and he pressed his hand to his heart. "These are delicious. My mother the Dowager Countess would give a body part for a box of these. Not sure you'd want one of her body parts, though. Sour old creature she is."

"I sent her three boxes just before we married," Orlando said. "She wrote back and ordered more."

"Good man." Oxley popped another into his mouth and closed his eyes in delight as he chewed. "Try one, Mistress Cowdrey. You've not tasted anything like it."

"I've tried them before."

"Susanna is a marvel in the garden, isn't she? Who says women can't be excellent gardeners? Not I. Who better to nurture plants than the very people who nurture by nature?" He chuckled. "Nurture by nature. Ah me."

"Lord Oxley," Lucy began, not bothering to hide her impatience. "I'll ask you again. What is it you know about Nick that you won't tell me?"

"Lucy…" Orlando massaged his temples. "It's better if you don't know."

That drew a sharp glare from Oxley.

"Why won't you tell me?" she pressed.

"Yes, Orlando," Susanna said pointedly. "That's a very good question."

Orlando winced. "Hughe? Help."

Oxley leaned forward and patted Lucy's hand. "Dear lady, you're overwrought. You've overtaxed yourself needlessly."

She shoved his hand away. "Two people invaded my house last night and tried to kill Nick in his bed. If that isn't reason enough to be overwrought, then what is?"

Susanna gasped. "Was anyone hurt?"

"No. Nick chased them away."

Oxley sat back in his chair and twisted his enormous ring. The only sign that he was troubled was the violent bob of his Adam's apple.

"That settles it." Susanna clamped her hands on the arms of her chair as if she would push herself up, but she did not. "Enough of this dancing around the truth. She ought to know."

"Susanna," Orlando warned.

"No. It's not like she's unaware that we're hiding something, and I believe she cares for Cole as deeply as she claims. Orlando," she said, softer, "you didn't keep it from me."

"I willingly told you. Cole hasn't."

"Nor will he," Oxley said with absolute conviction. "Don't worry, Mistress Cowdrey, we'll remove Cole from your home. I won't have you put in danger."

Lucy choked. He understood nothing! "I don't—"

"And put him where?" Orlando cut in. "He can't come here, not with Susanna like this."

"A room at the Plough," Oxley said. "He ought to be able to travel to Sutton Grange if he goes slowly."

"Stop!" Lucy felt like a shrew for shouting, but the thick-headed man didn't seem to understand a single thing of what she'd said. "Nick isn't going anywhere. He's staying at Cowdrey Farm until… " *He realizes he loves me.* "Until he's well enough to leave."

"I don't think that's wise." There was nothing frivolous or foppish about Oxley now. His face was set like marble, and those blue eyes were as icy as glaciers. She shivered. "I'm his friend, Mistress Cowdrey. I'll tell you what needs to be done to ensure his safety, and your own."

"You may be his friend, my lord, but I love and care for him. I want him to be happy. Do you?"

It was like she'd pricked him, and he'd suddenly deflated. He rested his elbows on his knees and dragged his hand through his hair. "Women," he muttered.

Susanna took Lucy's hand and gave her a grim smile. "I think you've worn him down."

Lucy expected one of the men to say something, but they didn't. Oxley appeared to be studying his silk slippers, and Orlando watched his wife with a gleam of pride in his eyes.

When it became clear that neither man would tell Lucy anything, Susanna spoke. "Hughe—Lord Oxley—is the leader of the Guild of Assassins," she said.

"Assassins!" The preening fop killed people? He was a leader of men who killed people? God's wounds, Lucy had misjudged him completely.

She suddenly felt sick. Assassins.

"The Guild is a small group of men who bring justice to those who escape it," Orlando went on. "I was one of them until I left to settle down with Susanna. Monk joined at that time, and Cole has belonged for four years."

Lucy wanted to throw up. Her Nick, a killer? But he was so gentle, so considerate.

Wasn't he?

Oh God, oh God. How could she be in love with an assassin? She, who wanted only to heal people. Who'd tried so hard to distance herself from her murderous cousins. Tried so hard to be liked in her new home.

"Lucy, are you all right?" Orlando asked. "You don't look very well."

Susanna's cool hand enveloped Lucy's. "She's received a shock. Give her time. Breathe, Lucy."

How could she when her chest felt like it was being crushed beneath a great weight? "You know," she said to Susanna, "yet you don't care."

Susanna squeezed her hand. "It's not like that. The people they assassinate are base creatures. They have no morals and no qualms about killing or hurting others. Most are in positions of authority and have avoided justice one way or another."

Lucy glanced at Orlando. This beautiful, smiling man had killed people? Lord Oxley and Monk too? Was no one as they seemed?

"You ordered Nick to assassinate Alderman Renny?" she asked Oxley. "Why? What did the alderman do?"

Oxley had been silently gazing at his feet, but now he looked up at her. His face had changed. The mocking smile was gone, the pale blue eyes weren't cold anymore, but they still leant an other-worldly quality to his handsome face, as if they could see beyond the here and now.

"I didn't order Nick to do anything. I assigned him this kill, but he could choose whether to take the assignment or not." He shrugged. "Every man who works for me has a choice in everything they do. Some choices will see them expelled from the Guild." His gaze slid to Orlando then back to Lucy. "I can't tell you what Renny did. That information was given to me in confidence, and I only passed it on to the Guild's *current* members because they need to agree with me that the target is guilty. If one of us is unsure, then we don't go through with it, or we try to find out more. Suffice to say, Renny's guilt was beyond question and his crimes were despicable. The victims have their reasons for not wanting to pursue the matter through proper legal channels. Renny is powerful in Larkham, and they are not."

The weight on her chest lifted a little but was replaced with the feeling that the world had been tipped on its head.

C.J. ARCHER

"They're good men," Susanna said. "I would not have fallen in love with Orlando if he wasn't."

"It's a lot to take in," Lucy said, "but it explains a few things." Like why Nick had been carrying so many knives, and why he had extraordinarily keen senses. "Thank you for telling me," she said to Lord Oxley. "I appreciate your trust in me."

"I'm sure you can understand our lives depend on the Guild's existence staying secret," he said.

"I understand. However, I do have one question. Orlando, you told Nick that he was an assassin that day you came to the farm, didn't you?"

"Yes."

"Did he believe you?"

Orlando shrugged. "I think so."

"Why?" Susanna asked Lucy. "What is it?"

"He seemed a little troubled after that conversation and in the days since," Lucy said, "but nothing compared to… " *Last night.* "Today. It's as if he woke up and decided to be a different person."

"I think the different person was the one *you* witnessed," Oxley said. "The Cole you spoke of is foreign to us."

She wasn't getting drawn into that discussion again. "Nevertheless, the fact remains that it wasn't discovering he was an assassin that flipped Nick back to his old self. It was— Oh. Oh no."

"What?" all three asked.

"He's been having nightmares about his past. Each one has revealed a little more about a period of time when he was eighteen."

"The point at which his memories stopped?" Susanna asked.

"Yes. And I think last night's nightmare filled in the final piece of the puzzle. It may have even triggered the return of all his memories."

"Hence the return to the true Cole," Oxley said.

"No," she snapped. "Not the true *Nick.* I refuse to believe it."

Susanna's hand tightened around Lucy's, but she would not be calmed. Why did the earl refuse to believe that there was more to

182

Cole than the man he'd known for only four years? It was as if he didn't want to entertain the thought that Nick may be as gentle-hearted and amiable as Orlando, for instance.

Oxley didn't show any sign that he'd heard her. He stared down at the floor, his elbows still on his thighs, his hands dangling between his knees.

"Do either of you have any clue as to what happened when he was eighteen?" Lucy asked both men. "What troubles him so?"

"I don't know," Orlando said. "He never confided in me. I didn't even know his full name until he told me the other day. Hughe?"

"I don't know either," Lord Oxley said without looking up. "He told me very little, and I was never able to discover much about him. Did he tell you anything about his dreams, Mistress Cowdrey?"

"Some. His father forbade him and his brother to leave the house and immediate grounds, but Nick escaped into the village one day. He was whipped for his disobedience." Lucy's stomach churned. "He was whipped again for going with two village boys into the wood. The scars are still visible on his back." She closed her eyes, breathed until the wave of nausea subsided. Susanna's reassuring hand squeezed again.

"Good lord," Susanna said. "How horrid. Why would his father do that?"

"I don't know. He hasn't spoken about the nightmares for two days."

"You think he had one last night that revealed more?" Oxley asked.

"I'm almost certain of it. What he learned must have shaken him to the core. Enough to change him."

Oxley sat back and rubbed his thigh. "Whatever happened, it's of concern, but I have a more immediate problem."

"Aye," Orlando said, grim. "His attacker."

"Attackers," Lucy said. "There were two."

Orlando swore softly. Oxley continued to rub his thigh as if it pained him. "Someone knows he killed Renny and wants revenge."

"But why not simply tell the Larkham authorities?" Lucy asked.

"A good question."

"Could it be a family member who doesn't think the authorities will succeed?" Susanna asked. "Or friends?"

Oxley shrugged. "Renny was a powerful man but not overly liked except by a very few who benefited from his leadership within the village. It may have been they. As to family, he had only a wife and young sons. There were no brothers, sisters or cousins to speak of."

"It must be his friends then," Lucy said.

Oxley didn't look convinced. "From what I saw of them, they were too well-fed and idle to be agile or quiet enough to sneak up on Cole. The man's never fully asleep even though he may appear to be."

"That's because he's not human," Orlando said and chuckled.

His wife shot him a glare, and he sobered.

"You've been to Larkham?" Lucy asked.

"Of course," Oxley said, standing. "I always investigate the targets thoroughly first. In disguise of course."

She eyed him up and down. What sort of disguise would hide that hair, the air of confident arrogance? Then she remembered the Larkham men had said Renny's killer was pale and bearded with long brown hair, nothing at all like Nick. Oxley and his men must be very good at hiding themselves in plain view.

Oxley strode toward the door and Lucy sprang out of the chair. "Where are you going, my lord?"

"To your farm. We need to get Cole into hiding as soon as possible."

She lifted her skirts and ran after him.

* * *

"REST A WHILE," Henry said. "Save your strength for your journey." He gave Cole a crooked smile that Cole managed to return despite the heaviness inside him. He passed the wineskin back, and Henry drank deeply.

"As soon as this field is done, I'll go," Cole said. "I shouldn't wait any longer."

"I still can't convince you to stay? These attacks may be a misunderstanding. I can't imagine you've done anything to warrant such ire. Surely it could all be resolved with a simple discussion."

"I doubt it."

"How can you be sure if you can't remember?"

Cole's blood throbbed, and his head ached. "It's better for everyone if I go."

"How will that solve anything? Do you propose to return for Lucy under cover of nightfall?"

The hot sun beat down on the top of Cole's head. He didn't wear a hat because he'd removed the bandage and didn't want it to rub on the raw wound.

Henry swore. "You're not coming back, are you?"

Cole said nothing.

"I should thrash you, but I doubt I could." He turned away, and Cole thought he was going to walk off, but he turned back again. His lips were pinched and white, and Cole had never seen such cold fury in Henry's eyes. "You're a heartless prick, Coleclough. My sister is the best of women, the kindest you'll ever meet and she's in love with you. Any fool can see it. Christ, I thought it was bad when Mallam broke their betrothal, but this is going to be so much worse."

Cole waited. Henry waited too as if he expected Cole to say something, perhaps defend himself. He did not. There was no defense for what he'd done to Lucy.

"She's going to shed a lot of tears, but you are *not* worth them," Henry snapped. "Neither you nor Mallam deserve a moment of her love. You're both the same. Both as heartless as the other."

"We're not the same." Mallam didn't care enough. Cole cared too much.

Fuck. Fuck, fuck, *fuck*!

He looked down at the newly plowed earth beneath his feet. He couldn't look at Henry any more and see the anger and frustration in his eyes.

The distant rumble of cartwheels made him look up. If Lucy had come to speak to him again, Cole would be undone once and for all. He couldn't continue to remain impassive if she pleaded with him to take her.

If it were his attackers instead…

"What is it?" Henry asked.

"I have to leave."

"Now?"

"Yes." He clasped Henry's forearm. He wanted to tell him to take care of Lucy, but it went without saying.

Henry's mutter was lost beneath shouts and hoof beats. Cole glanced at the track and swore. The cartwheels had drowned out the sound of the horses galloping ahead in an advance party. Four horses in all. Two carried the Larkham authorities, Sawyer and Upfield, and riding behind were two boys. They must be no more than thirteen or fourteen. He recognized one as the lad who'd come to the barn looking for work.

Everything clicked into place like two cogs turning slowly in harmonization. Hell. He needed to get out of there, but he couldn't outrun them through the open fields. He'd have to fight. Not an easy task with both men and boys unsheathing their swords. The boys shouldn't be a problem, but the men were an unknown.

Henry went to meet them as the cart rolled to a stop. "Good morrow," he said as the horses came to a halt in a cloud of dust. "Is there a need for weapons, sirs?"

"Move aside," Upfield snarled. The older of the Larkham men had a vicious, untamed look about him. Cole would deal with him first.

"We've come to arrest him," Sawyer said, pointing the sword at Cole.

Henry seemed to take the words like a blow to the stomach. He stepped back and glanced over his shoulder at Cole. He blinked hard as if he couldn't quite see, or didn't believe what he saw. "On what charge?" he asked.

"Murder."

One of the boys moved his horse forward, but Sawyer held a hand out to stay him. "He killed Alderman Renny," the boy said. "Our father."

CHAPTER 15

*C*ole's bruises had never ached so much. His head throbbed fiercely too, as if his brain was trying to break through the crack in his head.

"*You* did it," he said to the bigger of the two boys, the one who'd spoken. "You attacked me in the meadow."

"We both did," the younger chimed in.

Two lads. That explained how they inflicted so much damage so quickly, and being light of foot, they'd crept up on him. He thought it had been Lucy approaching, and coupled with his exhaustion, he'd not remained as alert as he should. Bloody fool. He deserved the crack on his head.

"Come quietly, and there'll be no need for violence," Sawyer said.

Upfield's lip curled into a warped grin. He looked like he had every intention of using violence.

"Stay back," Cole said to Henry. "Keep your men away." The farm laborers had ceased working and watched the performance. They were far enough away that they couldn't hear, however, or interfere. One less thing for Cole to worry about.

"Will you come with us willingly?" Sawyer asked. "No one will be hurt that way."

Only Cole when a trial found him guilty, which it undoubtedly would.

"Wait." Henry held up his hands, placating. "You have witnesses?"

"Many."

"What did they see?"

Sawyer shrugged. "This man killing Renny."

"*This* man? Did they describe him exactly?" Spoken like a true lawyer.

"Exactly?" Sawyer's horse shifted and turned, making the other three twitch restlessly too.

"Come now," Henry said in the placating tone Cole had heard him use on Lucy to good effect. "I know you cannot be positive it was Coleclough here, otherwise you would have arrested him the first time."

"He used a disguise!" the older boy shouted. "Frankie saw him take it off."

"I was sitting on the bank of the stream near the mill when I saw a man run up that night," the boy said. "I got scared and hid. You came up real close, but I didn't make a sound, not even when you took off your hair and beard. Almost fell in the stream, I was that surprised. Then you bent down near me and washed your face. It was too dark to see proper, but your face was darker than before you washed it."

A good lawyer would question the lad, put doubt in his head, but Henry remained silent. He looked down at his feet, shook his head and said absolutely nothing.

He had abandoned Cole. As he should if he wanted to keep his family and workers safe. It's what any law-abiding Englishman would do faced with such compelling evidence.

"He came home and told me," the older boy said, "but I didn't believe him."

"Fool," Frankie said with a roll of his eyes.

"I thought it was just something he made up. Anyway, I hadn't heard about Pa then." His voice cracked, and he pursed his lips, a young lad trying to be brave in front of men.

"When they told us what happened, I knew Frankie spoke the truth." He started to cry and swiped his nose with the back of his hand. "You killed our Pa."

It was a bloody nightmare. This was why Cole always left money for his target's families. Why he never wanted to see them, connect with them.

As if money could ever be enough. Of anyone, Cole knew it meant nothing compared to the loss of a parent.

If the boys knew what their father had been like, perhaps they'd think differently. They seemed like good lads. Yet he couldn't tell them he'd been given a clean death, which is more than what he deserved. They shouldn't have to hear that. It was better to think of one's parent as a good soul when alive, instead of a mad one.

Cole knew that all too well.

Upfield dismounted and raised his sword. He had a steady stance, a good grip. He knew what he was doing. "Enough talking! Get in the cart, Coleclough."

Cole nodded and ambled up to him. "Where are you taking me?"

Upfield opened his mouth to answer, but Cole slammed his fist into his jaw before he'd uttered a single word. He snatched the sword off Upfield while he was too busy picking his barrel-like frame off the ground.

"Dismount," Cole said to Sawyer.

"Stay back!" Sawyer shouted at the lads as he set his feet on the ground.

Neither of the brothers moved. Their horses shifted as if sensing danger.

Sawyer engaged, and Cole parried the first two blows easily enough. The man was a middling swordsman, but he didn't use his feet well.

"Peter, give me your sword," Upfield ordered the oldest brother.

Peter shook his head, his wild gaze fixed on Cole, his teeth bared in a snarl. He was bent on revenge, and Cole suspected he wouldn't be sated until he got it.

Upfield swore then turned to Frankie. He held out his hand, and the younger boy handed over his sword. He swallowed heavily and gripped the reins tight.

Upfield stepped into the fight, and Cole had to concentrate. He blocked strike after strike and managed to get some good ones of his own in, nicking a sleeve here or a doublet there. He didn't want to kill either of them, although he had a mind to scare the wits out of Upfield.

"Stand still," the older man growled. He pressed his hand into his side and breathed hard.

Cole had turned so much that Henry was now in his line of sight. Cole was right where he wanted to be—near the two horses. The lads were a little behind him, but he would hear them coming if they decided to attack.

Indeed, Peter made a lot of noise. He sounded like an ancient warrior, his battle cry high-pitched and loud. When Cole gauged him to be right behind, he ducked and rolled to the side in the dirt. He hit the ground harder than he'd hoped and pain speared through him, up into his head.

Then everything turned to fog. Shadows rolled in. He thrust out the sword, struck nothing but air, but the shape moved back. White-hot pain seared his skull, and he fought the panic as darkness flirted with him.

"Frankie, no!" That was Peter, the older brother.

Where the hell was Frankie? If Cole struck out and hit the boy, he'd never forgive himself. He put the sword down and held up his hands. "I can't see," he said.

"Could be a trick," said Upfield.

"Don't be a fool." That was Henry. He was closer than Cole expected. His face slowly came into focus, grim set. The world brightened again, but the screaming pain in his head remained.

He was hoisted up by Upfield and the driver. Cole could have fought them off, but there was no point. Sawyer would mow him down, perhaps the oldest lad too. And more people were coming. He heard wheels and horses approaching fast.

"Someone comes," said Sawyer. "Get him on the cart."

"Lucy." Henry swore.

Cole closed his eyes to gather himself. He would need all of the iron will he was renowned for, and more.

"Who's with her?" Henry asked at the same time Cole opened his eyes. "Are they your friends?"

Hughe and Monk. A bit bloody late.

"Nick!" Lucy screamed. She jumped off the cart before it had completely stopped and ran toward him.

"Lucy, don't," Henry said, catching her.

She struggled against him, but he held her and she finally calmed. Her wide eyes, however, filled with desperation. "What's happening? Where are you taking him?"

Hughe and Monk rode up, and Henry briefly explained the situation to them all. His friends remained passive, did nothing, as Cole expected. They couldn't risk becoming too involved.

"No!" Lucy cried. "You can't take him!" She struggled anew, twisting in Henry's arms, stamping on his foot until he let her go.

She ran toward Cole, tears streaming down her face. Without letting go of Cole, Upfield thrust out a hand and shoved her in the chest. She fell backward and landed on the ground. Her hat slipped off, and her hair tumbled about her face.

Cole wrenched himself out of the driver's grip, swung, and smashed his fist into Upfield's nose. Blood sprayed and Upfield bent over double. He cupped both hands over his face and made strangled gasping sounds.

Unfettered, Cole stepped forward and shrugged off the driver as he went to recapture him. The driver didn't try again. Cole held out his hand to Lucy and she took it. Dusty tears streaked her cheeks, and her lip trembled.

"Nick," she sobbed and buried her face in his chest.

He stroked her hair. Such a beautiful color in the bright sunlight. She was crying uncontrollably, her whole body heaving with every sob. Could she hear his thundering heartbeat through her sorrow? Did she know it beat for her? Only for her. She must be able to feel it. Must know that her tears were about to break him. He closed his eyes and drew in a shuddering breath.

Then he opened them and pushed her away.

She gasped and blinked at him. At least she'd stopped crying. "Nick?" She shook her head over and over. Her mouth opened and closed, but no sound came out.

Henry put his arm around her and tried to steer her away, but she didn't budge.

"Go home, Lucy," Cole said. "This is not your business." God, it hurt. Every word burned his throat. Her lower lip wobbled again and he couldn't do it, couldn't look at her anymore. She was going to undo the wall he'd tried so hard to build up between them. He thought he'd completed it, but seeing her so vulnerable and soft and loving… the bloody thing was crumbling all over again. He fixed on a point to the left of her.

"But Nick… "

"I don't answer to that name." He pushed past her, and she heaved a sob. He concentrated on emptying his mind, stilling his heartbeat. It worked, but it took enormous effort and inflamed his headache.

"Let's go," he said to Sawyer. "There's nothing for me here."

Lucy wanted to scream at him. How could he do this? How could he say those things? The ground shifted under her feet, and she couldn't keep her balance. Her legs felt weak and she wanted to lie down but something held her upright. Henry. It must be he.

"Come now, Sis," he said. "I'll take you home."

Home. No. She should be with Nick.

But Nick didn't want her. Didn't love her. He'd been telling her that for a day or more, but she'd not believed him. Refused to hear it. How could he not care after the intense lovemaking they'd shared?

Foolish, foolish Lucy Cowdrey. Duped again by a man who only wanted to tumble her. Pathetic creature.

"Wait here." Henry left her to run after the Larkham men. They loaded Nick onto the back of their cart. Upfield tied a rope around Nick's wrist as Henry spoke to Sawyer.

The party left with Nick in the back of the cart, his head bowed, and the Larkham men and boys riding beside him. Oxley and Monk rode with them too.

Henry returned and steered her to her waiting cart.

"He wouldn't fight," she said. Her voice sounded small. "Why wouldn't he fight them? He could have been free."

Henry blew out a breath. "To keep his friends safe, perhaps?"

Keep their disguises intact. Yes. That must be it. Odd how her mind was working fast, thinking through everything both Nick and his friends had told her, and yet her body felt like a weakened vessel with cracks running through it.

"They're taking him to Sutton Grange," Henry said. "There's a small jail cell attached to the Plough Inn. He'll await the assizes there."

"That's something, isn't it?" She had no idea what she was saying, let alone what she meant.

Henry stopped alongside the cart and turned her to face him. "Did he do it, Lucy?" Poor Henry. He seemed as exhausted as she felt. The dark skin beneath his eyes sagged like empty sacks, and the furrows on his brow were so deep they'd probably become permanent.

The sun slipped behind a cloud and she felt instantly colder. She hugged herself. "Yes."

Henry swore. "The cur. He deceived us. God, Lucy, I'm so sorry."

She ought to tell him Renny deserved to die, that Nick wasn't all bad, but she could no longer be sure of that. He must be bad to some degree because he'd crushed her heart and not blinked an eye.

* * *

"Murder," Hughe said to Sawyer with a shake of his head. "I can't believe it. I just can't believe it."

"How well do you know him, my lord?" Sawyer asked.

"Not well, as it turns out, wouldn't you say?" Hughe laughed his tinkling dandy laugh. It was utterly convincing. If Cole hadn't known it was all an act, he'd have believed the man riding the white horse was the most ridiculous fop to ever have visited Hampshire.

Monk rode behind the cart, directly in Cole's line of sight. He rolled his eyes, safe in the knowledge that the Larkham men and boys had their backs to him. Cole looked away and stared at the passing fields, but that only brought Lucy's sad, tear stained face to mind.

His stomach clenched into a tight ball. He groaned and pulled his legs up to stave off the nausea. It shouldn't feel like this. He'd walked away before, but he'd never been hit so hard.

Lucy was different. She shone a light on the small corner of his soul that wasn't completely overwhelmed by the dark. It was the corner where the happy, trusting youth he'd been before he'd killed his mother cowered, just waiting for someone's hand to guide him out.

Cole loved her.

That's why he had to let her go.

"You well?" Monk's voice startled him.

"Well enough if I ignore the splitting headache," Cole said.

"No talking to the prisoner," Upfield snarled.

Cole didn't know what he was worried about. It wasn't like they could discuss escape plans out in the open. It wasn't like escaping was even an option. Cole sat against the back of the cart, a rope tying each of his hands to cast iron rings on either side of him. He couldn't even scratch himself.

"How in God's name did you find him?" Hughe asked.

"You're his friend, are you?" Sawyer asked. "I'm afraid we can't discuss particulars with you. I apologize, my lord." Cole almost felt sorry for him. Sawyer seemed like a good man, but Hughe's presence obviously confused him. Most men would let someone of that rank take over, but Sawyer had not offered to step back and let Hughe give the orders. On the other hand, Hughe gave no sign that he was interested in giving any.

"Come now, I simply want to know how you managed to do it. And 'friend' is a term much bandied about these days. We're acquaintances, no more. He's worked for me from time to time, much as Monk does. The likes of them and I being friends is laughable." He laughed. Nobody else joined in.

"*We* found him," the younger of the boys, Frankie, said.

"Did you now?" Hughe sounded impressed. "And how did you do that, pray?"

Frankie told him how he'd seen Cole remove the disguise then run home to tell his brother. "Then we heard about Pa."

"My sympathies, lads." It sounded utterly sincere and knowing Hughe, it would have been. "Why didn't you go to the authorities then?"

"A bloody good question," Upfield growled. "Wouldn't have wasted so much time if they had."

"Come now," Sawyer said. "They're just children."

"I am *not* a child," the oldest boy, Peter, said. "We *did* tell someone. We told the first grown up we saw when we left our house. Mr. Wright."

Cole's gaze slid to Monk's. Wright was the father of one of the girls who'd been raped by Renny. He had every reason to keep the villagers off Cole's trail.

"You should've come to one of your Pa's friends," Upfield grumbled. "Wright's got no authority in the village. He doesn't get things done."

"He still should've followed up on their account," Sawyer said, thoughtful.

"He probably assumed the lads were larking," Hughe said. "Or were just so distraught about their father that they were making it up. Don't blame him."

"You're right, my lord," Sawyer said.

Upfield responded with a grunt.

"It is quite an unbelievable tale," Hughe said lightly. "A disguise, eh? I'd never have pegged Cole as the sort to dress up. Tell me, what did you do next? How did you find the villain?"

Villain? Cole scowled. Hughe was acting the part of unsympathetic employer a little too well.

"We followed him," Frankie said.

"My lord," Sawyer corrected him.

"My lord," Frankie added. "Ma thought we was in bed, but we slipped out. My lord."

"Aye, and when she discovered you both gone in the morning, she fell into a panic." Sawyer clicked his tongue. "Don't do that to her again."

"Go on," Hughe urged.

"There's two ways out of Larkham," Peter said. "Since Frankie saw him at the mill, we guessed he'd gone the Sutton Grange road, so that's the way we went. We know most of the lads working on the farms along the way, so we woke 'em up. Most sleep in the barn, so it weren't hard to do in secret. We asked if they'd seen a big man with dark skin passing." He shrugged. "No one thinks to ask children, you see."

"We thought of it, didn't we, Peter?" Frankie said, beaming at his older brother.

"Aye. We only needed to talk to two lads, and we knew we was going the right way. One said he let the man fill his wine skin from the water in the well, and the other said he'd seen him pass. The farm lad was with his wench in the bushes, half asleep, and this man walked right by 'em."

Monk *tsk tsked*. He seemed to be enjoying hearing about Cole's mistakes. Ordinarily Cole would have responded with a barb or a withering look, but he didn't have the heart to banter with him.

"Looked to us like the man had left the Sutton Grange road, so we did too."

"But we got lost," Frankie said. "There were fields and meadows everywhere. They all look the same, my lord, especially at night. My lord."

"I imagine they do."

"We got really tired a little after dawn," Peter said. "Frankie couldn't walk much further, so we found a hedgerow and pushed aside the branches and leaves to make enough space to lie down in."

"Once we was settled, we was well hidden, my lord." Frankie beamed. "No one could see us."

Cole nodded. He certainly hadn't seen anyone when he settled near the hedgerow. Admittedly he hadn't been looking for small boys hiding out.

"I woke up first," Peter said. "I couldn't believe my eyes when I saw him so close. He was asleep, so I crept out of the hedgerow quiet as can be. I picked up a stick and just as I was about to hit him, he woke up. I still got a good crack in before he turned round."

"I can see that," Hughe said. "Quite a cut on his head. It made him lose his memory."

"Really?" Peter sounded pleased.

"I woke up then," Frankie said. "We was really angry with him, Peter and me. Terrible angry. We kicked him. A lot."

"Don't feel bad, lad," Upfield said. "He killed yer Pa. You had a right to do what you did."

"Why did you stop?" Cole asked. "Why didn't you kill me?"

"Shut it," Upfield snapped. "You don't speak."

"Let the man talk," Hughe said.

"He's my prisoner, and I'll—"

"I *said*, let the man talk." Steel edged Hughe's voice, leaving no one in any doubt that he would use his rank if he had to.

"As you wish," Upfield muttered.

"My lord," Hughe prompted.

Upfield hesitated only briefly before repeating the title, just as Frankie had repeated it upon Sawyer's urging earlier.

"Answer the prisoner, Peter," Sawyer said gently. "Why *did* you stop?"

"I began to think, what if it's not him? What if Frankie got it wrong?"

"I didn't," Frankie said.

"I know that now, Toadstool. But at the time, I couldn't do it. He was just lying there, and we was kicking him, and he didn't get up." He sniffed then tried to cover it with a cough.

"It's all right, lad," Cole said. "I don't blame you. I would have done the same thing in your place."

"Don't talk to me!" Peter shouted. "I hate you."

Cole tipped his head back, but that just made his head bump against the barrier separating him and the driver. He already had enough of a headache. He didn't need to make it worse.

"Then the lady came," Frankie said, "so we ran off."

"Did you go home?" Hughe asked.

"Aye," said Peter. "But we told no one. I thought we'd killed him. I got worried that maybe he wasn't the murderer, and we'd be in trouble, so we kept quiet for a day or two, until I couldn't stand it no more. I wanted to know what had happened, if we'd killed him. If he was the right one."

"There was talk in the village about a special knife he'd used to kill Pa," Frankie said. "The blade's hidden inside the handle, real clever."

"So we decided to come back and 'vestigate," Peter said. "We told Ma we was camping down by the creek for a bit to clear our heads. We used to do it a lot with Pa before… "

"She was worried about you out there on your own," Sawyer said. "But she told me she had to let you go, that you needed to remember the good things about your Pa. If she'd known what you were really up to, she'd have wrung your necks. She probably still might when my message reaches her."

"You found me at Cowdrey Farm easily enough," Cole said to the boys.

"Aye, once we realized whose land we'd seen you on," Peter said, apparently forgetting he didn't want Cole to speak to him. "Frankie hid out in the loft at the barn, and I asked for a job. When I saw you walking about with a bandage on your head, I realized you was alive. Me and Frankie planned to look through your pack and see if you had that knife. If you did, we'd know you was the one who killed Pa."

"But then Mr. Upfield and Mr. Sawyer arrived," Frankie said. "When we found out they was staying the night, we decided to do nothing until the next night."

"We didn't want to tell them yet," Peter said. "Not until we had proof."

"Should've said something then," Upfield muttered. "Could've saved everyone a lot of time."

"You got that proof the following night?" Hughe asked.

"Aye, my lord sir," Frankie said. "We stole his pack. That special knife was inside. When we found it, we headed home, but met Mr. Upfield and Mr. Sawyer on the way. We told 'em everything."

"What industrious lads you both are," Hughe said. "I could sorely use men like you in my employ. Tell me, what do you think of girls?"

Monk smiled at Cole. Cole rolled his eyes but couldn't hide his smirk. Even in the most adverse times, Hughe the dandy could lift his mood.

Hughe ruffled the boy's hair. "It's most fortunate I was visiting my friend Holt," he said to the men. "With Lord Lynden away, I can oversee the arrangements in his stead. When is the next assizes to be held in Sutton Grange?"

"A fortnight," Sawyer said.

"Too bloody long," Upfield growled.

"And how far away is the coroner?" Hughe asked.

"It'll take about three days to get him here," Sawyer said. He cleared his throat. "Ah, forgive me for saying this, my lord, but I think it's best if you refrain from participating at all."

"Oh?"

"I wouldn't want your reputation to come into question, since you know the murderer."

"Not very well it would seem. I'm taken aback to learn of his crime."

"I haven't been found guilty yet," Cole reminded him.

"You will be," Upfield said. "We know you did it."

"I'm afraid he's right, Cole," Hughe said, matter-of-fact. "There *are* witnesses."

It was enough. More than enough. Cole wasn't going to be found innocent by a jury, even with Hughe using all his influence behind the scenes. Witness testimony was enough to convict a man. Cole was going to hang.

If he wanted to save his neck and his life, he'd have to escape, but that meant never returning to this corner of Hampshire or to Coleclough Hall. He'd be running and hiding for the rest of his days.

Avoiding Coleclough wouldn't be too difficult, since he'd been doing it for eleven years. Besides, the last place he wanted to be after Sutton Grange was his father's house. Too many demons there.

As for leaving Hampshire, leaving Lucy, he would do it. He *had* to. He'd already set the foundation for it. All he had to do was to continue to build the wall higher. Lucy's future depended upon him having the strength to keep that wall as impenetrable as a fortress.

CHAPTER 16

*H*enry had wanted Lucy to rest after returning home, but she couldn't. She needed to be active, so she helped the cook bake some pies, after which she cleaned up. Or tried to—the maids shooed her out of the scullery before she could get her hands wet. Instead, she went for a long walk with Brutus at her heels until the supper bell rang.

Brutus left her when he saw his bowl full and she continued up to her rooms. She sat in the small study adjoining her bedchamber and tried to sew, but it was hopeless. Her stitching was terribly crooked. The walk may have tired her body but not her mind. She couldn't stop thinking.

Matilda entered carrying supper on a tray. Brutus slipped in behind her and padded over to Lucy. He sat on her feet and put his head in her lap. For some reason, that made Lucy want to cry.

"Leave the tray on the desk, thank you, Matilda. I don't feel very hungry just yet." She stroked Brutus's ears, and she could swear he smiled at her.

Matilda set the tray down but didn't leave. "Can I get you something else, mistress?"

"No, thank you."

"Do you want the windows closed?"

"Leave it open. The breeze is lovely."

Matilda sighed. "You did too much today."

Lucy simply shrugged in response.

The maid sighed again. "I don't understand."

Lucy didn't want to talk about it. Not with Henry, Matilda, or even Brutus. Talking about Nick made her think about him and recall his final words to her. Worse, it made her think about what lay ahead for him.

She shivered.

"You're cold. I'm shutting the window." Matilda crossed the room and pulled the casement window closed. "Poor pet," she said. "I can't believe it."

"Thank you, Matilda," Lucy muttered.

"The thing is, he seemed like a nice sort, a good man." Matilda shook her head. "I can't believe he's a killer. And to deceive you so, too." She clicked her tongue. "First yer cousins and now this. The farm is cursed."

"It's not the farm, Matilda, don't think that. I'm determined to make Cowdrey a wonderful home for all of us. Anyway, Nick may have had a reason to kill that man. We shouldn't judge him."

"If you say so, mistress, but he *did* deceive you and the master. We all thought he was a baron's son and that his intention was to…" She cleared her throat. "Well, we believed him to be honorable."

"He is a baron's son."

"Aye. Well. What about the other thing? How could a man who carved such a lovely thing be so cold hearted?"

"Carving? What carving?"

"He didn't show you?" She *humphed*. "Course he wouldn't. Wait here. I'll fetch it."

She bustled out and returned a few minutes later, her hand outstretched. A little wooden dog sat on her palm. A little wooden *Brutus*. Nick had captured her hound's likeness perfectly, from the fine detail of his fur to his tongue lolling out the left side as he gazed adoringly up at something. He'd even managed to infuse the face with Brutus's enthusiasm.

"One of the maids found it in the guest bedchamber," Matilda said. "She thought maybe he forgot it. I said to her, 'How can he forget his one and only possession?' What say you, mistress? Do you think he left it behind on purpose?"

Lucy stroked the smooth wooden head with her thumb and the real Brutus's head with her other hand. She shrugged because her throat was too clogged with unshed tears for her to answer. She liked to think he'd left it for her, but that couldn't be. He'd made it clear she wasn't in his thoughts at all anymore, and probably never had been.

"'Tis a fine piece of work, ain't it?" Matilda said. "Shame he turned out to be a murderer."

A shame too that he'd taken advantage Lucy. It was an even bigger shame that she'd let him. She should have known better.

Matilda left and Lucy tried to sleep, but couldn't, not with Nick cooped up in a small cell. She spent most the night trying to turn her heart against him, telling herself he was a cur, that he deserved whatever the Larkham men did to him. But her heart wouldn't be swayed, and the thought of what could happen next turned her blood to ice.

Nick might be a cold-hearted beast where she was concerned, but he didn't deserve to be hanged for bringing justice to those girls.

She hoped and prayed that Lord Oxley could do something, but hopes and prayers didn't ease her mind.

"I still can't believe it," Henry said over breakfast. He'd joined her in the small parlor after urging her to get out of bed. She'd not been able to sleep, yet she didn't want to face the world either. "To think, he murdered someone! And we harbored him here in this house. I even let him court you!"

Lucy set her knife down firmly on her trencher. "You have it wrong."

"He didn't kiss you?"

"Uh, yes, he did."

"He didn't murder the Larkham alderman?"

"He did that too, but he had a reason." She got up and closed the door.

"He had a reason for committing murder?" Henry blinked slowly. "Surely you're not going to defend his actions after the way he treated you?"

"What I am going to tell you must remain a secret. You cannot speak of it to anyone." She recounted everything Orlando and Lord Oxley had told her about Nick and his assassination of Alderman Renny. When she finished, Henry stared at her, his mouth open. "I don't know what Renny's crime was," she said, "but I suspect it was heinous."

"This is shocking," he said. "Yet I do believe every word, if only because of Holt. If it had come from Lord Oxley alone, I would have had doubts. From what I've seen of him, he's a fool who likes attention. Worse even that Lord Lynden. But Holt I trust."

"Lord Oxley acts that way deliberately. I've seen him in his true guise, and he is as sharp as a blade. His men trust him, and he them."

"Then why didn't he try to release Coleclough?"

"How could he? They had witnesses. He cannot say that Nick was with him because that would clearly be a lie and would only implicate himself. Nor can he vouch for Nick's character for the same reason. It's hopeless."

"Not completely. Perhaps Oxley can talk to the coroner or assize judges. He would have some sway with them, and Coleclough is a nobleman's son too. That must count for something."

"Perhaps. But the judges aren't due for two weeks, the coroner in a few days. Anything could happen in that time, and Lord Oxley needs to keep his disguise intact until then."

"You think he values his disguise over his friend's life?"

"I don't know. I truly don't."

He suddenly stood. "I'm going to Sutton Grange. I can't sit here and do nothing after what you've said, no matter what I think of the man personally."

"I'm coming."

"Thought you might."

* * *

LUCY CLUTCHED Henry's arm as they approached the Plough Inn, and he sucked air between his teeth.

"Not so hard, Sis." He pulled gently on the reins and eased the horse to a stop alongside the green opposite the inn. "He might be all right. Mayhap they've released him."

They would not have released him. The Larkham men wouldn't allow it. Upfield seemed determined to avenge his friend's killer, and the more restrained Sawyer looked equally determined to see justice done, if only for justice's sake.

Or Nick may have succumbed to his injuries. Lucy clutched Henry's arm harder.

"We'll go inside. Milner will know where he is."

Lucy kept her arm looped through her brother's as they walked beneath the swinging sign of the Plough and into the taproom. There weren't many patrons, but that was hardly surprising considering the early hour. Lucy counted perhaps a dozen in all, and aside from Milner and his daughter, they were in two distinct camps. Sitting on stools in the far corner was Upfield and a few other men Lucy didn't recognize. Sitting around a table at the opposite end of the room was Mr. Monk, Widow Dawson and Anne Lane, the chandler's wife.

Widow Dawson hailed them and Monk pulled up two more stools. Henry sat. Lucy did not.

"Where is he?" she asked. "Is he—" She swallowed hard but the lump in her throat remained.

"He's well enough," said Widow Dawson.

"I want to see him." Lucy looked around the taproom but of course he wouldn't be there. They wouldn't let murderers drink with the patrons.

"He's in the storeroom," Monk said. "Since Milner is constable, it gets used as a jail cell from time to time. Some wanted to keep him in the stocks." He tilted his head toward the Larkham men. "But Hughe wouldn't allow it."

"Lord Lynden would have agreed on the storeroom if he were here," Anne said with a knowing nod.

"Where is the storeroom?" Lucy asked.

Widow Dawson caught her hand. "Leave him," she said. "He rests. I've seen to his wounds, and he has everything he needs."

"But…"

Anne caught Lucy's other hand. "Sit with us until he wakes."

Lucy plopped down on the stool with a heavy sigh. "Where is Lord Oxley? Is he with Nick?"

"No," said Monk. He didn't elaborate, and no one else seemed to know his whereabouts.

Milner brought two ales for Henry and Lucy without being asked and set them on the table. "Coroner's been sent for, and he'll go direct to Larkham to view the body. There seems to be no doubts about what happened, so the inquest is just a formality. Mr. Coleclough will stay in my storeroom till the assize judges get here."

"Mind you take good care of him," Anne said. "He's the son of a baron."

"I know, I know." To Henry, he said, "Widow Dawson here says the murderer's been stayin' at yer farm. She said he's got no memory."

"I said he had no memory of the *last few years*, Mr. Milner," Widow Dawson said. "If you're goin' to gossip, get the facts right."

The innkeeper wrung his hands in his apron. "Fact is, if he was the murderin' sort, Mistress Cowdrey here would know it after spendin' a few days with him. She's a good judge of character. What say you, ma'am? Is he the sort to have done it?"

Lucy felt all eyes upon her, trying to see into her mind, her heart. None drilled harder than Monk, but she didn't feel threatened by him. If Lord Oxley were with them, she may have found it more difficult to say what she wanted to say.

"He's not the sort to commit such a terrible deed without good reason."

Monk's only reaction was a twitch of muscle in his cheek. He wasn't happy that she'd said that much, but so be it. Nick's life was at stake. Lucy had to do everything necessary to save him. He may not love her the way she loved him—or at all—but she couldn't stand by and watch him hang.

"What reason?" Milner asked, leaning in.

"I wish I knew. He won't say."

The innkeeper straightened. "Pity. He'll tell the judges when the time comes, no doubt." He glanced at the Larkham men. "Do they know what the reason could be? A duel p'haps, or a slight?"

"I wouldn't ask them if I were you," Henry said. "I don't think they have as much faith in my sister's judgment as we do. Mayhap they think their man innocent, or they wouldn't be here."

Upfield drained his tankard and slammed it down on the table. "Wench!" he shouted at Milner's daughter. "Bring your fat arse over here."

"Enough of that!" Milner shouted back. "You treat my girl with some respect, or you won't be served."

Upfield stood. He wasn't tall, but he was solid and looked like he'd be difficult to knock over. One of his friends stood too, a huge man with a red face shaped like a brick. The two of them approached, scowling at Milner.

"We don't want trouble," Henry said, hands up. Always the peacemaker. He stood, however, and Monk too.

"Seems to me you're askin' for trouble bein' a friend to a murderer," Upfield said. "He should be swingin' on the gibbet where he belongs."

"You should be in a pigsty," Monk said, "but none of us are holding it against you."

Lucy held her breath and willed Monk to sit down and be quiet. If he was hoping Henry and Milner would back him up, he was in for a rude shock. Henry had never been in a real fistfight in his life, and Milner wasn't exactly a young man.

"Sit down, Mr. Upfield," Monk said. "We don't want—"

Upfield swung. Monk ducked, landing a punch in Upfield's stomach as he did so. Upfield reeled back and fell onto the floor with a heavy thud, wheezing like a bellows. The other big Larkham brute came at Monk, his blocky face set with fierce determination. Monk stood his ground and slammed his fist into the man's nose. Blood sprayed and he roared with pain. He was too occupied with holding his nose to come at Monk again.

Lucy expected the others to aid him, but they seemed shocked to see both their companions nursing injuries so quickly.

"You'd better go now," Monk said, flexing his hand.

They got up and left, but their scowls and spits were a sign that they'd not given up entirely. "He won't get away with what he did," Upfield snarled. "We'll see to it."

Lucy shuddered. She felt sick to her core. "Do you think they'll try to avenge Renny's death before the assizes?"

"We'll have to wait and see," Monk said.

It wasn't an answer that instilled much hope in her.

"Where's Sawyer?" Henry asked. "He seems like a sensible man. He might be able to keep them calm."

"In his room, I think," said Milner, heading back to his bar. "So where'd you learn to fight like that, Mr. Monk?"

"Here and there," Monk said, picking up his tankard.

"S'pose that's why Lord Oxley employs you. His lordship seems like the sort who'd need a good pair of fists in his employ. I remember when he first came to Sutton Grange, time before last, he had this big fellow with him. Huge he was, in height and girth. Tanned skin too, a little like Mr. Coleclough, but his hair were different."

Lucy's gaze slid to her brother's, but he didn't notice. He'd arched a brow at Monk. He sipped his ale slowly and ignored them all. Susanna had said she'd met Nick months before. Lucy supposed he could have been in disguise.

"I can't sit here any longer," she said, rising. "I have to see him."

Widow Dawson sighed. "Aye, but if he's asleep, don't wake him."

"I'll take you," Monk said.

Henry caught her elbow, and Lucy thought he would warn her to be careful, or perhaps even suggest he come with her, but he did not. He simply squeezed and gave her a grim but reassuring smile. Poor Henry. His new life at Cowdrey Farm had not been an easy one so far.

"Don't fret," Lucy heard Widow Dawson tell Henry as she walked off with Monk. "He's too weak to do anything but talk."

"Weak?" Lucy said to Monk. "Why is he weak?"

"The journey was rough. I'd wager the cart driver deliberately drove over every bump and dip. Upfield was tasked with helping Cole out of the back of the cart when we arrived, and I use the word help in its loosest form."

Oh God.

They crossed the inn's yard where an ostler led away a horse and a dusty traveler washed his face in a pail by the stables. The yard was surrounded on three sides by the double story building. The uppermost floor housed rooms for travelers and an undercover gallery overlooked the cobbled yard.

Monk led her toward the far corner near where the kitchen, larder, and other service rooms were housed in the furthermost wing. The stables were to its right, and the dining hall and taproom to the left. Monk held the door open for her and she stepped inside.

It took a moment for her eyes to adjust to the gloom. With the door closed again behind her, the only light came from a small, high window in need of cleaning. They stood in a narrow corridor that stretched to both left and right, and there was another door straight ahead.

"Mr. Monk, Mistress Cowdrey," said Sawyer, coming toward them from the left. Behind him, something moved, but Lucy couldn't see who or what it was. "Are you going to see the prisoner?"

"Aye," said Monk.

"Have you been in to him?" Lucy asked. Sawyer may seem like a sensible man, but he was from Larkham. He couldn't be trusted.

"No." He tugged on the brim of his hat. "Good day, ma'am, sir."

He left via the door through which they'd just entered. Once it was closed again, the narrow space fell into shadows. "This way," Monk said. He slid the bolt back and opened the door opposite. "I'll wait out here. Call if you need anything."

The room smelled of damp earth and wine, and it was much cooler than outside. The light was just as dim in the storeroom as it was in the corridor and it took Lucy's eyes a few moments to focus. Then, she saw him.

"Nick!"

He sat on a pallet on the floor at the far end of the small room, his back against a large barrel, his feet outstretched. His eyes had been closed, but he opened them when he heard her voice. At least, he half-opened them. They were too swollen to widen more.

"Dear lord," she said on a breath as she knelt beside him. "What have they done to you?" She touched his cheek gingerly. He flinched and she drew her hand away. "Did Upfield do this?"

"What are you doing here?" he snapped. "You should be home."

She sat back on her haunches and regarded him. "I did go home. Now I'm here. Let me see your face."

He jerked away.

"Let me see your face."

"Widow Dawson has already dabbed vile stuff over me and wound my head up tight, I don't need you fussing too."

His tone was harsh, but it didn't affect her. He was playing the part of uncaring assassin, just as he'd played the part of Oxley's servant, or wandering traveler. He was trying to push her away with this coldness, but she wasn't going to let him. They had very little time together, and she wouldn't waste it arguing.

The thought brought fresh tears to her eyes, but she refused to let them spill. Tears, like arguing, was for another time.

"I see you have everything you need," she said, looking around. A large tankard of ale sat a little apart from the pallet, a trencher of bread and cheese beside it. It wasn't infested with weevils and the pallet and blanket on which he sat seemed clean. Milner was treating him well enough. She probably had Oxley to thank for that.

"It's as good as any inn room," he said grudgingly. "But Milner needs to replace his rat trap." He shifted back on the pallet and a chain rattled. It was attached to his left wrist. She'd not noticed it before. The other end looped through a large iron ring in the wall and was locked with a padlock. The chain was long enough for Nick to freely walk around most of the storeroom, but not quite long enough for him to reach the door.

She pulled a face, both at the rat comment and the chain. "Is that necessary?"

"Sawyer and Upfield insisted. Seems they don't trust your Sutton Grange friends."

"Perhaps it's your friends they don't trust. Oxley in particular is not the man he presents to the rest of the world."

A beat passed, two. "He told you."

"Yes."

"How much?"

"Everything," she lied. If she had to resort to lies to get the truth then so be it. "You don't deserve this, Nick."

"Cole."

"Don't! You are Nick to me. Cole is not who you are. He's the disguise you've been wearing for eleven years. It's time to shed him."

He said nothing, and his face was too battered for her to make out his expression. Most likely he wouldn't reveal his thoughts that way anyway. He was too good at maintaining the mask. She was foolish to think she could get him to drop it now.

"Sweet, innocent Lucy Cowdrey." When he finally spoke, the sneer in his voice was like a knife through her gut. "You've learned nothing, have you?"

"On the contrary. I've learned much." She'd won over an entire village after her cousins' deaths. She could win back this man too.

She refused to believe that *her* Nicholas Coleclough was buried so deep that he was irretrievable. She wouldn't give up. Not yet. Not while there was still a chance of saving him from the gallows.

"You just want to be liked," he went on. "You hate to have someone somewhere thinking ill of you. You try to be the person they want, you go out of your way to please people, but to what end? This deep desire blinds you to what they really think."

"I don't know what you mean."

"Don't you? You visited Susanna Holt almost every day. Has she come to you?"

"She's with child!"

"She could have been to see you in the early weeks. There is no law against expectant women traveling short distances. When I went to Stoneleigh before I even met you, they spoke of you. Spoke of how innocent and eager you were, of how they tolerated your presence because they wanted to foster goodwill with their new neighbors. Not because they liked having you there every day."

Lucy shook her head. He was good. He was very good. If she let her guard down for only a moment, she might even allow herself to believe him. But it was time to keep her wits about her and her guard up. He'd closed his heart and was using his head. She could do that too.

"I don't think the Holts would like to hear you slander their good name like this," she said as coolly as she could manage.

"And what of Widow Dawson? You think she likes you tending her patients? I'm sure she loves having the sister of a gentleman farmer take away her livelihood."

"Stop it, Nick, it won't work. Do you know why? I already told you, I have learned much since leaving my family home. Perhaps I was naïve then, but not anymore. I know when someone is speaking the truth. Susanna has spoken the truth when she asked me to visit as often as I could. Widow Dawson spoke the truth when she thanked me for seeing patients she could not. And you, my sweet Nick, spoke the truth when you

C.J. ARCHER

told me that I knew you and you knew me and nothing else mattered."

The air was as dense as a winter fog. His face was still in shadow, but she could just make out the line of his mouth. It wasn't set as firmly as she'd thought it would be, but twisted a little, and once, she thought she saw his nostrils flare, but it was too dark to be sure.

"That's the thing about us men," he finally said. His voice was soft with an amused edge to it. "We're good at knowing how to get a wench to spread her legs. Some of us better than others. Mallam, for instance, needed to promise marriage. I don't recall ever having to resort to that lie."

She didn't believe it. Not a single word. If she hadn't spent five intense days with him, she may have fallen for it, but the real Nick Coleclough wasn't cruel. He was a gentleman, a man who believed in justice. The man who'd made a rattle for his friend's babe and not wanted due thanks for it, and the one who'd lovingly carved Brutus's likeness and left it for her as a parting gift.

Getting him to let go of that iron will and drop the mask, however, was going to be difficult. She needed to use every weapon in her arsenal.

"You'd like me to run away now, wouldn't you?" she said. "I'm not going to, Nick. That is the first thing you must come to terms with. Fortunately for me, *you* can't run away. I should thank the Larkham men for chaining you up in a private room."

"What are you playing at?" The uncertainty in his voice was the first sign that he was unsettled by her approach.

"You said I haven't learned anything." She shifted forward on her knees. "Well, that's not true. I've learned what true love is, and it wasn't what I felt for Edmund Mallam."

She could have sworn she heard the sound of him swallowing. That was the second sign. She could take that path of thought further, but it wasn't the right time or place. Instead, she crept closer to him on all fours.

"Stay there, Lucy."

214

She paused. "We all care for you. Me, yes, but Orlando and Susanna, Monk and Oxley too. None of us will sit by and watch you swing for killing a man like Renny."

That produced a snarl from him. "They feel responsible, that's all. Especially Hughe. He doesn't want my death on his conscience. It's already too crowded, you see, he can't fit one more."

"He cares for you, and you need to accept it," she said. "He's quite distressed that he's going to lose you, in one way or another."

"What do you mean?"

"To the Larkham mob, or to me."

He went very still. She crept closer again on her hands and knees, but he pulled his legs up. She touched his ankle and felt him shudder.

"I warn you now, Nick, I am *very* determined that I'll be the one to take you away from Lord Oxley."

"Yes," he whispered. "I can see that."

She smiled. She had him. "I don't plan on losing."

"I can see that too."

She moved closer, closer, until she was touching his knee, his shoulder, his mouth. His poor, split lip.

"Don't, Lucy," he whispered. "Don't touch me. I'm trying everything… I can't… please."

Just like that, the little game they'd been playing ended. She leaned in and gently kissed his mouth, beside the cut. "You usually win when you plead," she said. "But not this time."

CHAPTER 17

*C*ole was defenseless. Lucy had removed his wall brick by brick until it could no longer stand against her quietly determined onslaught. Each airy kiss shattered him anew, and finally he gave in and simply held her and kissed her with the ferocity that he'd wanted to ever since she walked in.

She hadn't forsaken him.

"We'll get you out," she said. She sat in his lap and kissed one of his swollen eyelids. "It shouldn't be too difficult to escape. Mr. Monk could get the key to the chain—"

"No." He lifted her off and set her down on the pallet. He couldn't keep up the pretense of hating her, but he still had to keep her away. If he could do nothing else for her, he could at least do that. "I'm not going to escape."

She glared at him. "Why not? With Monk and Oxley's help—"

"Escaping will solve nothing." He focused on her mouth, but it pouted in the most delicious way, so he looked elsewhere. "It won't clear my name. I'll have to run and hide forever."

"You mean *we* will."

"No."

"But Nick—"

"No!" He drew up his knees and before she could speak, he said,

216

"It will also throw suspicion onto Hughe and Monk. I can't risk their reputations. Their work is too important."

"Not more important than your life!"

"There is another way," he said. "Hughe has influence. He may be able to convince the assize judges that I'm innocent."

She narrowed her eyes. He had to admit it was impossible. A person accused of murder never escaped the noose when there were witnesses. It wouldn't matter that the case hung on a child's account. It was enough.

"It's two weeks before the court sits," she said. "If you think Upfield has the patience to wait that long, you're mistaken. He's baying for your blood, Nick."

Tears pooled in her eyes, and he desperately wanted to fold her into his arms again. Instead, he circled them around his knees and stared down at the pallet. "Upfield will beat his chest and make a lot of noise, but he won't do anything." He wished he could be as certain as he sounded. Upfield had taken everyone by surprise when he'd attacked Cole while he was still chained up in the cart. Cole had got a solid kick in, but not until after Upfield had landed some hard punches. Monk and Sawyer had dragged him away while Hughe looked on. If anyone had seen the earl, they would have thought he was unmoved by the scuffle, but Cole knew differently. He'd never seen such cold fury in Hughe's eyes.

"Be patient, Lucy. My fate will be decided in two weeks."

She clicked her tongue. "This isn't like you. You're a man of action. You get things done. I cannot believe you're going to await your fate down here like an obedient dog. What's wrong with you? Why are you being so accepting? It's almost as if you welcome this."

Her words reached into his heart and squeezed. He was trapped, caught in her bright light, and there was nowhere to run. How could she have guessed at something that had taken even Hughe a long time to work out?

Ah yes. Love. That grand illuminator.

He'd hesitated too long. He should have spoken sooner, but she was looking at him now with those wide eyes, and he saw the moment the final, fatal piece clicked into place.

"No," she whispered, shaking her head. "No, Nick. I'm here and I love you. Don't throw away what we have." She began to cry and he hugged his knees harder, digging his fingernails through the hose into his skin.

He should tell her that he didn't love her in return, but she was much too clever to believe it.

She cradled his face in her hands with such tenderness that his heart lurched violently. He didn't deserve the gentleness. Didn't deserve her. If he was capable of speaking, he would have told her that.

"There is everything to live for." Her voice cracked and she sucked in a breath. "You're a good man. Despite what you think, your soul is good, Nick. The people you've assassinated were animals. You've done nothing wrong."

"Is that what you think?" He shook his head. He didn't want to go on, didn't want her to know how truly black his heart was.

His resolve mattered not a whit. She had a look of sheer determination about her. "Then what is it? Tell me!"

She gripped his shoulders and shook him. It must have loosened something inside him because the words just tumbled out. "I killed my own mother."

Her jaw dropped. She let go of him and covered her gasp with her hands. She looked away, but not before he saw the horror and revulsion in her eyes.

So be it.

He breathed once, twice, surprised that it didn't hurt, that his heart still beat inside his chest. He'd often wondered what would happen when he said those words out loud, and now he knew. A strange numbness seeped through him, slowing the blood in his veins and the thoughts that had been racing around his head moments ago. It was like he was watching a play from the safety of the audience. He could see the moment Lucy thought of her next line.

"Monk!" he called out before she could speak. "Monk!"

The door opened and his friend appeared. "Have you throttled him yet, Mistress Cowdrey? He can make you want to sometimes." He came inside and his smirk died when he saw Lucy. He turned a hard glare onto Cole, shook his head. "Come." He held his hand out to Lucy. "I'll escort you to your room."

Cole didn't watch her leave. If she turned to look at him, he didn't know. It was better that way. After the door shut and locked, he lay on the pallet and closed his eyes.

Hopefully Lucy wouldn't want to see him for the next two weeks. Hopefully none of them would.

* * *

"What did he say?" Monk asked when they were outside in the fresh air of the innyard.

Lucy shook her head, not because she didn't want to tell him, but because she couldn't believe what Nick had said. He'd killed his mother. It was so shocking. A heinous crime. Surely he was mistaken, or there must be a reason for it.

Now that her mind could function again, she wanted to return and ask. "I must go back," she said.

"I don't think that's a good idea." Monk rounded on her and gripped her shoulders. "I've never seen Cole look so miserable. He's always been so unemotional. I don't think he'll want you to see him like this."

"That's precisely why I need to go to him."

But he did not let her go. "What did he say?"

"What did who say?" asked Lord Oxley, joining them. He was grinning but it slipped off when he saw Lucy's face. "You've been to see Cole?"

She glanced back at the door that led to the storeroom and inclined her head. Nick probably wouldn't want her to tell his friends what he'd just told her. She had the very strong feeling he'd never told anyone. That, she supposed, was part of the problem.

Nick was too bloody minded to share his burden even with those closest to him.

She had no such qualms. To help him, drastic measures needed to be taken. "He told me he killed his mother."

Monk's hands fell to his sides. He stared at her. Oxley's lips closed firmly, briefly. He opened them to swear softly.

"It must have happened when he was eighteen," she said.

"The event blocking his memories from returning," Oxley said.

"Except in his dreams." She folded her arms over her chest. It was cold, despite the airlessness of the yard and the summer sunshine beating down on them. "It obviously affected him greatly. Affects him still."

"Aye," said Monk. "Well, it would, wouldn't it?"

"It certainly explains many things." Oxley removed his hat and rubbed a hand through his hair. "His unwillingness to talk about his past, for one thing."

"He hates himself," she said. "Hence the carelessness with his own life."

"More than once I thought him mad when he stepped into an affray that had nothing to do with us," Oxley went on. "It explains why he worked in the coal mines and fought in those organized matches." He huffed out a humorless laugh. "It must have frustrated him that he won all the time."

"And there was his disregard to save for a future after the Guild," Monk said. "He used to give all his money away. I never understood why. Until now."

"He thought he had no future." Lucy bit her bottom lip to stop it quivering. "Even with me."

"Especially with you," Lord Oxley said. He took her hand and kneaded the knuckles. "Mistress Cowdrey, Cole loves you, that's why he's trying to keep you away."

"I don't understand."

He sighed and looked heavenward. "He thinks himself unworthy of you. He thinks you'd be better off without him."

"He's probably right," Monk said. She gave him a sharp glare, but he simply shrugged. "His future is not looking stable, you must admit that."

"Do you think I care, as long as we're together?"

"The point isn't that *you* don't care," Oxley said, "it's that *he* does. Why would a man want the woman he loves throwing away her future for him? He thinks you will be better off without him."

"He's wrong." She pulled away. "I must go back and tell him."

"Don't. It may be better for Cole if he thinks you've given up."

Perhaps he was right. She itched to talk to Nick again and hold him, but it may not be wise to push him. He was desperate enough already, and it may make him more miserable than ever.

Lord Oxley let go of her and slapped his hat back on his head. "I have business to attend elsewhere. Good day, dear lady." He bowed and strode off toward the taproom.

Just as he disappeared, three men entered the yard through the arch leading out to the street. Upfield, his oversized friend, and another Larkham man.

"The innkeeper asked you to leave," Monk told them.

Upfield and the others blocked their path. The big man crossed his arms and puffed out his chest. Considering he sported two black eyes and a crooked nose, Lucy thought him rather foolish to be so cock-sure. On the other hand, it was three against one.

Yet Monk did not back away. Would Lord Oxley hear her if she screamed?

"Let Mistress Cowdrey pass," Monk said. "If you want to pick a fight with me, I'm more than happy to oblige once she is safely inside."

It seemed Nick wasn't the only one who liked to step into situations where the odds were against him.

"She's a murderer's doxy," Upfield said, stepping up to them.

Lucy leaned back. The man's breath was truly foul, and the stink of his body even worse.

A face appeared at the window leading to the taproom, then suddenly disappeared. She'd only caught a glimpse, but Lucy could have sworn it was Milner. Yet he didn't come into the yard to tell

Upfield and his mean to leave. She didn't blame him for being scared. He was no match for any of these men, and Lucy understood his fear. It crawled up her spine and made her scalp tingle.

Monk pushed her behind him. She searched for a weapon and spotted a broom leaning against the stable wall. It was as good as any. The ostler was nowhere to be seen.

"Apologize to Mistress Cowdrey," Monk said.

Upfield spat on the cobblestones. Lucy stepped back from Monk until the broom was directly behind her.

Monk sighed. "You shouldn't have done that. Now I have to defend her honor."

"She's the lover of a murderer. She ain't got no honor."

"What do you want, Mr. Upfield?" Lucy asked quickly. She couldn't allow Monk to get hurt because of her. "What are you doing here?"

"Use that little brain God gave you, wench, and think."

"Mr. Monk!" she cried as his hand balled into a fist.

Monk grunted in what sounded like frustration, but he did not strike Upfield.

"He left two boys without their father," Upfield went on, "and Larkham without a good man."

"Good?" she spluttered.

"Lucy!" Monk snapped. He'd never used her first name before—it would seem he was as determined as ever that Renny's true nature not be made public.

It was a point she would have to bring up with Oxley later. As far as she could see, telling them what Renny had done was the only way to clear Nick's name.

"What do you know, wench?" Upfield sneered. "Renny was a proud man. He got things done in Larkham, took care of his friends. Your lover don't deserve to live after what he did."

"He deserves a fair trial," she said.

"Two weeks is a long time." Upfield grinned, baring his blackened teeth.

"Don't you go near him," Lucy bit off.

"Easy," Monk said, turning to her.

The big brute saw his opportunity and slammed his fist into Monk's jaw. Monk reeled back, but didn't fall. He quickly recovered and put up his fists.

The three Larkham men drew their swords.

"Bloody hell," Monk muttered. He wasn't armed.

Lucy grabbed the broom. Perhaps she should throw it to him, and he could use it as a weapon. She was about to call his name when he bent down then quickly straightened again. The blade in his hand glinted. It must have been in his boot.

"Enough!" came a shout from the archway. Milner rushed in looking fiercer than Lucy had ever seen him. Behind him were four men. No, make that six… ten… Good lord, half of Sutton Grange had followed him into the yard! "There'll be no bloodshed here."

Upfield lowered his sword and blinked at the mob. "We only want justice for one of our own," he said. "You'd do the same for a Sutton Grange man."

"Aye," said Lane the chandler, holding a very solid looking brass candlestick in his hand. "But we'd see to it he got justice the right way, not like this."

There was a sea of nodding heads behind him and a chorus of "Ayes." Lucy recognized every single one of the faces. Her friends Anne Lane, Widow Dawson, and Joan Freeman were among the women off to one side, but she also recognized the baker and his son, the blacksmith and his three apprentices, the glover, the butcher, the two Taylor brothers, and even the grammar school master. There were a half-dozen more men too, all carrying weapons of some sort.

Upfield fronted up to Milner. He still held his sword, but it was pointed down, unthreatening. "Why are you defending the cur?" he asked, genuinely confused. "He's not even a Grange man."

"Mistress Cowdrey is a Grange woman," Widow Dawson said. "If she thinks Coleclough deserves a fair trial, then we'll see to it that he gets one."

Lucy bit her wobbly lip. She did so love this village. *Thank you*, she mouthed to them.

Upfield gave a low, long groan of frustration then slammed his sword back into its scabbard. "If he escapes—"

"He won't," Milner said. "I'll see to it."

Oh, Milner, please don't promise that.

"Are you the only one with a key to the chain?" Upfield jerked his head at Monk. "I don't trust him. I don't trust his lordship neither."

"I'll get the key off him then," Milner assured him. "None of you are to come back here, understand? If you want to stay in the village, then the White Hart has rooms. Otherwise, go back to Larkham."

"We'll be stayin'," Upfield said. "Now get out of my way."

The villagers parted for him, and the three Larkham men left.

"Are you all right, Mistress Cowdrey?" Monk asked.

"Yes." She smiled. "Thank you, you were most brave."

He nodded at the crowd, some of which had already dispersed, while others headed into the taproom. Widow Dawson, Anne, and Joan remained. "It seems you have a good circle of friends here," Monk said. "I'm glad of it."

She smiled at each of them as they came up to her. "So am I."

THEY HADN'T GIVEN Cole a candle. It was a starless, moonless night and nothing but inky blackness could be seen through the high storeroom window. He couldn't even see his hand in front of his face. The only sounds came from his own breathing and the scratch of rats as they searched for holes in the grain sacks. They'd probably found his untouched supper and devoured it already. How fitting that he should spend another night alone with the creatures.

He leaned his back against the wine barrel and pinched the bridge of his nose. Despite the tonic Widow Dawson had given him, his head throbbed like the devil. Exhaustion dragged at his body, but he didn't close his eyes. The nightmares would come if he did, as they had last night. They'd been worse than ever. Most of his memory may have returned, but the dreams hadn't ceased.

They always started the same way—Carter whipping him, then Cole's escape, only to find his hands were smeared with his mother's blood. But after that, the dreams changed. The woman lying on the ground wasn't his mother, it was Lucy. He'd killed her.

He'd prefer to stay awake all night, every night, than see that. At least she was safe now. Perhaps she'd gone home to the farm. He wished it hadn't taken him telling her about his mother, but perhaps it was for the best. If the look of pure horror on her face was a sign, then her affection for him had come to an abrupt end. So be it. Better she knew what he was really like than believe him redeemable.

The *clunk* of the bolt sliding back sent the rats scurrying away. Cole stood, rattling the chain attached to his wrist, and set his feet apart. No matter how low he felt, he wouldn't give in without a fight. Not to a cur like Upfield. The notion made his blood boil.

The door opened and a circle of candlelight illuminated Hughe's face. Cole swore under his breath. "What are you doing here?"

"Don't you want your supper?"

"I've got supper."

"Here's more." Hughe stepped in and closed the door with his booted foot. He held out a trencher laden with meat and bread and nodded at the bowl of broth on the floor. "Not hungry?"

"The rats will eat it," Cole said, taking the trencher. "You think I'm working up an appetite in here doing nothing?"

"I needed an excuse to visit you dressed like this." He wore a belted tunic over breeches and a brown cap covered his fair hair. He hadn't darkened his skin tone or padded his clothes, but such extremes weren't necessary in the dark. He would easily be mistaken for a servant delivering supper to the prisoner.

"You getting worried about being seen with me?" Cole sat back down on the pallet and indicated Hughe should sit too.

"I can't come in plain sight anymore as Lord Oxley. Upfield will hear about it and accuse me of skullduggery come the trial. I don't want to jeopardize it."

"You think it's going to make a difference?" Cole snorted softly. "I'm not going to walk free from this one, Hughe, no matter how many strings you try to pull when the judges get here."

Hughe stretched his legs out and rubbed his thigh. It had been injured years ago, although Cole had never asked how and Hughe had never talked about it. Whether it pained him from time to time or whether he massaged it out of habit was also unclear. It certainly never hindered his movements.

"You should have tried to escape when they came to arrest you," Hughe said. "We could have helped you then. A little confusion, some timely incompetence on my part, and you would have gotten away."

"And destroy your disguises? That would be foolish, Hughe, and you know it."

"Stop being so dramatic. It wouldn't have *destroyed* anything."

"All that was needed was a seed of doubt to be planted in their minds, and they'd accuse you and Monk of helping me. They already know you and I are acquainted. Perhaps you could have gotten away with it, but could Monk too?"

The silence weighed heavily as Hughe fixed a glare on Cole. Neither man looked away first. "It would have been easier to escape then than now," Hughe said quietly.

"I couldn't be sure Lucy wouldn't try to come with me."

"Ah yes, sweet little Lucy Cowdrey." Hughe sighed heavily. "You know she—"

"Don't," he snarled. "Don't talk about her. Don't even mention her name."

Hughe's lips pinched together, and he looked to the ceiling. Cole knew it must be difficult for him not to say his piece. Hughe liked to let his men know when he thought they were being fools. "Seems I've exhausted all my conversation topics," he said instead.

"I want you to leave Sutton Grange," Cole said. "You and Monk. It'll be better for me if I'm on my own."

"No, it won't. Stop thinking you're alone, Cole. You're not. You have friends. People care about you whether you want them to or not."

Cole folded his arms across his chest, and the chain around his wrist pinched. "Nice try, Hughe.

"They do. Must be your charm and wit we all can't get enough of."

Cole merely grunted.

"Lucy's right," Hughe said.

"I said, don't mention her."

"I'll speak about her if I bloody well want to. Lucy was right when she said you're a good man. You wouldn't be working for me if you weren't."

"Don't idealize what we do, Hughe. We kill people for money. We're the worst kind of mercenary. Doing what we do does not require a good heart or soul, just a good aim."

"If that were so, you'd have kept all your payments."

"Even I suffer from a guilty conscience once in a while."

"I'm aware of it," Hughe muttered. "Cole, I know you don't think our work is wrong, so don't pretend otherwise."

Cole said nothing since it was true.

Hughe sighed again. "What troubles you? Why do you not want my help? Give me an honest answer this time."

"Very well, I'll tell you. I don't want my friends getting caught up in this mess. It'll be better for you and Monk if you leave. You're right, I do believe in what we do, which is why I don't want you to be associated too closely with me. I don't want to be the one to bring a halt to your scheme. There. Noble enough for you?"

"Are you worried about our work or our lives?"

Cole wasn't going to answer that. It was too close to the bone, and he already felt raw enough.

"You think I'm going to leave you here to face trial alone? You think Monk will?" Hughe shook his head. "If we leave, Orlando will act in our stead. You know that."

"He's moved on. His wife takes priority now, as she should."

"True enough, but he won't sit idly by and let you swing for the Guild. So stop pretending that you're alone when you're not."

Cole drew his knees up and regarded his leader. His friend. The shadows played across Hughe's face, made him look ghostly, ethereal. There was no use arguing with him anymore. Cole wasn't going to win. Hughe was better at oratory than Cole could ever be.

"Lucy won't stay away either," Hughe said.

"I told you not to mention her."

Hughe smiled. "I don't follow orders very well."

"You're wrong about her. We had a conversation earlier." Icy fingers wrapped around his heart and dug in its claws. "She won't be coming back."

"Is that what you think?" Hughe gave a short, humorless laugh. "Fool. She doesn't care what you did when you were eighteen."

Did Hughe know? It was impossible to tell. His face gave nothing away.

"If you want to do something for me," Cole said, "then keep her away from Sutton Grange until after the trial."

"I can't do that. She's got a mind of her own, and a willful one from what I've seen."

Cole scooted forward. He would have grabbed Hughe by the throat if he didn't think the other man would move faster. "Do it for me, for her." He threw up his hands and the chain clanked. "I'll ask nothing else of you. Please, Hughe."

Hughe blinked slowly. "I'll do what I can." He reached behind his back and pulled something out of his belt. A sheathed dagger. "In case Upfield decides he can't wait for the judges." He held it out to Cole. "Take it," he growled, shoving the handle into Cole's stomach.

Cole took it and dropped it on the pallet.

Hughe stood and heaved a breath. "I'll leave you with the candle. Don't burn the place down."

Cole stood too. "I'll try not to."

Hughe clasped Cole's shoulder and, after a moment, Cole returned the gesture. The earl might be a prick at times, but he was a true friend.

Hughe left, locking the door behind him, and Cole sat back on the pallet. After a moment, he unwound the bandage from his head.

CHAPTER 18

"*I* can't stay here any longer," Henry said, turning away from the window to look at Lucy. His hair gleamed in the afternoon sunshine, but his face seemed paler than ever. If she had to guess, her brother had slept as ill as she had. "The farm needs me."

"The farm doesn't *need* you, Henry." Lucy set her pen down in the stand and blew on her page to hasten the drying of the ink. "But if you must go, then go."

"Not without you."

"I'm not leaving."

"Lucy," he said with an exasperated sigh. "I cannot leave you here alone."

"For goodness sake, I'm not alone. I have my friends, and there's always Lord Oxley to keep the Larkham louts in order."

She'd not told Henry about the incident in the yard the day before, nor did she plan to. He would be even more determined to take her away from Sutton Grange. From Nick. She'd been surprised when Monk hadn't mentioned the confrontation, and she'd expected one of the others to say something too, but none had. She couldn't hope for her brother's ignorance to last much longer if he remained in the village.

"Don't make me order you, Lucy."

"For goodness sake, Henry, stop being a beast, and take this letter for me." She folded the paper and handed it to him. "Ask Milner for some sealing wax and find out if anyone will be heading to London soon."

He took the letter. "Who is it for?"

"The queen."

He burst out laughing. "You jest."

She glared at him and he sobered. "I'm in no mood for jokes," she said.

"You cannot honestly think the queen will read this and intervene in Coleclough's trial."

"I have to try, Henry. And unless you've been deeply and madly in love, then you'll not understand." She sniffed and turned away. "Now please, go and talk to Milner and put that in the hands of someone going to London. It must leave today or tomorrow at the latest."

"It's too late for anyone to begin traveling now." He came up behind her and gently massaged her shoulder. "I'm sorry, Lucy, I know this is important to you. I can see how much you care about him. You certainly weren't this upset when Mallam broke your engagement, and that was after the man humiliated you."

"The way I felt about Edmund Mallam is nothing compared to what I feel for Nick." She placed her hand over his. "The thought of not being with him, of knowing he's gone…" She wiped away a tear. "I'm sure I'll never breathe again."

"Ah, Lucy." He kissed the top of her head. "I'll take the letter now." But he didn't make it further than the window overlooking the road. "Bloody hell," he muttered. "What are they doing?"

Lucy stood and peered out too. Her heart stopped dead. A mob of twenty men marched along the street toward the inn, Upfield at the helm. She recognized the big thug next to him and a few of the others, including Renny's sons, Frankie and Peter. Every man and boy carried a club or piece of wood. A few had drawn their daggers, and almost all had swords strapped to their hips.

She clutched Henry's arm. "Oh God," she whispered. "Nick."

"I'll get Oxley," he said, heading for the door.

"He's not here!" she cried, running after him. "When I didn't see him in the dining room, I asked Milner, and he said he hasn't seen Oxley or Monk since dawn. Henry, they're going to…"

He gripped her shoulders and shook her. "Calm down. I'll speak to them. You stay here." He raced off toward the stairs leading to the taproom.

Once he'd disappeared, Lucy ran along the gallery and down the set of stairs that led to the yard. She hurried across the cobbles, glancing once, twice, over her shoulder. She couldn't see them, but their shouts were loud and clear. Henry could not hope to be heard above them.

"Justice!" someone cried. "Justice for Renny!"

"Aye!" chorused the mob.

There followed bangs and thuds—clubs smashing into walls and posts, most likely, as the mob forged onward. There was no way Henry could hold them off on his own.

Lucy slipped into the corridor then pulled the bolt back on the storeroom door. It was a brighter day than yesterday, and the beam of light streamed through the high window and fell across Nick's pallet.

"Nick!" His head jerked up at the sound of her voice. "Get up!" she shouted, running toward him. "You must go NOW!"

He jumped to his feet and caught her. "What's wrong? Lucy, are you all right?"

"They're coming for you." She pulled away and grabbed his hand. The chain rattled and she cried out in frustration. She'd forgotten about it.

Nick bent to her level. "Lucy, be calm. What's wrong?"

"They're coming. A mob of Larkham men." Just as she said it, a shout of "Justice!" followed by a roar of agreement came from the innyard. Too close.

She jerked free and pulled on the chain. "Can you get this off?"

"Not without a key."

"Where is it?"

"Milner has it, or perhaps Oxley."

"Then why hasn't he set you free before now! Nick," she sobbed. "Nick, please, try and get free. They're coming for you."

Even as she said it, the bang of clubs and calls for justice sounded closer. A much smaller cry of "Stop" was swallowed by the angry shouts. Henry might as well be whispering in a gale for all the good it did.

She scrabbled at the chain on Nick's wrist, breaking her fingernails to the quick. Tears streamed down her cheeks, and she could hardly see what she was doing. He grabbed her and roughly pushed her away. "Go! Lucy, get away!"

"No." She planted her feet a little apart and crossed her arms. Her heart drummed in her chest. "I'm not leaving you."

"Bloody hell!" He glanced over her head. Angry voices rose and fell like a tide. They were so close. "I cannot do what I have to do unless I know you're safe."

"What do you have to do?" Free himself at all costs, or… ?

"Go, Lucy." His voice was quiet, but she heard it, even with the mob's cries echoing around the yard. She raced to the storeroom door and slammed it shut. It blocked out a little of the noise, but it wouldn't hold them back. There was no lock on the inside.

"I'm not leaving you," she said, returning to him.

"You can't stop them. Nor can I."

"You could try!" She bunched his jerkin in both hands and shook him as hard as she could. "Please, Nick."

He gently grasped her wrists. His dark gaze met hers, two swirling orbs that burrowed through to her soul. He seemed oddly serene considering the situation. "I'm not going to fight them."

She pulled herself free and thumped his chest, over and over, until she remembered his bruises. She pressed her forehead against the hard muscle and let her tears soak into his jerkin. "Why not?" she gasped between sobs. "Why are you just giving up?"

"It's for the best."

"Not for you!"

"But it is for you."

She paused. Why was he so calm, so compliant? "It is *not* the best for me."

"Lucy, you have no future with me. Even if I got out of this, which I won't."

"You might! With Oxley's help, you could escape."

"Perhaps, but then I'd be a wanted man, and I'll not drag you around the country while I run and hide. That's no life for the woman…" He sucked in a deep breath. "No life for you."

"I don't care!"

The outer door crashed back on its hinges. "*Justice, justice, justice for Larkham!*" chanted the mob in the corridor.

Oh God, oh God. She stepped closer to Nick. He stepped back, out of her reach.

"Lucy." He glanced at the door and ran a hand through his hair. He no longer wore the bandage. "I killed my mother." His nostrils flared, his jaw shuddered. The calm façade had cracked like an eggshell.

"*Justice! Justice!*" The storeroom door opened. A club smashed against the doorframe. Wood splintered. Upfield and two others pushed through, and more men surged in behind them.

"I don't deserve you," Nick said quietly. He shoved her away.

She fell on all fours to the floor, out of the way of the mob pouring into the storeroom. Nick's gaze met Upfield's at the head of the tide. The Larkham man grinned and slapped his club into his palm.

"Don't!" Lucy cried, getting up. "Don't touch him!"

Upfield ignored her. A few of the others glanced her way, including the two Renny boys. The younger one looked to his brother, Peter and frowned. Peter snarled.

She ran to Nick, but Upfield grabbed her arm and tossed her backward like a ragdoll. She slammed into the corner and sank to the floor, dazed.

Nick ran at Upfield, but four men grabbed him and held him back. Another two joined in, then another. Muscles strained as they tried to hold Nick. In the end, only a punch to his jaw quieted him, and Lucy's voice telling him she was unharmed.

"Do that again and I'll kill you," Nick said, menace dripping from every word.

"Fool," snarled Upfield.

The men let Nick go, and he wrapped the chain around his hand. Lucy expected him to pull it free, but he didn't try. It was more like he was holding on for balance. "I'll go with you," he said. "Take me wherever you want. But no one else gets hurt."

"No!" Lucy cried. "Nick, stop it! Don't give in."

He ignored her. Upfield hesitated a moment then inclined his head. "Agreed. It's you we want."

"Lucy?" It was Henry, his voice coming from beyond the mob. "Lucy, are you all right?" The crowd parted, and he was spat out into the storeroom. "Thank God," he said when he saw her. He knelt and wrapped her in his arms.

"They're going to take him," she said, pulling away. "Can't you do something?"

He shook his head. "They want his blood, and they're not going to stop until they get it."

The crowd parted again. "Move aside, make way. This is my inn, and I'm in charge here." It was Milner, and right behind him came Widow Dawson.

"Where's your bandage?" the wise woman asked, squinting at Nick.

"Release him," Upfield snapped at Milner. "He's ours now. We only want justice for one of our own."

"Your own?" Lucy said. She didn't care anymore. Nick was going to be lynched or beaten to death if she didn't do something. And since he wasn't going to help himself, she had to do it for him. "Your *own* was a vile man."

"Lucy," Henry whispered. "Be careful."

"Don't," Nick warned her with a shake of his head. "It'll change nothing."

She stood in front of Upfield where he couldn't ignore her. He laughed in her face, his foul breath making her wince.

"Get out of the way, *wench*," he said. "He ain't worth getting beat up for."

Behind her, Nick growled. Henry came up beside her. "Don't touch my sister," he said.

"If you do," said Widow Dawson, "this entire village will come after you."

"Aye," said Milner.

Upfield's gaze flicked from one to the other, but he said nothing, nor did he tell her to move again.

"Listen to me," Lucy said. "There is something about Renny that none of you know. If you did, you wouldn't be here defending his honor. The man had none."

"What're you saying?" Peter growled, stepping forward. He held a dagger in his hand, unsheathed, but not poised to strike. That didn't mean he wouldn't.

"Renny was a good man," Upfield said. "What do you know of him, anyway?"

"I know that he committed terrible crimes." She forged on, even though her heart broke for the boys. Peter glared at her, his arms crossed, but the younger, Frankie seemed to shrink in on himself. "Crimes so awful that his victims are too damaged to accuse him, even now."

"Lucy," Nick said, sharp.

"Shut it, Coleclough," Henry said. "Or I'll beat you myself. She'll speak if she wants to, and neither you nor I can stop her."

Lucy kept her back to Nick, but she could feel his glare boring into her. She could do this. She had to. "They hired Nick to... assassinate Renny." The word stuck in her throat, made her mouth dry.

Several people in the mob gasped. Frankie grabbed his brother's hand, but Peter shook him off. His face was hard, as hard as Nick's had ever been.

"What'd he do?" someone near the back called out.

"Aye," said the big man next to Upfield, his nose and eyes swollen from when Monk had hit him. "If his crime was so bad, why don't we know of it?"

"Because his victims wanted to keep it quiet. What he did… " She gulped, shook her head. Henry's arm wrapped around her shoulders. She couldn't go on. Those poor girls.

"If you can't tell us," Upfield said, "how can we believe you?"

"She can't prove it," someone said.

"You." Peter pointed his dagger at Nick. "You tell us what my Pa is supposed to have done."

Nick remained silent.

"See!" Peter shouted. "Pa did nothing. He was a good man."

To Lucy's surprise, it took a moment for anyone to say, "Aye," and that was only Upfield. A few more chimed in, but not the entire mob.

The big, blocky man put a hand on Peter's shoulder. "Give us names, witnesses, and we'll not trouble you today. We'll let your fate be decided at the assizes."

"No, we bloody won't!" Upfield snapped. "It's lies! Must be. Peter, lad, you know your Pa."

Peter said nothing, but he continued to glare at Nick.

"Where's Sawyer?" Henry asked. "He seems a reasonable man."

"Not here," Upfield said.

"He left for Larkham this morning," Milner added.

"Prob'ly staking a claim on Renny's widow," Upfield said with a sneer that earned him a fierce glare from Peter.

"Don't sully my Ma's name," Frankie said, indignant. "She's a good woman. The best."

"Aye," said several of the mob.

"Which is why she needs justice," Upfield said. "You too, lads. This man killed your Pa. Anyone here got doubts he did it?"

Feet shuffled. "No," one said.

"None," said another. "Too many witnesses."

"Renny's boy himself saw this man remove his disguise," Upfield went on. "You talk of vileness, wench, but *he* did the lowest thing. He took the life of a good townsman, a father and husband. Left his wife and children with no master. How can you defend him?"

She was losing them. The mob had wavered for a moment, but now Upfield had them again. They echoed his words, smacked their clubs into their open palms.

And then Upfield himself stepped around her and grabbed Nick by the jerkin. Milner had unlocked the chain—perhaps to free Nick so he could defend himself—and Upfield shoved him forward through the crowd.

"Stop!" she shouted. "Stop it!" She tried to run after them, but Henry held her so hard she could barely move.

"Hush, pet," said Widow Dawson. The hopelessness on her face was as plain as day.

The crowd followed Upfield and Nick out. Lucy could no longer see him, but that didn't stop her screaming until her throat burned and her voice expired. She beat her fists against Henry, scratched at his hands and arms, but he held her firmly until she felt too weak to even stand. He sank with her to the floor and she curled into a ball. Her stomach churned. Her heart felt like it was being sucked out of her chest. Her sobs filled the empty storeroom.

Nick was gone. He hadn't even tried to fight them off.

She'd lost him.

CHAPTER 19

*C*ole could still hear Lucy's cries even after he was marched out of the innyard to the street. They ripped through him, made him want to run back and beg her forgiveness. Made him want to fight for her, for himself.

But he couldn't hope to beat so many captors, and, once he'd blocked out her sobs and come to his senses again, he remembered that she was better off being free of him. She *would* find someone else. How could she not? She was eminently desirable.

He should know. He desired her beyond reason and above everything except her own safety and happiness. Perhaps it was madness. He certainly felt like he no longer had a grip on a world that had tilted sideways. He was sliding off into an abyss, but at least Lucy wasn't going with him. She *would* recover.

"Move!" Upfield growled, pushing Cole forward.

They were heading out of the village, in the direction of Larkham. Would they walk all the way, or would they kill him on the road somewhere? It seemed they didn't want to do it within spitting distance of Sutton Grange. He couldn't blame them. Lucy had too many friends there. Some were even following. He caught a glimpse of Widow Dawson with two women and some men, but not enough to confront the mob. Perhaps if Hughe and Monk were there it would be different, and definitely if Orlando was added to the mix. But all of his friends seemed to have abandoned him.

It was up to Cole. The irony almost made him laugh. Until that morning, he'd welcomed whatever was in store for him, as he'd welcomed it every day of his life since he'd left Coleclough Hall.

Or thought he had.

Now that his life was closer to ending than it had ever been, he wanted to live. It must have always been that way, only he'd not realized. He supposed that's why he'd never lost a fight. There was something inside him that had never truly given up.

The only thing he had given up on was Lucy. Nothing changed the fact that she was never going to be his. She was much too precious to be shackled to a man like him. A hunted, hated man with no prospects beyond being an assassin.

"Move faster." Upfield slammed his fist into Cole's back, right on a bruise that one of Renny's boys had inflicted in the meadow.

Cole ground his back teeth and kept going. The pain eased after a moment, unlike the one piercing his head as sharp as a blade, making thinking up a plan of escape difficult. At least he had time before they reached Larkham. Something would come to him by then.

"Stop here," Upfield said. "It's far enough."

Fuck.

The men surrounding Cole halted. Upfield pushed him down onto the dusty road. A sharp stone scratched his knee, and a boot kicked him in the back. He needed a weapon, but there were only small stones scattered across the road surface, no large rocks. He wished he'd hidden the knife Hughe had given him in his boot instead of under the pallet where it still lay.

"Don't do this," pleaded Widow Dawson. She sounded close, just out his line of sight. "Please, sir, it's wrong."

"Go back to Sutton Grange," Cole said. "Take care of Lucy. There's nothing you can do here."

"God and the judges won't look well upon you, Mr. Upfield," she went on, ignoring Cole. "Don't think we won't tell 'em."

"Widow Dawson!" Cole snapped. "Go!" The foolish woman was only going to bring trouble down on her head if she spoke like that.

"Peter," Upfield said. "Take my sword. Remove his head from his shoulders. Do it fast, or take your time. Up to you."

He was asking the lad to kill? The man was base.

"Do it for yer Pa."

Cole braced himself. He didn't want to attack the lad, but it would be easier than trying to bring down Upfield. He listened for the first step on the packed earth. The boy was light, Cole needed to concentrate.

Still nothing.

"You do it, Upfield," said one of the other men. "The lad's not ready."

Upfield grunted. There was a shuffle of feet, a rustle of clothing. Cole closed his eyes. Held his breath. Waited.

Someone—maybe Widow Dawson—screamed. It covered the sound of Upfield's step but not the whine of a blade through air.

Cole ducked to the side, swiveled, and lunged at Upfield's legs. Upfield crashed backward and landed on his back. The breath *whooshed* out of him as he hit hard, and he let go of the sword. He did not get up, but lay there, fighting for air. He would recover in a moment or two. Cole didn't have much time.

He scanned the faces, full of anger and indignation. He could not possibly fight them all. "What will it be?" he asked, settling into his battle stance. "One at a time or all together?"

The biggest man growled. "You're cock-sure for someone surrounded by dozens of armed men."

Cole caught sight of something down the road, a distant movement, and he felt the vibration of hooves through the earth. It didn't come from the Sutton Grange direction like he expected. Whoever it was, he silently thanked them for the distraction.

"Ah, here they are," he said.

Heads turned to follow his gaze. Cole seized the big man around the throat and wrenched the sword out of his hand. The man tried to call out, but could only manage a gurgle. It took the others a moment to realize what had happened, and when they did, they turned on Cole.

The blows to his ribs broke bones, but it was the club smashing into his head that finally felled him.

The drumming of hooves grew louder. People shouted, but Cole couldn't make out words through the fire blazing inside his skull.

Then a voice rose above all the noise, clear and commanding. "Disperse!" Hughe.

Cole closed his eyes because it hurt too much to keep them open. Blackness swallowed him. Hands cradled his head, inspected the new wound methodically yet gently. Widow Dawson. He should thank her, but the words jumbled through his brain, and he couldn't put them together into a sentence.

"Shhh, don't try to talk," she said.

"Who did this?" Hughe demanded. "Who's responsible?"

Careful, Hughe, or they'll realize you're no fool.

"So help me, I'll thrash every one of you."

Don't let them think you care.

"You. Upfield is it? On your knees."

Cole cracked open an eyelid, but the world blurred and the sunlight stung his eyeball. He saw Monk and Sawyer on horseback beside Hughe, and a set of female arms wrapped around Sawyer's waist. Not Lucy's. He closed his eye again.

"Nick! Dear God." Lucy. She was there after all. Hell. He didn't want her to see him like this.

She was suddenly beside him, her familiar hands taking over from Widow Dawson's, gently stroking his hair, inspecting each of his new cuts and bruises. She sobbed once, then pressed her cool lips to his hot forehead. Her kiss lingered long enough for her tears to dampen his skin. She made no more sounds, but he could feel her entire body shuddering.

He would give anything to hold her, comfort her, let her know he was all right. He struggled to sit, and a pair of strong hands helped him. Monk, he realized when he opened his eyes again.

"Do you know who you are?" Monk asked, frowning into Cole's face.

"I'm a cantankerous, cold-hearted devil."

Monk gave a shaky laugh. "Glad you're still with us, my friend," he said quietly. "You had us worried."

"Us too," said Henry. He passed Cole a wineskin.

Cole drank and handed it back. He lifted his gaze to Lucy's. The fear and worry on her face hurt him more than his physical pain. He looked away. She remained close, but did not touch.

"I told you to kneel," Hughe said from where he still sat on his horse.

Upfield knelt. "We only wanted justice, my lord."

"Like this? Are you barbarians in Larkham?"

"We care for our own."

"Do you? I'm glad to hear it."

Cole knew that tone. Hughe had something up his sleeve.

"We must get Nick back to Sutton Grange," said Lucy. "His injuries need to be tended to."

"Aye," said Widow Dawson. "Mayhap he can take yer horse, Mr. Monk, if the beast can be instructed to walk gently."

Monk nodded, just as Sawyer dismounted, revealing the woman sitting behind him.

"Ma!" cried Frankie.

Peter gasped. "What're you doing here?"

"You ought to be home, grieving," Upfield said. "Not facing this cur here. What'd you bring her for, Sawyer?"

Cole knew. *You damned fool, Hughe.*

But Hughe wasn't looking at Cole. He too had dismounted and regarded one Renny boy then the other. "Take them to the Plough," he ordered Monk.

"What?" Peter said. "Why?"

The younger boy, Frankie, began to cry. "Ma?"

"Go with Mr. Monk," she said, leaning down and lovingly touching her younger son's head. "I'll come and find you later. There are some things that need to be discussed here, and they're not for your ears yet. Or yours, Peter."

"No!" the older boy said, crossing his arms.

"Let him stay," Hughe said. "After what he did to Cole in the meadow, he's old enough to hear this."

Cole wasn't so sure about that. It was one thing to beat up the man who'd killed your father, it was quite another to learn what your father had done to deserve the death.

Widow Renny dismounted with Sawyer's aid, then Monk and Frankie mounted and rode off to Sutton Grange. Once they were out of earshot, she turned to Upfield. He stood again, the scowl on his face gone. The man seemed genuinely curious. Cole glanced at Hughe, shook his head slightly. *Don't do this. Don't tell them. The girls...*

Hughe ignored him.

Cole closed his eyes against the nausea. He'd heard the details once already. He didn't want to hear them again.

"Release him," the widow said. "He doesn't deserve this."

A ripple of gasps washed over the mob. They all looked at one another, at Upfield. "What!" their leader blurted. "What have they said to you?"

"Only that the man who killed my husband is facing a trial. He should not."

"But you said yerself, he killed Renny!"

Lucy grasped Cole's fingers, and he soaked up the comfort she offered. Then he let go. Out of the corner of his eye, he saw her blink rapidly at him, then she turned to watch Widow Renny.

"My husband wasn't the man you thought him." She pressed her lips together, and Sawyer touched her shoulder. "He was depraved."

Lucy stood mesmerized by the brave woman standing in front of the mob of men she must have known all her life. She couldn't begin to imagine what courage it took. She only wished the older

Renny boy had gone with his brother. It would have been easier for their mother.

"I knew him better than anyone," Upfield snapped. "He was a good alderman, upstanding. He did much for the village."

Two or three heads nodded.

"He was good to his friends, yes. You benefited from his decisions, Mr. Upfield, and others too. I understand why you're angry now. Your livelihood may suffer for a short time, but I trust it will recover soon enough."

"So?" Upfield jerked his thumb at Nick. "Renny may have made some decisions that didn't benefit all, but was that reason to kill him? Or to let his killer walk free?"

"There's more, Mr. Upfield. Much more." Widow Renny glanced briefly at Peter, and tears pooled in her eyes. Sawyer's hand on her shoulder squeezed, and she bit her wobbling lip. A hush blanketed the mob as they waited. There was not a breath of wind, nor a rustle of leaves to break the silence.

"My husband committed a terrible sin against two girls. I have no wish to enter into details, but the things he did… " She shook her head, closed her eyes. "Not a single one of you good people would be unmoved if you heard what he'd done. You would be sick to your stomachs, and you would have run my husband out of town if you'd known, or worse."

"Surely this is a mistake," said Upfield, but he didn't sound confident anymore. "What girls do you speak of? How old were they? Mayhap they begged him to do those things. Some wenches—"

"Enough!" Cole bellowed. "*No* woman wants that." He looked like he would thump the man. Hughe too, if the hard set of his jaw was any indication.

"He's right," Widow Renny said quickly before Upfield could argue. "Raping young virgins then doing what he did afterward… " She choked on a sob and shook her head, unable to go on.

Upfield shuffled his feet and rubbed a hand over his chin. "I cannot believe it," he said without malice. "Are you sure?"

"I'll not identify the girls or their families, as is their wish, but when Lord Oxley came to me this morning and told me, I went to see the girls and gently questioned them. He spoke the truth, they said. Moreover, I was already suspicious." She shot another glance at her son. Peter stood silently near Upfield, his head bowed, his shoulders heaving with every breath. "You see, my husband treated those girls in much the same manner he treated me in our marriage bed. If anyone doubts that Renny was a monster, I'll show them my scars. I have nothing to hide anymore. He's gone, and I'm… " She spluttered a sob. "I'm so relieved."

Peter's head jerked up. His face was red, his cheeks damp from tears. "Ma, why are saying this?" he shouted at her. "Pa wasn't like that."

But no one echoed his words. The lad looked around, his eyes wide, desperate, but none met his gaze. His face crumpled, and he ran off. Sawyer made to go after him, but Widow Renny held him back.

"Not yet," she said. "He'll need to be alone for the rest of the day to work off his anger. I'll speak to him later."

"The path ahead won't be easy for him," Oxley said. "Or for you."

"I'll take care of them all." Sawyer gave Widow Renny a tentative smile.

"You're a good man, Mr. Sawyer," Lucy said. "All of you are good men, and we understand that you only wanted to see justice served. But it has been served, in its own way, and now it's time for Mr. Coleclough to be released."

Lord Oxley gave her a brief, approving nod. Then his face changed ever so subtly. His eyes brightened, his mouth softened, and the tension left his body. He was back to being the dandy again now that the danger had dispersed.

"There's no need for an honest man to pay for this crime," Widow Renny said. "If he is guilty, then you could say the families who hired him are too."

"We don't want to lay this at their doorsteps," Upfield muttered.

"Aye," said his big friend. "If Coleclough promises not to show his face in Larkham again, we'll let him go."

"You have my word," Nick said. "I'm leaving Hampshire altogether anyway."

"When he's healed," Lucy added. She tried to catch his attention, but he wasn't looking at her. It made her heart dive again, when it had just begun to soar.

Upfield approached Lord Oxley, and even bowed to him. "And you, my lord, how did *you* know Coleclough was hired by those families?" The question was insolent. A mere townsman should not speak thus to a nobleman, and a nobleman certainly didn't have to answer him.

But Oxley merely fluttered a gloved hand as if sprinkling dust in the air. "Oh, he told me everything last night. I took it upon myself to ride out to Larkham at first light and speak to Renny's widow to discover if there was any truth in the claim. I'm just an innocent bystander, Mr. Upfield. Wrong place, wrong time." He pouted. "Or is that right place, right time? No matter. It is mere coincidence that I was in the area now. This man hasn't worked for me for some time, and I can assure you he never performed *these* kinds of duties in my employ."

He didn't blink an eyelid, didn't give a hint that he was lying through his teeth. Lucy had never met anyone quite so accomplished at it.

"I have Mr. Monk now," Oxley went on. "Much more sensible fellow. Not prone to moodiness either."

Nick must be used to Oxley's ways because he listened without flinching. He stood unmoved, not really looking at anyone or anything. He was back to being closed off from the world, from Lucy.

At least she had time in which to get through to him. His injuries would take weeks to heal.

"I'm LEAVING," Nick said. He stood in the doorway of one of the Plough's guest rooms, blocking the entrance so that Lucy couldn't get past. "Today."

"You can't!" She pointed at his head, once more bandaged by Widow Dawson. "You're not well enough."

"Don't do this, Lucy. Don't make it any more difficult than it already is."

"Stop being so pig-headed and let me in. I want to talk to you." If he wasn't already bruised and battered almost beyond recognition, she would have grabbed his arms and shaken him until some sense rattled loose in his head. She'd have to rely on words instead. Kisses might help too. Coupling certainly would, but she didn't think he'd allow it. The man had a will of iron when he put his mind to it.

He pinched the bridge of his nose. "Have you not heard enough to make you want to run in the other direction yet, or do I need to say it again? I cannot be the man you deserve."

"Let me decide that."

He went to shut the door, but she put her foot inside. The heavy oak closed on it. "God's blood!" she cried.

The door opened again and he crouched down. "Are you all right? Show me your foot." He removed her shoe without waiting for her answer and inspected it through her stocking. He stroked her instep, her heel, and cupped her calf. His thumb gently massaged.

"I'm sorry, Lucy," he whispered. "I'm so sorry." He pressed his forehead against her knee and cradled her lower leg against his chest.

She gripped the doorframe for balance with one hand, and stroked his cheek with the other. "Don't go, Nick. I love you, and I will until the end of my days. You leaving won't change that."

His shoulders shuddered. Twice, he began to say something then stopped. Finally, after drawing in a querulous breath, he said. "I killed my mother, Lucy. What sort of man does that?"

"You were eighteen."

"Still a man."

"You haven't yet told me the circumstances."

"They don't matter. I can hardly live with what I've done. How can I ask you to?"

She removed her leg, which he seemed to take as a signal to get up. He turned inside and picked up his pack from the table. He'd gotten clean clothes from somewhere and washed the blood from his hands and face. Widow Dawson had not wanted Lucy inside when she'd patched him up, but once she'd left, Lucy had decided it was time they talk.

She snatched the pack off him. "You're not going anywhere."

He took the pack back. "I have to."

"You don't *have* to do anything. You're a free man with a free will. Stay. I'm ordering you."

One corner of his mouth lifted in that almost-smile. "What happened to my free will?"

She grabbed the pack off him again and put it behind her back. "Kiss me and then tell me you're leaving. If you can do that, I'll give you back the pack and let you go."

A beat passed, two. "Very well."

She lifted her chin, waited for his kiss. "Then do it," she said when he hesitated.

His chest rose and fell rapidly three times. "Give me a moment."

"No." She wouldn't give him any time to steel himself. "Kiss me now."

Somebody behind her cleared his throat. Lucy spun round to see a tall man of middling age and little hair standing in the doorway. He wore a tailored brown doublet and a gentleman's traveling cloak, and carried his hat in his hand. Behind him stood another man with gray hair and familiar almond-shaped eyes. Nick's eyes.

"Greetings, Son," the older man said. "May we come in?"

CHAPTER 20

*L*ucy's gasp echoed around the room. "Lord Coleclough?"

Cole rocked back on his heels and scrambled to gather his wits. "What are you doing here?" And then he remembered the letter he'd written when he first arrived at Cowdrey Farm with nearly half his memories missing. His father and brother must have left for Hampshire immediately upon receiving it.

And to think, he'd almost missed them. If only Widow Dawson had worked faster, he could have been spared this.

Hughe stood on the gallery landing, leaning lazily against the railing, a smirk on his face. "Everything all right?"

"Perfect," Cole snarled. Hughe nodded, shot a quick glance at Lucy, then left.

Thomas came into the room and paused in front of Cole. He looked him up and down, his eyes narrowed to slits, his forehead creased. "Your letter said you'd lost your memory, but it didn't say how badly you'd been injured. Bloody hell, who did this to you?"

"It doesn't matter."

Thomas shook his head and, as if he'd suddenly remembered he hadn't seen Cole in eleven years, broke into a grin. "Greetings,

Brother." He pulled Cole into an embrace. "Where have you been? What have you been doing all this time?"

"Working, traveling." Cole stepped back, out of his reach. He was acutely aware of Lucy watching him, but he didn't want to look at her face. It was difficult enough dealing with his sentimental brother, it would be nigh impossible to remain impassive if she began to cry.

"He was about to leave," she said, a hint of anger in her tone that proved she wasn't near tears after all. "Perhaps you can convince him to stay, sir. He's not well enough, as you can see."

"I'm more than ready," Cole said.

"That's not the same thing." She crossed her arms, and he steeled himself for a battle of wills. He thought about sending up an appeal to God, but he doubted the Almighty was still listening to him after such a long absence.

A slow smiled spread across Thomas's face. He bowed to Lucy. "My name is Thomas Coleclough, Nick's brother, and this is our father, Lord Coleclough."

She curtseyed to both men and introduced herself.

"Have you been taking care of him?" Thomas asked.

"As much as he allows. He's incredibly obstinate when it comes to his own health and happiness."

"I can well imagine." He chuckled and she smiled.

Cole bristled. "If you've come to ask me to return to Coleclough Hall, it's been a wasted trip. Indeed, it's a wasted trip anyway." His gaze connected with his father's. The old man still blocked the entrance as if he could stop Cole leaving. "I've remembered everything."

His father remained unmoved, giving Cole the opportunity to size him up. His appearance was rather shocking. Thomas at least looked more or less the same, just a little harder around the jaw perhaps, but their father had aged considerably. He seemed to have shrunk a few inches, and he was certainly thinner. His back was a little crooked and his fingers more so, which probably explained why he didn't wear riding gloves like Thomas. He had much less hair and far more wrinkles than eleven years ago. The eyes, however, were still as unforgiving as ever.

"Then we have much to talk about," the baron said. To Lucy he said, "Send someone up with refreshments when you leave."

"If you don't mind, my lord, I'd like to stay."

He cocked an eyebrow at her. His mouth twisted from side to side in a way Cole knew all too well. It meant his father's anger was simmering just beneath the surface. If Lucy pushed any further, it would boil over.

"I don't think so," the baron said.

"If she wants to stay, she can," Cole said. "You have no authority here."

His father walked into the room, his steps slow and shuffling. He ignored Lucy and eyed Cole closely. "You've grown."

"You've shrunk."

The baron made a *humphing* sound. "She can stay."

"As if you had any say in it."

His father's mouth twisted again, side to side. Cole caught Thomas studying him. He expected his brother to warn him not to irk their father as he used to do, but he merely shrugged and shook his head, as if their father's anger were not worth worrying about.

The baron lowered himself into a chair, gingerly at first, then falling the last part of the way as if his legs could no longer hold him up. He settled back with a sigh. It was the way an old man moved. An unwell man. No wonder Thomas didn't seem concerned. Their father couldn't possibly expect to dish out a thrashing the way he used to when they were boys.

"Tell us more about the last eleven years," Thomas asked. He sounded like an eager puppy, and looked a little like one too with those big, trusting eyes. "Lord, I can't believe you've come back to us after all this time. We thought you…" He stopped smiling and swallowed loudly.

Cole said nothing. How could he respond to the raw emotion

imprinted all over Thomas's face? If there was one thing Cole regretted about leaving, it was that Thomas had remained behind. But he looked to have turned out well, not at all afraid of the baron or under his influence.

"You should have written," their father said.

"I will from here on." To Thomas he said, "I wasn't sure how well my letters would be received."

"How well? Fool, I was desperate to hear from you after you left." He clasped Cole's arm hard. "We worried about you so. We both did."

Out of the corner of his eye, he saw Lucy cover her mouth with her hand. She blinked back tears. She and Thomas were so alike, sentimental to a fault.

"How is the estate?" Cole asked to stave off the awkward silence that threatened to overwhelm them.

"Carter's dead."

Cole nodded. To his surprise, the news didn't affect him. He ought to be more pleased, but it was likely the man had aged as poorly as the baron, and it was difficult to find pleasure in that. "You didn't replace him with someone just as hard and quick with the whip?"

The muscle in the baron's cheek twitched. "There was no need," he said. "You had gone, and your brother was always a good boy."

"Don't, Father," Thomas warned. "Nick—"

"I go by Cole now," Cole said, and Lucy clicked her tongue.

Thomas sighed. "It's time to set aside past differences, and for you to come home where you belong."

"I don't belong there."

"Then where do you belong? Where's your home now?"

The air in the room fairly throbbed it was so densely charged. Cole didn't answer, so Thomas turned to Lucy. "Do you know?" he asked her.

"His home will be here," she said, stepping up beside Cole. She didn't touch him, however. A small blessing.

"Lucy, don't," he muttered.

"But not until some things have been aired," she went on as if he'd not spoken.

Cole silently groaned. Perhaps if he walked out now, she would follow him. No, that wouldn't work, they'd probably all follow and the conversation would simply be continued in a more public place.

"Nick thinks he killed his mother," she said. "I want to know what really happened, from your lips, my lord."

Cole expected his father to snarl and snap, to stand over her because even shrunken as he was, he was still taller than she. But he remained sitting. He simply sighed so deeply, his body seemed to cave in upon itself.

"Nick killed her," he said. "He remembers correctly."

Lucy stiffened. "But surely he had a reason."

"Why does it matter?" Nick rounded on her. "The fact doesn't change—I did it, and I have to live with that."

"No, Nick, *we* have to live with it. And we will." Her fingers reached for his, tentative. He should pull away, but he could not. She was a whirlpool and he a mere leaf, unable to stop the pull toward her. He curled his fingers around hers. "You are not alone, Nick, and we can face this and move on from it. Together."

His throat burned. God, he adored her. How could he ever deny her anything? He'd been a fool to think he could, but he must continue to try. "I'll listen," he said. "But it changes nothing." He nodded at his father to go on.

"Start at the beginning," Thomas said. "From when you and Mother wed."

The baron set his hat on the table and indicated Lucy should sit in the only other chair nearby. She did, but didn't let go of Cole's hand. He held his breath, held everything inside as tight as possible lest it all unravel.

"You met in Florence, didn't you?" she prompted.

Lord Coleclough nodded as he stared at his hat. "I adored her instantly. She was a beauty. Hair as black as midnight, her eyes too.

When she danced, I couldn't take my eyes off her. The way she moved, with such abandon, her eyes closed, her lips parted as if she could taste life and she couldn't get enough of it. I knew I had to marry her. It took some effort to convince my father to agree to the union, but my mother talked to him. She saw how much I loved Maria, and she me.

"After we married, we came to live in England. My parents both died within the year and I inherited Coleclough. That first year had been wedded bliss, but afterward..." He shook his head. "Things changed. I don't really know why or how. It began slowly. She would cry a lot and for no reason that I could determine, or fly into a rage over the smallest things. I may have forgotten to say good morrow, or looked at one of the maids in a way she thought meant I had… you know."

Lucy knew. "Go on." She didn't want him to stop now that she was finally getting a rounded picture of Nick's life. He stood beside her, still holding her hand in his. It was a small gesture, but she felt relieved beyond measure.

"Maria refused to go to court with me, saying she didn't agree with our queen's protestant religion. We began to have heated discussions on theology after that, which of course were fruitless. Then Thomas was born. She wanted to bring him up Catholic in secret, but I refused. It was much too dangerous to be Papist even in private." He stared straight ahead, seemingly lost in his story. "She changed rapidly after his birth. I don't know whether it was the pressure of being mistress of Coleclough, or that she missed her religion or her family, but she became unpredictable. One moment she said she loved me, the next she would fly into a rage and scratch my face. She accused me of having mistresses, then of keeping her prisoner in the house. I admit, I was no saint, but I was faithful to her, and I did not lock her away."

"Not then," Nick said.

Lord Coleclough nodded. "The situation was bad, but it became worse after you were born, Nick. She went from angry and weepy to quiet. She would sit by your cradle or in her rocking chair, and sing to you. I thought her cured, happy again. I was overjoyed. Then one day her maid came to me in a state. She told me she'd caught Maria pressing a pillow over your face. The maid stopped her in time, thank God, and took you away."

"She tried to kill him?" Good lord. Lucy had heard of mothers who'd lost their minds after the birth of a child and tried to harm themselves or the babe, but it still shocked her to the core. "Did you know any of this, Nick?"

He'd gone white, his bruises stark against pale skin. "I knew she was mad," he said. "After I saw her in the cottage and then in the house, but I thought she'd gone mad *after* you banished her. I thought that's *why* she went mad."

Lord Coleclough shook his head. He looked so old and frail, it was difficult to reconcile this man with the one Nick had talked about. "I hid her away in the wood because she tried to take your life twice more, and I was terrified that one day the maids wouldn't be there and couldn't save you. I had to get her away from you, and the old woodsman's cottage seemed perfect. I hired Carter too to oversee arrangements. It was the only way to keep you safe without banishing her from the estate entirely. I couldn't do that. She was my wife. Lady Coleclough." He shrugged, as if that explained his reluctance.

"She didn't try to return to the main house?" Lucy asked.

"She did, twice. The first time, I simply sent her back to the cottage. The second time, I had Carter beat her. It was the only thing she understood. She didn't try again."

"You had her beaten," Nick said, voice dark. "You could think of no other way?"

"What was I to do? She wanted to kill my son! Should I have tried to talk her out of it? Do you think that would have worked?"

Nick and Thomas exchanged grim glances.

"Is that why you ordered the boys not to leave the property?" Lucy asked. "Were you afraid they'd wander into the wood and find her?"

"Yes. She would have killed Nick if she'd seen him. I didn't know if she wanted to harm Thomas too, but I wasn't willing to wait and see. So I kept them at home. It was easy enough when you were small, Nick. You hardly went anywhere, or wanted to. But as you grew, I had to give strict orders. The villagers didn't know what had happened to Maria, but there was talk of the witch in Bowen Wood, and I knew you'd try to learn more if you spoke to them. You were always so curious and clever, both of you. But you, Nick, were defiant whereas Thomas was not. By the time you were eighteen, a grown man, you were strong enough in body and mind to defy my orders outright.

"Even Carter's whippings didn't stop you. You still went into the wood. The second time..." His mouth twisted. He closed his eyes and drew in a deep breath. "The second time, Carter went too far. I...allowed him to. I was sick afterward when I realized how much damage he'd inflicted."

Lucy's hand tightened around Nick's. He was quite still, his head bowed.

"You were very headstrong," the baron said. "You had decided that your mother needed saving, and so you went to save her. But she hadn't given up on her intent to take your life. She poisoned you."

Nick frowned, nodded, his gaze on his father but his focus more distant. "I was ill for days afterward. The broth?"

"I suspect so. I couldn't keep Maria in the cottage after the village boys had seen her there, so I brought her back to the Hall and kept her locked away in her apartments. I admit I didn't know what to do." He wiped his brow with the heel of his hand. "I told Thomas everything while you were recuperating. It was he who suggested she wanted to end your life, so she could take you with her."

"With her?"

"To heaven, hell, or wherever she was going in death."

"Oh my," said Lucy. "She loved you after all, in her own way."

"Her own *mad* way," Lord Coleclough said. "She tried to kill one of the maids one day when Nick was almost fully recovered. Thomas reached her first, then Nick and I."

"She was going to kill me," Thomas said. "Nick saved me."

"By taking her life," Nick whispered.

Thomas gripped Nick's shoulders and peered into his eyes. "You saved me, Brother. Do not think otherwise. You had no choice."

"There is always a choice."

"No." Lucy slipped her arm around his waist. "There isn't. You cannot be blamed for saving your brother from a madwoman."

"Our mother," he said, voice thick.

"Our mad mother," Thomas said.

"You're a good boy, Nick," Lord Coleclough said. "You always were. I should not have let Carter whip you. I should never have let you think any of this was your fault. Perhaps some of the blame should lie at my feet, but I am certain that none of it should lie at yours." He pushed himself out of the chair and shuffled over to Nick. Thomas stepped aside and let their father face his younger son. "I'm sorry. I suppose I could have been a better father, but I..." His nostrils flared the way Nick's did when he was trying to stifle his emotions. "I did what I thought was right at the time."

Nick seemed to be studying the floor as if he'd lost something there and needed to find it.

Please say something, Lucy silently begged. *Forgive him.* She released his hand, and he turned his head a little to see her. She winked and to her great surprise, he winked back.

"It's been a long day," Nick said, resting his hand on his father's shoulder. "I need a drink. Will you join us in the taproom?"

Lord Coleclough's mouth twitched into a small smile. He breathed deeply and the smile widened. "I'm parched."

"As am I," said Thomas.

Lucy knew enough about men and families to know that all was forgiven as best as it ever could be. The rift might remain raw for some time, but the healing had begun. It only remained to be seen if healing this wound could heal all, and Nick could be hers again.

"Will you be joining us, Mistress Cowdrey?" Thomas asked.

"Of course she will," Lord Coleclough said.

"We'll meet you down there," Nick said. "In a moment or two."

His father cocked an eyebrow. "Take as long as you need."

Thomas scooped up his father's hat and held the door open for him. Lucy watched them go, her heart in her throat. As soon as the door closed, Nick wrapped his arms around her and pulled her against his chest. His heart beat loud and fast. He kissed the top of her head, and plucked the pins out of her hair so that it tumbled down her back.

"Are you all right?" she asked, peering up at him.

His warm brown eyes swam. "That depends. Are you?"

She cupped his face. "Of course."

"Then so am I." He kissed her.

It was sweet and a little timid, as if he were unsure of her feelings or afraid of hurting her. This big, fierce warrior of a man had turned as gentle as a puppy, and she adored him with every piece of her. She'd never been happier. Never thought such happiness could exist.

He broke the kiss and got down on one knee. "Lucy Cowdrey, you've brought light into my world, and for that I cannot thank you enough." She opened her mouth to speak but he shushed her, so she began to cry instead. "I have to say this now, or I may never." He cleared his throat. "I have dark corners, Lucy, but the shadows recede a little more every day you are with me. I can't live without light. I can't live without you. Will you put up with me for the rest of our lives?" Her tears turned to laughter at his proposal, and he frowned. "Is that aye or nay?"

"Aye! Aye! You big, lovely, wonderful fool. Get up. You're battered enough as it is without hurting your knees too."

He rose and took her into his arms again. His heart had slowed to a steadier rhythm that was as strong as ever. "I'm sorry that wasn't very romantic. I don't know how… "

"Hush. It was the most romantic proposal I've ever had."

He narrowed his eyes, then he laughed. Laughed! It was the most wonderful sound. She'd missed it.

"I'm sorry for so many things I said to you," he said, sobering. "I meant none of it."

"I know. You were trying to do what you thought was best for me." She traced the curve of his mouth with her fingertip. "But Nick."

"Yes."

"From now on, I decide what is best for me."

"The best for both of us. I'm going to need your advice on the farm."

"What farm?"

"The farm I'll either buy or lease." He sighed. "For once I wish I hadn't given away most of my wages. I'll ask Hughe for a loan, and we'll settle near here."

"As long as we're together, I don't care where we go."

He kissed her again, his mouth lingering and soft against hers. It tugged something inside her, deep down, something primal that made her want to take him right there in one of the Plough's rooms.

"We mustn't," she said, pulling away with more than a little regret. "They'll be waiting for us."

He groaned. "Cruel wench."

* * *

NICK FELT like a great weight had been lifted from him. He hadn't realized it before, but he'd never truly breathed until now. Lucy had accepted him. Him! And after all the things he'd said to push her away too. He'd need a lifetime to make up for saying them. He'd take that lifetime, and gladly.

She was his.

All was right in the world.

If only Hughe wouldn't scowl at him like that. He sat on a stool in the taproom next to Monk, Henry, and Thomas. His father sat a little apart with Widow Dawson who inspected his crooked fingers.

Monk signaled to Milner to bring more ale and the innkeeper had them on the table almost before Nick and Lucy sat.

"How's your head, Cole?" Monk asked.

"Better," Nick said. "Everything's better. And I'd like you to call me Nick from now on. Cole is no more."

Monk nodded. Hughe merely sighed and drained his tankard. "I knew it," the earl muttered.

"I'm leaving your employ."

"I knew that too. Bloody hell."

"Don't worry." Monk slapped him on the back. "You still have me."

Hughe looped his arm around Monk's shoulders and grinned sloppily. "Thank God for that, my friend." Either he was drunk or he'd slipped back into dandy mode already.

"Is there something you wish to tell me, Sis?" Henry said, eyeing Lucy.

She reached for Nick's hand and smiled. "We're betrothed."

A round of cheers, kisses, hugs, and good wishes followed, but Henry held back. He didn't seem unhappy, as such, merely thoughtful. When Widow Dawson and another of her friends cornered Lucy, Nick approached her brother.

"I'll write to your father," he said. "Do you think he'll object?"

"Not at all," Henry said.

"I'll take good care of her. I know it'll be difficult for a few years, but once I can get the farm—"

"What farm?"

"I'll lease some land and graze sheep. The wool prices have been good in recent years."

"No." Henry set his tankard down hard on the table. "I won't allow it."

Nick ground his back teeth to stop from shaking the man. He would not allow anyone to stand in his way of wedding Lucy, and that included her brother. But he did want his blessing because it would hurt her deeply if they didn't get it.

"You must," he said. "Please, Henry, for Lucy's sake. I know I'm not the man you would have chosen for her—"

"It's not that! God's wounds, man, you're the only one for her. No, it's the farm. Take Cowdrey."

"What!" Nick laughed. Henry didn't join in. Bloody hell, he wasn't jesting. "I can't take Cowdrey. It's your inheritance."

"I don't want it. I want to study law."

"Ah. Far be it from me to tell a man to go against his heart's desire, but I don't think your father would like the idea."

"He'll get used to it. Instead of making the farm my inheritance, he can make it Lucy's dowry. I doubt he'll object. It'll stay within the family after all, and he wouldn't want you to begin your lives together with nothing."

Nick blinked at his future brother in-law. "Are you sure?"

Henry slapped him on the shoulder, and Nick winced as he struck a bruise. "I'm sure. Lucy, come here, your betrothed has something to tell you."

Lucy slipped in beside Nick, a curious smile on her face. "Is it good news?" she asked, eyeing first Henry then Nick.

"The best," Henry said and laughed. Nick couldn't recall having seen the man laugh once since they'd met.

"I've already had the best news," she said, tightening her hold around Nick's waist. He kissed the top of her head and she smiled up at him. "Well? Don't keep me in suspense."

"Your brother is going to return to London to study law, and we're going to live at Cowdrey Farm."

Her jaw flopped open. "We're going to stay here?" She threw her arms around Nick's neck and kissed him hard, then she threw her arms around Henry and kissed his cheek. "Father is going to try to talk you out of it."

Henry cocked his head to the side. "Mother will speak to him and all will be well."

Lucy nodded and laughed, as if it were a known fact that their father would not go against their mother's wishes. Nick fingered a strand of Lucy's hair and smiled at her. He completely understood how a husband could be incapable of refusing his wife anything. There was not a thing in the world he wouldn't agree to if Lucy asked. Not a single thing.

And that's just how he wanted it.

LOOK OUT FOR

The Saint

The third Assassins Guild novel.

What happens when Monk comes face to face with the woman who rejected him? Find out in the next Assassins Guild book.

To be notified when C.J. has a new release, sign up to her newsletter. Send an email to cjarcher.writes@gmail.com

A MESSAGE FROM THE AUTHOR

I hope you enjoyed reading this book as much as I enjoyed writing it. As an independent author, getting the word out about my book is vital to its success, so if you liked this book please consider telling your friends and writing a review at the store where you purchased it. If you would like to be contacted when I release a new book, subscribe to my newsletter at http://cjarcher.com/contact-cj/newsletter/. You will only be contacted when I have a new book out.

ALSO BY C.J. ARCHER

SERIES WITH 2 OR MORE BOOKS

After The Rift

Glass and Steele

The Ministry of Curiosities Series

The Emily Chambers Spirit Medium Trilogy

The 1st Freak House Trilogy

The 2nd Freak House Trilogy

The 3rd Freak House Trilogy

The Assassins Guild Series

Lord Hawkesbury's Players Series

The Witchblade Chronicles

SINGLE TITLES NOT IN A SERIES

Courting His Countess

Surrender

Redemption

The Mercenary's Price

ABOUT THE AUTHOR

C.J. Archer has loved history and books for as long as she can remember and feels fortunate that she found a way to combine the two. She spent her early childhood in the dramatic beauty of outback Queensland, Australia, but now lives in suburban Melbourne with her husband, two children and a mischievous black & white cat named Coco.

Subscribe to C.J.'s newsletter through her website to be notified when she releases a new book, as well as get access to exclusive content and subscriber-only giveaways. Her website also contains up to date details on all her books: http://cjarcher.com She loves to hear from readers. You can contact her through email cj@cjarcher.com or follow her on social media to get the latest updates on her books.

facebook.com/CJArcherAuthorPage

twitter.com/cj_archer

instagram.com/authorcjarcher

pintcrest.com/cjarcher

bookbub.com/authors/c-j-archer

Made in the USA
Columbia, SC
01 December 2019

84168172R00167